LA FINCA

La Finca

Published by The Conrad Press in the United Kingdom 2019

Tel: +44(0)1227 472 874
www.theconradpress.com
info@theconradpress.com

ISBN 978-1-911546-71-9

Typesetting and Cover Design by:
Charlotte Mouncey, www.bookstyle.co.uk

The Conrad Press logo was designed by Maria Priestley.

Printed and bound in Great Britain
by Clays Ltd, Elcograf S.p.A.

LA FINCA

BEA GREEN

For my gorgeous, gentle and kind daughter Ashley, who loves the sun and will forever be the sunshine in my life.

'Ya el sol, Platero, empieza á sentir pereza de salir de sus sábanas, y los labradores madrugan más que él.'

(Platero, the sun begins to be reluctant to leave his bed, and the farmers get up earlier than he does.)

Platero y yo by Juan Ramón Jiménez

1

July 2017

Approximately five minutes before the olive tree farm was officially his, Sebastián felt a wave of nausea hit him.

It was six o'clock on 16th July 2017, a sultry Monday afternoon. Businesses here in the small city of Ronda, located within the province of Málaga, wouldn't be closing until eight o'clock, if not later.

Trying to ignore the churning in his gut, Sebastián watched in silence as Adolfo, the solicitor, walked confidently into the office and sat at his desk.

Poker-faced, Adolfo looked quickly through Sebastián's file one last time to check everything was in order. Finally he put it down and pushed back his chair so he could open a drawer in his desk, all the while seemingly oblivious to the discomfort Sebastián was in.

'And here are the keys to your farm, Las Nevadas,' said Adolfo with a flourish, reaching down into the drawer for the heavy sack of keys and putting it on the table.

The metallic clunk of the keys landing firmly on the wood resonated throughout the quiet room.

Sebastián tried to speak but he was suddenly feeling faint and the room was starting to spin. He felt beads of sweat gathering on his forehead.

Gasping for breath, he looked at Adolfo, who was saying something to him that he couldn't hear. Sebastián had suddenly become deaf, as though he were underwater. He quickly pushed back his chair, bent his head down towards his knees and tried to take some deep breaths.

He felt a hand on his shoulder.

'*¡Jesús!* Sebastián, are you all right?' asked Adolfo.

Sebastián nodded, not trusting himself to speak. He heard Adolfo sigh with relief.

'*Hombre*, you gave me a fright! You should have seen your face. It went white, really white!'

Sebastián waited for another minute, until the roaring noise in his ears died down slightly, and sat up tentatively.

Adolfo hovered nervously in close proximity for a moment and then went to sit back down.

'Are you ill?' Adolfo asked, with his usual bluntness.

Sebastián shook his head, which at last felt firmly connected to his neck.

'No, I'm fine. I think it was a panic attack. It's passed now.'

'*A panic attack?* Are you serious?'

'Yes, I've had one before.'

Adolfo stared at him and then looked at the bag of keys. He was speechless for the first time since Sebastián had met him.

'It's because of the purchase,' said Sebastián, reading his thoughts. 'This whole thing has been so much pressure, so much effort and time.'

Adolfo said nothing in response but Sebastián could detect a faint glimmer of surprise in his eyes.

Sebastián, in turn, couldn't help but feel annoyed.

Adolfo, like Sebastián's own father, had played the role of Job's comforter throughout the lengthy process of buying the olive tree farm.

Now, on completion of the purchase, Adolfo was looking perplexed when told by Sebastián he was overwhelmed with the responsibility of taking on a dilapidated farm and, of course, the colossal task of restoring it to productivity.

The irony of this wasn't lost on Sebastián.

'It'll all be fine,' said Adolfo, trying to be reassuring but actually sounding as though he was trying to convince himself. 'As you know, it was built in 1856 by the Governor of Granada, the illegitimate nephew of Queen Isabel the Second. You're preserving a piece of Spanish history. It's a noble cause.'

'Don't give me that nationalistic nonsense, Adolfo. You know perfectly well that the farm is riddled with *carcoma* and the building's falling apart. There's not a straight floor in the place. The previous owners had the irrigation system switched off so the olive trees are in a very poor condition. In fact many of them appear to be dead. So don't you dare tell me I'm getting a good deal here.'

Adolfo threw Sebastián an icy look.

'Well, why did you buy it then, Sebastián?' he asked, reasonably enough.

Sebastián put his elbows on the table and his hands to his head.

'I'm really starting to wonder. I was looking to invest in a country estate. I wasn't looking to take on what's likely to be a three-year project.'

Adolfo said nothing.

'The place had something special about it, I guess,'

volunteered Sebastián, after a significant pause.

He gazed out of the window, as though by looking outside he'd bring the farm into sharper clarity in his mind.

'There's a magical atmosphere to it,' he continued. 'It's still living and vibrant, even as it's fighting for its last breath... You can sense it's a place where people were happy to live, long ago.'

Sebastián looked at Adolfo, noted the confusion on his face and straight away knew he'd lost him.

He could clearly see Adolfo wasn't up to the poetical nuances of his speech. This didn't surprise him much. Adolfo's entire focus in life seemed to consist of the bottom line. Deals, commission, sales targets, these were the things Adolfo understood. The rest of life passed him by.

Sebastián sighed.

He picked up the deeds and the large bag of keys, a bag that was surprisingly heavy until he remembered all the locked doors at the farm.

He stood up.

'Right, thanks for everything, Adolfo.'

Adolfo nodded his head.

'Let me know how you get on.'

'Oh, I have no doubt you'll hear all about it on the Ronda grapevine. As you've told me before, Ronda is a small community.'

Adolfo laughed and they parted on relatively good terms, given the length of their business association. On and off it had taken near enough a year to see this purchase through.

Sebastián stepped outside into the heat of the day and made his way slowly back to his hotel.

He needed time to pull himself together. Most people on

receiving keys to their new property would be rushing to enter it. Sebastián knew that he needed a little space to come to terms with the huge commitment in time and money, as well as emotion, he'd just made.

Later on, as he sat in the bar of the hotel, nursing a cold beer with the sound of the radio in the background, he reflected back to the moment the olive tree farm had first captured his heart.

2

It all began in the summer of 2016 when Sebastián booked a second viewing of Las Nevadas... He knew as soon as he picked up the phone to call the solicitor for another viewing that he was going to buy the place.

It was during this second viewing of the property that he first discovered the olive press.

He'd felt a bubble of excitement building up in him as he looked at the old press, with its fibre disks piled neatly on top of each other.

It was a large, heavy-looking, circular contraption dominating one half of the room.

It had two big cone-shaped millstones for grinding the olives, and, positioned above the two millstones, a hollow inverted cone made of metal.

In a bygone age the freshly picked olives would have been poured into the metallic cone. Stacked against the wall were rusting 5-litre tins with *Las Nevadas Aceite de Oliva Virgen* (Virgin Olive Oil) written on them.

The more he saw of this old olive tree farm the more Sebastián felt captivated by its history and uniqueness.

Sadly, today its olive-processing factory was outdated and redundant but this small slice of Spanish history enthralled him. More than ever he wanted to restore this decaying farm-house and its surrounding acres.

He wanted the farm despite the undeniable fact that it was sadly neglected. The olive trees, which were neatly planted at regular intervals across the farmland, were in terrible condi-tion, having been abandoned to nature several years ago, and the normally bright rust-coloured earth of the farm was now covered with overgrown yellow grass.

Sebastián had looked back out towards the open door. Outside this dark and enclosed ground-floor room the sun was burning inexorably into the white courtyard.

The air outside was still with the fierceness of the heat but the swifts hidden in the cool leaves of the huge palm tree were still chattering with vigour, undeterred.

Today was 5th August, and it happened to be one of the hottest days of the year in Andalucía.

In the refreshing chilliness of the ground-floor factory Sebastián could feel the wet patches of sweat on his white shirt cool and stick uncomfortably to his skin. No doubt his shirt would be covered with dirt too, now, after exploring this abandoned farmhouse. Little satellites of dust floated in the sunlight streaming through the open doorway.

Sebastián walked up to the doorway to call for his brother.

'Felipe!' Sebastián yelled, and waited for a moment for his brother to reply. There was no answer.

Sebastián was in a dark and windowless external room to one side of the courtyard. His brother, meanwhile, had disap-peared to inspect the decaying stables at the back of the old farmhouse building.

After a couple of minutes Sebastián stuck his head out of

the door, squinting in the glare of the sun, and yelled again.

'Felipe!'

'Calm down, calm down, Seb! I'm here. What is it? What's all the excitement about?' Felipe said, as he jogged over to the doorway.

'Come in here and have a look.'

Felipe bent his head and entered the room.

All he could see, initially, was a dilapidated desk and chair on the black and white tiled floor. As his eyes became more accustomed to the darkness after the bright sunlight outside he saw another door against the wall.

He walked up to it and peered into the adjoining room.

'*¡Madre de Dios!* Is that an old olive press?'

'Yes. And it looks like it works, too.'

'Well, I'm glad something is working in this wreck of a place. I still think you're mad to be thinking of buying it. The estate might only be worth a million-and-a-half euros but I reckon you'll end up spending three times that bringing it back to its former glory.'

Sebastián didn't say anything in response.

He didn't need to reply; he already knew his entire family was dead against him buying this *finca,* all 150 hectares of it.

However, from the moment the solicitor had showed him photographs of Las Nevadas he'd fallen in love with it. It was ideally situated, only a mile and a half from Ronda, and had spectacular views to the surrounding mountain range, Sierra Blanquilla.

The house was only a shell of its former self and would need huge amounts of money and manpower to restore it. Wooden beams in the building showed signs of infestation from *carcoma*, or woodworm as it was called in English, and would need to be treated.

Every tiled floor in the house dipped alarmingly and Felipe had actually managed to put a foot through the dining room ceiling when he was inspecting the attic quarters off the kitchen.

Yet every room, from the sitting-room to the bedrooms to the chapel, showed traces of its former majesty.

This house breathed history and had somehow remained relatively unaltered since 1856, when it was built.

The thick interior and exterior walls were bleached white; black painted metal railings covered all the windows. The shutters were painted a traditional bright green and the roof was covered in terracotta tiles. It was a very traditional Spanish *finca*.

After inspecting the old olive press, Felipe and Sebastián walked out of the dark olive factory into the blinding sunshine of the courtyard.

3

In the middle of the courtyard stood the stalwart palm tree, its trunk thickened with age. Within its branches, swifts filled the courtyard with their deafening shrieks.

Sebastián stretched.

'I'm going to have to come back with an architect and a builder so I can get some estimates for the costs going forward.'

Felipe looked at his brother with concern.

'Seb, no, really, you can't. You cannot be seriously contemplating buying this place. It will suck you dry. You'll never get any return for the money you spend on it. And who's going to supervise all the work that needs doing? We don't know anybody in Ronda, or Andalucía for that matter, who is trustworthy enough.'

Sebastián smiled.

'I plan to supervise it all myself.'

Felipe gaped at him, stunned momentarily into silence.

'What about your business? I take it that needs no supervision?' he eventually asked, sarcastic.

Sebastián continued smiling patiently; he had owned a successful public relations company in Madrid for the last eleven years.

'I've someone in mind to hand over the reins to.'

'But why, Seb? I still don't understand it, none of us do. It's like you're having a mid-life crisis or something. What's going to happen when this place drains you of all your money? You know Dad won't help you out.'

'I know that. He won't need to. I'm going to make this place self-funding.'

'How, exactly?'

'I want to provide hospitality for tourists. An elite market. Ronda can cater for a huge section of society. The winter months will attract the serious walkers, cyclists and mountaineers, the spring and summer will be a magnet for those escaping a cold climate.'

'What about the olives?'

'I need to meet up with some other local farmers and pick their brains so I can see what I can do with the olive trees. The trees might be too far gone to be of any use.'

Felipe pondered this.

'It would be a huge risk.'

'I know.'

Felipe grinned.

'Well, don't say you weren't warned by your family.'

'I won't,' Sebastián said shortly, wanting to change the subject. 'Shall we head into town for some tapas?'

'Where will you stay if you're going to be supervising your hospitality project?' asked Felipe, still unable to take his thoughts away from Sebastián's new venture.

'I'll stay at the small villa on the right hand side of the estate, the one we saw at the bottom of the driveway. Do you remember it?'

Felipe nodded.

'It was built relatively recently and happens to be in pretty good condition, despite the fact it's been lying empty for the last eight years. At least that's what Adolfo says. I haven't seen it myself.'

Sebastián tried to recall all the information the solicitor had given him about the small villa.

'Apparently the man who owned the Las Nevadas *finca* had a daughter married to an Englishman. So that they would keep their ties to Spain, he gave them a plot of land on the *finca* to build a holiday house, which they did. Forty years ago. When the olive farm was sold eight years ago, the villa was sold with it.'

'Of course it was. Nobody would be mad enough to buy the *finca* with a privately owned house slap bang in the middle of it. Oh, well. It's clear you have an answer for everything. Let's go and forget about this place.' Felipe shook his head. 'Let's drown ourselves in some Rioja before we head back to Madrid tomorrow. After all, you soon won't be able to pay for my bar tabs.'

Sebastián playfully hit his brother on the shoulder as they walked down the cobbled driveway to where his red Alfa Romeo car was parked in the shade of some trees.

Outside the main farmhouse, the gardens were like a jungle. Two empty decorative pools, filled with decayed leaves, languished on either side of the driveway.

In the distance, on the right hand side, there was a deep pool of rancid water and a tennis court nearby with its metal fencing torn and crumpled, its surface covered in weeds, and grass forcing its way through the tarmac.

Sebastián averted his gaze.

One thing at a time, he thought to himself. There'll be plenty of time to focus on the grounds later. Restoring the farmhouse was the priority just now.

Sebastián and Felipe got into the car, which was as hot as a sauna despite having been left in the shade. Turning on the air conditioning Sebastián reversed the car and drove out of the metal gates at the end of the cobbled driveway.

In front of him, descending in a gentle slope, was the grey gravel road leading out of the estate.

Giant eucalyptus trees lined the road, their pale grey bark peeling and revealing the trees' cardinal red skin underneath. The long viridian green leaves hung down in gentle fluidity, looking slightly wilted, emphasising the brutal dryness of the surrounding landscape.

Sebastián had wondered why the farm seemed to be known locally as *Los Pinos*. The most notable trees were the numerous olive trees and these graceful eucalyptus trees lining the road to the farmhouse.

However, the solicitor had explained that on the west side of the estate there was a small copse of rare Pinsapo pine trees, an ancient tree that was now officially protected by law in Spain.

'So, when are you next coming back here?' asked Felipe, breaking the silence in the car.

Sebastián exhaled loudly and sank his shoulders to release the tension in them.

'To be honest with you, I don't know. It depends on the solicitor.'

Feeling this was an unsatisfactory answer, Sebastián proceeded to explain.

'The seller of the estate is an American pension fund. An average small-town solicitor, working with a global enterprise, could take forever. The wheels of the law turn so slowly here in the south. It's a wonder they manage to run any businesses at all.'

'It's just another way of living, Seb,' Felipe rebuked his brother gently, looking out at the passing landscape. 'It doesn't mean it's wrong. We live life at too fast a pace in Madrid. We could learn a lot from Andalucía.'

'Well, you can see why the rest of Europe blames the southern countries for inefficiency and laxity. The south of Italy has the same problem.'

Felipe waved his hands irritably.

'Don't get started on politics, Seb, for heaven's sake. I like the way southerners savour life. We don't need to be puritanical about it. If you're going to settle here you're going to have to get used to it. You just have to harness the best of the southern mentality and use it to your advantage. It'll certainly suit tourists escaping hectic lifestyles.'

'Yes, that's true,' agreed Sebastián, as they drove into the crowded streets of Ronda. Ronda had an inexplicable one-way system in place and he struggled to grasp it. Ignoring the sudden blast of car horns he turned abruptly towards their hotel, cutting across a number of cars heading in the opposite direction.

'By the way, do yourself a favour, Seb, and get yourself a driver. Your driving isn't getting any better,' muttered Felipe, extricating himself with obvious relief from the car.

Sebastián smiled complicitly at his brother as they walked into the hotel. Sebastián's driving skills were the subject of a great deal of hilarity within their family. His mother tended to be the most vocal in condemnation of his driving skills, mostly because she worried about him the most.

4

Sebastián liked the Hotel María Cristina because it gave him a view of the street called Carrera Espinal, or La Calle de la Bola as the locals liked to call it.

He felt in its own way this long street was the beating heart of this small city, in the same way La Rambla was in Barcelona or the Gran Vía was in Madrid.

On the outskirts of Ronda, in the industrial sector, there were various large multinational stores including, of all things, an Aldi supermarket. But here in Carrera Espinal the tourists, the serious shoppers and the loiterers lingered.

It was a street to potter along, nobody would be in a hurry, and at certain times of the day half the town's population would gather here to catch up on gossip.

Apart from siesta time, from half past two to five o'clock in the afternoon when the shops would shut, this street was always busy with people, especially in August when the tourist season was in full swing.

However, with the latest heatwave hitting Andalucía hard, shops were opening even later than normal in Ronda and the city had become a ghost town during the hottest hours of the day.

At nine o'clock at night, in the coolness of the evening, the city came to life again, with all ages enjoying the milder temperatures outside and strolling the streets once more.

Sebastián often asked himself if anyone ever did any work when he saw the locals gathered in numerous groups outside the cafés, chattering away as if they didn't have a care in the world. Unemployment in Andalucía was high but he'd still to see the industriousness and commitment to work he saw in his office in Madrid.

Maybe Felipe's right, he thought. We all need to take life a little less seriously and learn ways to take away the stress that's so detrimental to our health.

However, he knew Felipe was hardly a good example to follow.

As if to run counter to his older brother, Felipe had managed to tank out of school with very few qualifications and had restlessly moved from job to job until he decided to invest the inheritance gifted to him by his grandfather on property in Romania.

He'd disappeared to Romania for eight years and then reappeared two years ago in Madrid, apparently unscathed by his experience and with enough income to be able to lead a life of relative leisure.

His family never questioned him but always received him with open arms when he turned up.

The Spanish culture of strong blood ties was very marked in their family, Sebastián thought, musing on Felipe's role. No matter what Felipe got up to, his engaging grin and magnetic charm would always guarantee him a place in the family. As for Sebastián, he valued Felipe's honesty and the way he didn't judge his fellow beings.

Sebastián, lacking family support for his latest project, had found a new appreciation for Felipe's easy-going temperament.

Sebastián shook himself as he felt the weariness from the hot afternoon hit him. He opened his bedroom window to let the air cool the room as the evening descended and made his way down the tiled stairs to the bar, where no doubt Felipe would have already got himself a glass of local Rioja and be chatting away to the bartender.

5

May 2017

It took a long nine-and-a-half months after they'd last viewed the property for it to be time to sign the contract for the olive tree farm.

Sebastián looked at his watch with resigned patience as he sat in the relative comfort of the air-conditioned solicitor's office.

Here in Ronda everything runs at a different pace, he thought to himself. He found the incompetence and inefficiencies of the staff at this particular office baffling.

Here he was, trying to close a deal he'd been pursuing since August 2016, and he still didn't know for sure if it was going ahead.

It was now May 2017 and he was sitting for the fifth time in this office, hoping the solicitor would tell him that the contract had completed between both parties involved in the sale and purchase of the olive tree farm.

The offer he'd put in for the farm, after viewing it for a second time, had initially received no immediate response as the owners were based across the Atlantic.

The farm had been bought at the height of the market in 2007 by an American pension fund for twenty-five million euros and now in 2017 Sebastián was about to seal the deal for a meagre one-and-a-half million euros.

A bargain.

Of sorts.

The olive farm had been left totally neglected and abandoned for the last eight years.

Combine the slow bureaucracy across the Atlantic with the torturously laid-back attitude of a provincial solicitor and, to be frank, many others would have given up the chase by now.

Sebastián bent his head and rubbed vigorously at his forehead, which thankfully still had a full thatch of hair and no receding hairline, unlike his older brother and father.

He began to daydream as he waited for the solicitor to appear.

May had brought an unprecedented amount of rain to Andalucía and the drive up to Ronda had revealed hills clad in a coating of green vegetation, unusual at this time of year.

The climate in Ronda was pleasantly warm, and killing time this morning he'd enjoyed wandering among the gardens in the nineteenth-century park, Alameda del Tajo, with its frightening and vertiginous views above the gorge.

The views from there were utterly amazing.

No wonder the Moors had established a fortress in Ronda in 711 AD, thought Sebastián. They must have displaced a good number of golden eagles in the process, too. On one side, the city of Ronda itself was like an eyrie, perched right on the edge of vertical cliff faces.

Sebastián stretched his arms out and yawned, releasing the tension in his shoulders.

Here in Casa Valiente estate agent and solicitors' office he'd been seated in the comfortable leather chair for forty minutes while Adolfo had popped in and out of the office to consult with his superior.

The solicitor's desk was very tidy, which did not suggest this firm was doing a brisk trade in property sales and rentals.

Maybe the American pension fund had been misled by the central location of this estate agent and its plush office environment. Casa Valiente also had an impressively slick website advertising its portfolio.

It was just a pity its customer service did not live up to expectations, Sebastián thought.

Finally, the door to the office opened and Adolfo appeared again, looking slightly bewildered, which for some reason intensely irritated Sebastián.

'OK, Sebastián. Good news! I've got the signed contract from the Abacus Fund. It was apparently faxed last week and the secretary put it away in the file without notifying me. Sorry for the wait. Now, once you've signed it you'll have a completed contract setting the date of entry as...' Adolfo faltered slightly and looked intently at the contract.

'The sixteenth of July,' Sebastián said with admirable patience.

Not willing to take his client's word for it, Adolfo continued reading the contract.

'Yes, that's right,' he finally said, reluctantly. 'The sixteenth of July.'

Adolfo opened the contract at the signature page and passed over a smart ballpoint pen for Sebastián to sign with.

Sebastián decided to have his revenge for Adolfo's endless procrastinations. He went to the start of the contract and proceeded to read it slowly while Adolfo sat down opposite him with pursed lips and began to tap his fingers impatiently on the desk.

Finally, after twenty minutes of giving the contract close

scrutiny (something his lawyer had already done for him a couple of months ago), Sebastián signed the contract and handed it over.

'Right. There's still a few things we've to discuss.'

Sebastián looked at Adolfo with mingled surprise and suspicion.

Why was he mentioning this now when Sebastián had just signed the contract?

6

Noticing the surprised look on Sebastián's face, Adolfo cleared his throat, seemingly ill at ease.

'As you probably know, Ronda's a small community.' Adolfo paused for a moment, as if unsure how to proceed. 'The family who owned the estate before the Americans bought it were well known here. Three generations of the same family have owned that farm. They had many people working for them, keeping it running.'

Adolfo paused for a minute to fiddle with his pen.

'One family worked for the original owners for many years, living in a small apartment off the main building. And this family is still living at the farm.'

Adolfo met Sebastián's eyes for the first time.

'They just carried on working for the Americans when they took over. They're still there.'

Sebastián felt utterly perplexed.

'Why was I not told about this before now?'

Adolfo shifted uneasily in his chair.

'It's not really relevant to the contract. The decision is yours to make.'

'What decision?'

'It's for you to decide whether you keep the family on at the farm or not. They've always kept an eye on things while the owners were away or abroad. The father, Emilio Gordillo, is an elderly widower now.'

Sebastián leaned forward and looked intently at Adolfo.

There seemed to be something strange about all of this but he couldn't read Adolfo's expression. When he chose, Adolfo seemed to be an expert at revealing nothing with his facial expression.

Even so, Sebastián sensed Adolfo was tied in some obscure way to these people.

'It's very clear no one's managing the farm now. So why exactly are they still there?'

'When the Americans bought up the farm, Emilio and his children stayed on at the downstairs apartment, basically to make sure no one broke into the house or caused trouble on the estate. The olive tree farm itself has been left to moulder and hasn't been maintained. The Americans weren't interested in the olive trees. It was purely a development opportunity for them.'

Adolfo looked out of the window for a moment and sniffed in disgust.

'The Americans had always intended to build a golf resort and helipad on the estate, but when the new mayor of Ronda came in planning permission was denied. Something about environmental concerns because of the golden eagles living in the area, or some such thing... Also, not long after the Americans bought the farm, property prices crashed in the south of Spain. Planning permission was then tightened for new developments, so the housing market wouldn't continue to depreciate.'

Adolfo turned to face Sebastián again.

'Anyway this family, they're still waiting to hear what their fate is.' He touched the tips of his fingers together. 'I suggest at the earliest possible opportunity, when you next visit the house, you meet with them and have a chat with them. Make whatever arrangements you think best.'

'What if they refuse to go? I need to know what their legal rights are.'

'Yes, I've looked into that. As far as Spanish law goes, at the moment, once they have completed their three-year tenancy (which they have) you are within your rights to ask them to leave, with notice of course. However, I know the family and I don't think they'll be difficult. You might even find it useful to keep them at the apartment while the repairs and all the construction to the main house are getting done.'

Sebastián nodded, taking this in, but refusing to commit to anything.

'You say "family". How many of them are there?'

Adolfo laughed superciliously, which had the inevitable effect of making Sebastián's temper rise.

'Emilio Gordillo had thirteen children, would you believe it?'

Adolfo caught the sudden look of apprehension and shock on Sebastián's face and hastened to reassure him.

'Don't panic. All of them are independent now, except for a daughter and son, Nuria and José Luis.'

Sebastián nodded numbly, taking all this in.

'You know, Emilio Gordillo was very friendly with the previous owners. He might be able to advise you on the original state of the house. He spent all of his childhood there,' carried on Adolfo, helpfully.

He brushed his arms deftly, smoothing the creases on his suit.

'He's an old man now. I know you're keen to conserve the

traditional aspects of the house, even if it's going to need quite extensive building work done to it. He'll be able to help you with that. He has a long memory.'

'Adolfo, I'm not sure Emilio would be keen to help me, especially if they're all going to have to move out of their home,' said Sebastián, voicing his scepticism.

Adolfo smiled patronisingly at him.

'Emilio would help anyone who'd restore Las Nevadas back to its former grandeur. He loves that place, irrespective of what becomes of him.'

Sebastián pondered this for a moment, unconvinced.

'Hold on a minute. I've visited the farm twice so far and I saw nobody there. They can't be keeping that much of an eye on the place.'

Adolfo chuckled.

'Oh, Nuria will have seen you. She's not keen on meeting visitors and we always phone before we take anyone up there. But she's never far from the farmhouse. Her brother's not all there and she likes to keep an eye on him. He seems to spend most of his time whittling away at wood in the workshop.'

Sebastián thought back to his last visit and wondered if he'd seen the workshop. He couldn't recall any part of the huge building that could've been called a workshop.

'You seem to know an awful lot about them. Do you know them personally?'

Adolfo nodded reluctantly, as though he were afraid of being implicated in some unanticipated legal argument. 'I went to school with Nuria. She was in my class until she dropped out at the age of sixteen.'

Sebastián nodded. It made sense. Ronda was a small place.

'She's no oil painting, but once you've met her you'll never forget her.'

Sebastián chose to ignore this cutting observation. He considered it to be made in poor taste, but having dealt with Adolfo for nine months he felt it was typical of the man.

He doubted Emilio would be disposed to help him with his renovations. Adolfo seemed to have the sensitivity of a bull in a china shop. With the best will in the world, Emilio would surely feel Sebastián was an upstart usurper of his childhood home.

Adolfo seemed to have no other pressing business to occupy him but Sebastián had left his business in Madrid in the hands of a relatively inexperienced manager and was anxious to get back as soon as possible.

He decided it was time to go and stood up.

'Thank you, Adolfo. I really appreciate all you've done. I hope to be back in the middle of June, as agreed with the Abacus Fund, to have a quick look at the house again with Piedra.'

'Ah yes, Piedra Tanote? An excellent builder. Even so it might be too big a job for his firm. We're just a small provincial town, after all.'

'He comes highly recommended and I'm sure his team will be up to the task. He seems keen, anyway.'

'Yes, of course he'll be keen. It'll be a very lucrative contract to rebuild the house. Still...'

'What?' asked Sebastián impatiently, eager to get going but wanting to know what Adolfo had to say.

'Nothing. It's not my concern.'

'Adolfo, for pity's sake, tell me.'

'Builders here go at their own pace and they don't always

work to schedule. It might be too big a job for Piedra's firm. Anyway, it's not my responsibility, thankfully.'

Adolfo shook hands with Sebastián, and as Sebastián left the office he could feel Adolfo's eyes on his back.

Sebastián could tell he'd not be surprised to see him, defeated and overwhelmed, back in his office six months after having bought the farm, asking for it to be put up for sale again.

They both knew it was going to be a Herculean task to restore the *finca* to any normality.

7

July 2017

All these flashbacks from the past raced through Sebastián's head as he lay on his hotel bed.

He spent the first half of that night staring at the sack of keys on the hotel dressing table. Every time he tried to sleep the keys made their presence felt.

Finally, at three o'clock in the morning he got up, lifted the sack of keys off the dressing table and put it on the cupboard floor, out of sight.

Then he started to write a list of things he had to do later that day, foremost of which was meeting the family currently living in the apartment at the farm.

He needed to make some quick decisions regarding the farmhouse and the surrounding acres, but he had no idea what to do with the Gordillo family. An old man, his son and daughter were hardly adequate guards for the estate, especially now there'd be building materials about the place.

He had a horrible feeling the whole situation would end up being a moral dilemma, not a practical business decision, which was hardly the start he wanted for the old farm. Ruthless decisions would have to be made.

He decided to head up to the farm later that morning, unannounced, and see if he could catch the elusive Gordillo family going about their business.

With this thought in mind he finally fell asleep.

The next morning, at half past eight, he was woken by the sound of shop shutters rattling as they opened, resonating outside his window. Calle de la Bola was getting ready for the day ahead. Sebastián got up to draw back the curtains and was blinded by the bright sunshine in the process. The light hammered his tired brain.

He stumbled to the bathroom and had a look in the mirror. Ignoring the dark shadows under his eyes that made him look on the verge of death, he took a long, hard look at himself.

He could see a middle-aged man with black hair, except at the sides where fine white hairs were starting to creep in. His face was square and suggested a firmness in character, except for his eyes.

His eyes gave him away.

They were the eyes of a dreamer. Light brown, large and with long eyelashes, they glimmered with health, but also with a strange kind of detachment. Eyes are meant to be the windows into the soul. And here he was, the dreamer, buying up a dilapidated old olive tree farm with what seemed just now a hopeless vision. It was a vision of making the farm self-sufficient, restoring some of its original antiquity and bringing visitors of all kinds to enjoy country life here in rural Andalucía.

Sebastián stretched out his broad shoulders, twisting his neck to the right and then the left, before bending down to the sink to splash cold water on his face.

8

At about ten o'clock Sebastián indicated right, turned off the road and drove into the driveway leading up to the Las Nevadas farmhouse. He parked, as usual, in the shade of the trees near the entrance and got out of the car.

The small door in front of him was open. It had been cut out of the gigantic, bright green double doors leading into the main farmhouse.

This was positive, thought Sebastián. It suggested someone was around.

Suddenly, out of the quietness, a motor started up loudly. Sebastián turned round in a circle, trying to gauge where the sound was coming from. It seemed to him to issue from a corner on the right hand side of the garden.

He walked in the direction of the noise. The motor stopped for a moment and he could hear the crashing of a branch falling down. As he pushed through some overgrown bushes, he saw a metal ladder set against a tree.

He looked up, taking his sunglasses off to get a better view.

At the top of a ladder there was a slender woman in dungarees, with her back to him, inspecting the tree where she'd just lopped off a branch. In her gloved hand was a small chainsaw; despite her slim frame she was clearly strong, for she carried it in one hand with ease.

Not wanting to startle her, Sebastián sat down on the shallow edge of the decorative pool and waited for her to come down. After starting up the chainsaw again and neatening up the stub left behind, the woman descended the ladder nimbly.

Sebastián waited until she reached the ground before speaking. 'Hi.'

The woman jumped and turned quickly to look at him.

Sebastián saw she was of average height, slight, but he could see the wiry strength in her arms and legs. This was a woman who was used to physical work. Her face was nut brown and lined, suggesting she was used to spending a lot of her time outdoors.

'I take it you're Nuria?'

She nodded slowly, appraising Sebastián.

'I'm Sebastián Ortez, the new owner of Las Nevadas. I take it you've been told about me.'

'Yes, I'd been told. I'm Nuria Gordillo.'

Nuria took her glove off and held out her hand.

Sebastián shook it, feeling the rough calloused skin on her hand. Nuria's grip was firm and strong.

'I need to have a chat with your family. I have builders arriving here next week and we need to come to an agreement regarding the apartment you're living in.'

Sebastián caught a fleeting look of anxiety in Nuria's black eyes.

Adolfo had described Nuria as no oil painting but he'd been very harsh.

Yes, Nuria was definitely unusual, but immediately Sebastián noticed that she was in fact extremely attractive in her own individual way. She seemed to be wearing no make-up but her dark skin was smooth and blemish-free, except where the lines around her eyes and mouth cut into her face. Her features were symmetrical; a harsh critic might have declared her mouth and nose too wide, but her eyes were large and very beautiful. They were so dark they shone like twin pools of obsidian.

'Yes. We were expecting you. Would you like to come and have a cup of coffee? My father will be at home and I'll probably find my brother in the workshop.'

'Ah, yes. I've heard of this workshop but I don't recall seeing it when we toured the farm.'

'It's easy to miss because it's behind the main entrance to the house. It used to be a garage but in the end nobody bothered to park in it because it's easier to park in the main courtyard. So the garage became a workshop of sorts.'

Nuria turned and took down the heavy ladder. Sebastián didn't offer to help as he sensed she would've been offended by the suggestion she couldn't manage by herself.

'If you don't mind me asking, why are you cutting branches off the tree?'

'These trees need to be trimmed, all of them. There used to be a multitude of beautiful *Mirabilis* flowers growing here among the trees but since the trees have been left to their own devices the flowers have all been smothered. For now, I only remove the branches that have died or are diseased. It's very basic maintenance. Could you carry the ladder?'

Sebastián nodded and accepted the ladder as Nuria turned, carrying the chainsaw, and led the way back to the farm courtyard. Nuria unlocked a door at the end of the courtyard and dumped the equipment in it. It was clearly used for storage; in the darkness Sebastián could see all kinds of well-kept gardening tools. Clearly, at one time, the gardens had been well maintained.

Sebastián, mentally noting the fact that Nuria had a key to the storage room, wondered how many other keys this family had access to.

Nuria, with a purposeful stride, turned left, walking down the side of the farmhouse until she reached the back of it. Sebastián followed, even though she hadn't invited him to come with her.

A large sliding door at the side of the wall, which had been locked on Sebastián's previous visits to the farm, was now half open.

Nuria walked up to it and disappeared through it. Intrigued, Sebastián followed her in.

The smell of freshly cut wood wafted in the air. Sebastián felt himself walk over a soft carpet of wood shavings. Several workstations were set up in this large room and, with rigid neatness, tools of every description hung on the walls. Shelves were stacked with wooden bowls and jugs.

On the floor, beside the sliding door, was a huge pile of wood. Sebastián, with a shock, realised that it was made up of the remnants of olive trees.

At the far end of the room sat a man who hadn't registered their presence at all. He was large and broad, dressed in denim and with shoulder-length dark brown hair. He was absorbed in carving the wood in front of him with a chisel.

'José Luis. This is Sebastián Ortez, who's just bought the farm.'

José Luis didn't move an inch. He carried on cutting away at the wood in front of him as though his life depended on it.

Sebastián went over to the shelves and had a look at the objects on them. He picked out a bowl. To his surprise for such a rudimentary workshop, it was beautifully carved. He carefully put it back.

'José Luis,' Nuria said impatiently, trying to get his attention. José Luis ignored her.

Exasperated, Nuria went up to him, took his chin in her hand and looked him in the eye.

José Luis quickly looked away but obediently stopped what he was doing.

'Do you want to come and have coffee with us?'

José Luis looked swiftly at Sebastián and shook his head.

'OK. That's fine. Me and dad will take care of it.'

Nuria turned and walked out of the workshop.

'I'm sorry about that. He doesn't like it when anything interrupts his work. He doesn't like meeting strangers either.'

'It's fine. I'm impressed by the work he does. It's certainly of a high quality.'

'Yes, he's become very good at it. He sells a fair portion of his work in the tourist shops in Ronda.'

'Where does he get the wood from?'

Nuria turned and looked at Sebastián, forthright.

'From here on the farm, of course. If you think any of these trees are going to be of use to you, you'd be deceiving yourself. These trees are diseased and decayed. They'll never return to health now. You'd be better off starting afresh.'

9

Nuria led Sebastián to the apartment, which was on the right of the arch leading to the two huge doors at the entrance of the courtyard. Sebastián had seen it before, but when he'd visited none of the Gordillo family were around.

By the window, in the sitting-room, Emilio Gordillo was seated in a large armchair. He looked up as they entered. His face was a mass of wrinkles but his eyes, black like Nuria's, looked at Sebastián intelligently. Clearly the old man was still sharp.

This should be interesting, Sebastián thought.

As they came in, bending their heads because the doorway was so low, Emilio stood up. He was a small man but he had a certain grace and dignity. He shook Sebastián's outstretched hand and sat back down again.

Emilio gestured at the sofa in front of him. 'Take a seat.'

'Thank you. I'm guessing Adolfo or the estate agent's office has already told you I'm the new owner of Las Nevadas.'

'Yes, of course they have,' assented Emilio, politely.

'I've some difficult decisions to make with this estate. I need it to break even, better still, make a profit. It's running at a loss just now.'

Sebastián leaned back on the sofa.

'I have the builder, Piedra Tanote, and his team of builders arriving next week to start work on the house. At the end of this week a pest control team are coming to see if we can save any of the beams in the house and rid them of any existing *carcoma*. I think, from what Piedra was saying, some of the exposed wooden beams will have to be replaced.'

Emilio nodded in agreement, his face expressionless. Sebastián unconsciously clenched his hands.

'Anyway, Adolfo's explained to me your situation. Because I can't be here all the time, I do need someone trustworthy to be a security guard at the farm, especially with all the building materials that'll be around.'

Sebastián took a deep breath.

'I'll be looking to recruit someone with experience, someone who's properly qualified. Otherwise, I doubt I'll be insured. I think it might be time for you guys to move on from this farm.'

'Yes, we were expecting you to say that.'

Sebastián felt relieved. This was going better than he expected.

He turned to look at Nuria who was sitting next to him on the sofa. She looked absolutely devastated. She got up quickly when she saw him looking at her and hurriedly left the room.

Confused, he looked back at Emilio.

Emilio smiled reassuringly at him.

'Don't worry about her. She's thinking of her brother. He's not good with change. But change always comes and we'll just have to deal with it as best we can. We expected this. José Luis and I are dead wood. We're of no use to anybody. However, I'd advise you not to write off Nuria. She's an excellent gardener and cook. She could be useful to you.'

Sebastián didn't say anything but he wasn't convinced. The gardens at the front of the farmhouse were a mess.

'She hasn't been working on the gardens here,' continued Emilio, as though reading his thoughts. 'She doesn't work for free. She works mostly on the gardens in the housing complex further along the Ronda–Ardales road. She has a great reputation as a gardener and, actually, for honesty too – a rare thing around here, let me tell you.'

Emilio waved towards the window.

'How else do you think we survive here? We've been given this apartment to live in but they paid me the minimum wage. Not that I'm any use now as a guard, as you've rightly pointed out. Having said that, who else would want to live out here in the sticks, on such low pay?'

Emilio fell silent and looked at Sebastián for a moment.

'What would you like us to do?'

Sebastián paused.

He looked around the small sitting-room. The walls were covered in photographs and a couple of rustic still-life paintings. The furniture was immaculate and there were a few well-polished ornaments on the sideboard. All of it suggested a home that was well-loved.

He felt a twinge of admiration for this old man, who was so bravely confronting an uncertain future. He was willing to engage with Sebastián, to discuss moving on, but Sebastián was the coward here, shying away from ousting this family from their home.

He looked back at Emilio.

'Would you know anyone who'd be suitable to work as a guard here?'

Emilio shook his head.

'I don't think it's going to be easy. Anyone young isn't going to want to be stuck here. They'll want to be in Ronda where the action is. We can ask around if you like.'

Sebastián nodded. He was stuck, as he'd foreseen, in a moral dilemma.

Nuria appeared with a tray, a coffee jug and three espresso cups.

'Would you like some coffee?' she asked Sebastián. He nodded and absently took the cup and saucer from her.

'Your father says you're a first-class gardener.'

Nuria smiled affectionately at her father.

'He exaggerates. It pays the bills and I enjoy it.'

'Well, I have to tell you I've something of a dilemma here. You've been here for a long time, out of misplaced loyalty to the estate, or out of necessity, I don't know. But I have to make some sensible decisions. I'm not even certain buying this place was a sensible decision. Time will tell.'

Sebastián took a long sip of coffee and drained the cup. He felt the caffeine hit the spot like rocket fuel. He put the cup down and sat forward with his elbows resting on his legs.

'Aside from an experienced security guard, I'm going to need an experienced gardener to take on the gardens, the tennis court and the pools. Quite frankly, I was focusing mainly on the house, but the gardens are the first thing you see when you arrive here.'

He cleared his throat.

'I'm happy to take you on as a head gardener, Nuria, and let you all stay on here in the apartment. I'll pay you a decent salary but you're going to have to hand in your notice for your current gardening jobs, and recruit at least another couple of gardeners to help you.'

Unsurprisingly Nuria and Emilio looked stunned. They looked at Sebastián uncertainly. He didn't blame them; he was feeling increasingly volatile in his decision-making. He smiled at them, trying to reassure them.

'I'll need a cook too if I'm going to be supervising the building work all day, so if you don't mind, Nuria, I'd really appreciate it if you'd be willing to help me with that once a day, at least until things settle down a bit. I'm a poor cook and I've a feeling Piedra's going to be calling on me a lot at the start.'

Nuria nodded, looking perplexed.

'What about José Luis?'

'What about him?'

'Can he still use the garage as his workshop? It's all he lives for.'

'For now, yes. I can't say so indefinitely. Actually, come to think of it, if I ever do get tourists in the door, I'm sure they'll be interested to see the workshop. But all of that's a long way away.'

Before he could say anything else, Nuria threw her arms around him and hugged him tightly. He could see tears glistening in her eyes but she was smiling at him.

'I'm sorry. It just means so much to us. You see, José Luis would never cope without his beloved woodcarving. He loves it here, it's the only place he can truly be himself. He's not really accepted anywhere else.'

It was Sebastián's turn to look confused.

'He's autistic, you see. People here are very provincial. Very narrow-minded. They've no understanding or tolerance of people who are different.'

10

A week later, Sebastián was looking at the exposed beams under the archway to the courtyard with Piedra the builder. Above this archway, inside the house, ran a long corridor that led to the main bedrooms and the chapel.

'Apart from a couple of beams, the rest of it looks stable. The floors upstairs are uneven because of the sand they used long ago as a filler between the beams. With time it has moved and filtered through the plasterwork,' Piedra said, gazing up. He pointed at the plasterwork between the wood.

'If pest control declare the beams safe from the *carcoma* infestation, I would conserve them. We can replace the ones that are too weak. It's part of the traditional style of the house, these exposed wooden beams. We could then take up the floors in the house upstairs and clean out the area between the beams and put insulation down instead. You'll need it in the winter. I would then suggest putting down a hardwood floor but that would be up to you to decide. If you wanted tiles we'd have to put down plywood flooring first.'

Sebastián nodded.

Piedra came highly recommended to him from a number of sources, but the main recommendation came from the manager of Ronda's provincial Unicaja Bank. Sebastián thought this could only be a good thing given he'd just taken out a large mortgage with them and the bank would clearly be interested in recouping its money safely. The manager wasn't going to recommend a building firm that wasn't trustworthy.

So far he was pleased with Piedra, although when Piedra started to talk about storage tanks, boilers and solar-generated hot water and heating Sebastián felt completely lost and wished he'd explain things in layman's terms. But the builder clearly knew his stuff.

He was a short, squat man with a creased face, not unlike a gargoyle's, but open and gentle in its expression. He was respectful but also blunt when needed.

Earlier on in the day he'd inspected the attic of the rambling farmhouse, shown Sebastián which beams would have to be replaced and suggested putting in steel girders to strengthen the roof of the house. The stables at the back of the house needed to be rebuilt.

All the wooden shutters and doors in the house would have to be repainted, as would the iron *rejas*, or grilles, on every window.

Much to Sebastián's relief, Piedra seemed to think the *carcoma* damage had been contained. There were telltale holes in the wood but they weren't of recent origin. It looked as though one of the previous owners had taken care to treat the holes before things got out of hand. Pest control would be the ones to confirm this later in the week.

An architect was taking care of the main body of the house. He was working on plans to divide up the space into eight en suite bedrooms. At the back of the farm, and outside the large walls of the farmhouse, planning permission was being sought to build a cluster of ten self-catering mews homes.

The swimming pool, next to the front garden, was going to be enlarged and remodelled to make it child friendly. Its maintenance would be left to Nuria and the two gardeners working for her.

On the right hand side of the farmhouse grounds there was a small orchard. Sebastián hoped this could be enlarged, enough to provide some of the provender for the guests staying at Las Nevadas.

At present there were a few plum, fig and peach trees, some in poor condition like the olive trees. The fig trees seemed to be the most robust; at present their branches were heavy with hanging fruit. Nuria had brought him a basket of the soft figs a couple of days ago.

Nuria was optimistic that with a new greenhouse keeping out the field mice and rats they'd be able to grow cucumbers, tomatoes, peppers and watermelon. She also suggested starting a vineyard as many other farms in the vicinity had done.

Like Piedra, Nuria was respectful towards Sebastián but both were clearly aware he was a city boy with minimum knowledge of the countryside. Because of Sebastián's huge gaps of knowledge both of them were keen to educate him, as well as advise him about what, in their opinion, was best to do with this old farmhouse.

11

Sebastián set up his office in the room next to the old olive press. He felt the press should be his inspiration for restoring this farm to productivity.

His desk was already covered in paperwork; all of it was related to the farmhouse. He was just trying to figure out Piedra's estimate for materials for the kitchen and dining room renovations when he heard a sharp knock at the door.

'Come in.'

Nuria poked her head through the door. As usual she was dressed in filthy dungarees, but with the addition this time of a couple of muddy streaks across her cheeks where she must have unknowingly rubbed the backs of her hands. He felt tempted to wipe them away for her, but he knew she was so independently minded she would no doubt take it as an affront.

'Hi Sebastián, sorry to disturb you, but we're wondering what you wanted us to do with the layout of the trees in the garden.'

Fed up with everyone constantly asking his permission to do things, he resisted the urge to say 'do anything you want' and got up.

'Yes, of course. Let's go and look at them.'

When he stepped outside he saw the two other gardeners Nuria had recruited, Iván and Jorge, patiently waiting with Nuria. They were both very young but obviously pleased to be working.

Too many young people here in Andalucía are without work, he thought. One of the few perks of this project was being able to give a job to those who clearly wanted to work and earn some money.

They walked out through the archway and the large double doors to the front of the farmhouse, the two young gardeners walking at a respectful distance behind them.

Nuria walked down the paved road until she stood exactly in the middle between the two gardens.

'Right, these gardens used to be symmetrical, as you can see by the fact we've two identical feature pools on either side of this driveway, with an ash tree planted in the middle of each in its own cemented container. It's clear the rest of the trees were planted to add to this symmetry but since the gardens have been left more or less to their own devices a few rogue trees have stolen in and are occupying space that would be better served for flower beds, as originally intended.'

Nuria looked at Sebastián to check he was following her line of thought. He nodded brusquely at her.

Nuria went up to the beginning of the garden.

'Here we have two almond trees on either side of the drive-way...' she walked down to the far end of the garden, 'and here are two more. Thankfully all of them are in good condition.'

She then made her way through the undergrowth and put her hand on a small tree growing at an awkward angle.

'This is a rogue ash tree. It has nothing to do with the rest of the garden. As you can see it isn't fully grown yet. I would suggest cutting this one down.'

She pushed through more undergrowth until she got to the far side of the garden.

'This is a holm oak and there's an identical one on the other side. Both of these should be conserved. There's also a carob tree on each side but again we have three of them growing where they shouldn't, and blocking light for the flowers.'

'Sorry, tell me again, which are the carob trees?'

Iván, anxious to prove himself, pointed the trees out to Sebastián.

'OK. I get the point. So we cut those down as well, then?'

Nuria nodded in agreement and pointed to a space on the left hand side, beyond the garden.

'And there's a cork oak tree, over there, on the other side of the cypress hedge lining the driveway. I've no idea what it's doing there.'

Sebastián looked across the driveway at the cork tree.

A distant memory of driving through a beautiful cork oak forest in the province of Cádiz sprang to his mind. Those trees had had a certain dignity and majesty, despite having strange red trunks where the outer layer of cork had been removed.

'It's not in the main garden so I'd prefer to conserve it. It makes me sad to take away too many trees. I get we need to have tidy gardens at the front of the house but this oak is growing away from the garden and I have a weakness for oak trees. It's very typical of here, a feature if you like.'

Nuria smiled to herself.

Is she smiling at my sentimentality, wondered Sebastián? He felt slightly defensive and tried to remind himself he was boss here.

Nuria, meanwhile, had moved on with characteristic decisiveness.

'OK, I wanted to suggest planting some orange trees on the

path to the pool area where there's a lot of sun and not much exposure, so they won't get the cold wind hitting them directly in the winter. There's no point trying to plant lemon trees at this altitude. They don't cope well with the frost and snow we get from time to time.'

Nuria looked towards the pool with its dirty brownish green water.

'I would also recommend planting a large willow tree in the area next to the swimming pool. It will provide a nice bit of shade for those that want it and they're very attractive trees. Also it'll benefit from the pool overflow, when the pool releases its water and is refilled.'

She took Sebastián by the arm right into the garden on the left hand side of the driveway. She bent down and scrabbled in the mud for a bit.

She looked up at Sebastián.

'See this?' she said, pointing to the ground with her soiled hands.

He looked down and saw what looked like a black plastic tube buried in the earth.

'Yes, what is it?'

'This is part of the old irrigation system. It'll be full of holes after all this time. I suggest we get as much of it out as we can and make use of the decorative pools. There's a miniature aqueduct behind each. In the old days, once a day, the overflow from the pool would travel along the aqueduct and then down funnels built into the ground to keep the gardens fresh. I think we could revive that old system without having to put in a new irrigation system.'

He nodded again.

'That makes sense.'

'And as for the flowers,' Nuria said quickly, sensing Sebastián was beginning to tire of the conversation, 'I was thinking of putting in mainly *Mirabilis jalapa*, the four o'clock flower as they sometimes call it, in a variety of colours. It's been planted in these gardens for decades.'

'The four o'clock flower?' repeated Sebastián, his interest caught. 'Why's it called that?'

'It opens up in the afternoon and stays open throughout the night. It emits a lovely scent. I'd also try and grow some jasmine on trellises under the windows because they also let out a sweet perfume. It'll be nice to smell it in the summer when the windows are open.'

'Yes, I agree, all of that sounds very good. I'm happy for you to get started as soon as you can, Nuria. Thanks, guys.'

Sebastián smiled and nodded politely to the two younger men and then walked back to his office at a fast pace before Nuria came up with any more ideas. She was full of enthusiasm for the garden project, no doubt born of the fact this place felt like home to her, but Sebastián could only cope with so much information.

He had the builders, joiners, plumbers and the architect consulting him on a daily basis. It was proving a little wearing.

12

Later on in the day, at around half past two, Nuria yelled out his name through the apartment window. This was his cue to join the Gordillo family for some lunch.

Sebastián looked forward to these lunches. Apart from the loneliness of being so far away from his own family, he liked the laid-back, unceremonial attitude of this family.

José Luis, having been rigidly silent for the first few meals, now felt comfortable enough to venture his own opinions during the lunchtime conversation. For someone who was a virtual recluse, José Luis demonstrated a surprising awareness of what was going on around him.

He didn't hang around for long, though; the workshop seemed to call to him like an obsession or an addiction.

Sebastián found Emilio Gordillo a wonderful source on the history of the farmhouse.

In another life Emilio would've probably been a historian. He was so intensely enthusiastic about anything historical. Sebastián soon found Emilio's sharp mind was able to remember things from the past in minute detail.

The most enjoyable time of the day for Sebastián was, when having eaten well and helped with the washing up, the pair of them looked over photographs of the old farmhouse before it was sold to the American pension fund.

In the photographs, rooms were full of classic, beautifully carved antique furniture. Huge mirrors hung on the walls of the sitting-rooms, as well as a life-sized full-length portrait of the matriarch of the family, Amaya Arismendi.

She was a beautiful woman with a rather severe expression, which apparently (according to Emilio) didn't represent her generous and kind nature. Sebastián suspected Emilio had harboured a secret passion for the woman.

'She was a beauty, so she was, the Spanish equivalent of Sophia Loren. That's who she reminded everyone of. She grew more and more beautiful with age,' said Emilio, lifting up the photo of Amaya to see it more clearly. 'She had five children and eventually, of course, they had to sell the farm because there's no easy way to divide it with so many children, and grandchildren too.'

He sighed.

'It was a sad day when the farm was sold. I just watched the lorries get loaded up with all the furniture, day by day, as the place was completely cleared out. I think they divided up the furniture among themselves, though how they managed to do it without arguments I've no idea...'

Emilio looked at Sebastián with momentary mischief on his face.

'They only came to stay here in the summer months, or occasionally in the winter for the olive collecting. So my wife and I, we used to sneak into the main farmhouse and have a look around it now and again. Lots of beautiful paintings they had, antique silk fans and embroidered tapestries on the wall.'

'Why were they only here in the summer months?' asked Sebastián, intrigued.

'Diego Casales had trained as a lawyer. After the civil war he ended up working as a judge in the Supreme Court. In Madrid, of course. All thanks to his father Pablo, really...'

Whenever Emilio talked about Pablo Casales, Sebastián could sense his unashamed admiration for him.

Emilio took a sip of water and looked at the stack of photos in front of him.

'Before the civil war kicked off, times were changing rapidly and Pablo soon picked up the winds of change, as you'd expect a successful businessman and landowner to do. He sent his younger son, Diego, off to Madrid to study at a private school, and then paid for him to train as a lawyer. This was unusual at the time. Normally a son would be expected to run the family business.'

Emilio looked hesitantly at Sebastián for a moment, as if weighing up how much he should share.

'Please carry on, Emilio. It's fascinating to learn about the people who owned Las Nevadas before me.'

'OK. Well, to be brutally honest, Diego was useless at business. He would've been a disaster if he'd had the time and leisure to manage this farm. Those of us who worked here managed things as best we could for him, but Diego still made a lot of stupid mistakes. Remember that bit of ground with no olive trees, where you're proposing to build the mews?'

Sebastián nodded.

'That ground was cleared of olive trees many years ago so they could build a small airport there. Apparently an investor discovered Las Nevadas had the perfect altitude for small planes to land. The only problem was they shook hands and agreed on it before planning permission was sought. Planning permission was denied because of the harm an airport would cause to the golden eagles that reside in these mountains. So Diego was left with a big piece of empty, useless land.'

'But Diego had a development built on this land as well, didn't he?'

'That development, which is further along the main road, was a travesty. Diego sold the land for peanuts and, on top of that, he failed to ensure the residents would pay for the water. There were years of litigation before they resolved that problem.'

Sebastián looked down again. He sifted slowly and quietly through the black and white photos of the farmhouse.

He liked the photograph of the dining room best. This was a huge room with a towering ceiling and it was also the first room you came to when you climbed the entrance stairway.

In the photograph a huge table stretched across one side of the room. Clearly meals were very much a family affair.

Emilio looked over Sebastián's arm at the photo.

'That room was used a lot in the summer. The Casales family always came. It didn't matter how dispersed they were, every summer they would meet up here in Las Nevadas. The very young children would eat in the room by the kitchen, the older ones sat with the elders in the dining room. They were quite a volatile family... There was always some tiff or argument developing. My wife worked in the kitchen so she knew exactly what was going on.'

Emilio sighed. He looked out of the window for a long moment. Sebastián, seeing the expression of sadness on Emilio's face, kept quiet.

He was beginning to realise his insensitivity towards Emilio. For him this was all interesting history but to Emilio this was a part of his life, as he once knew it. All of this rich tapestry long gone now, of course. What must it be like to be the last one standing?

13

'Diego Casales and Amaya Arismendi... As a couple they were very different. Diego was a supporter of General Franco and she was a beautiful woman from the Basque Country in northern Spain. Arismendi, of course, is a Basque surname. She was proud of her surname and her roots, despite living in Madrid with Diego for most of her life.'

The mantel clock ticked loudly and comfortingly from the dresser in the silence that followed Emilio's speech.

Sebastián had dropped in on Emilio, taking some respite from all the paperwork in his office, and they'd had a coffee together. It hadn't taken long for Emilio to bury himself in the past again, remembering the family he'd worked for all those years ago.

Sebastián leaned back on his chair, his eyes fixed expectantly on Emilio. He didn't feel the need to disguise his rampant curiosity about Diego and Amaya because, for now at least, Emilio seemed to be basking in his interest.

'Diego and Amaya's relationship happened during the Spanish Civil War. Believe it or not their romantic story started in the Basque Country.'

Emilio shut his eyes for a moment, trying to decide where to begin.

'As you probably already know, the Basque Country endured

the first aerial bombardment against innocent civilians by the Nazis. It was to be the great example of psychological warfare in Spain, a present from Hitler to Franco if you like, as they were allies and both dictators. It was the bombing of Guernica that shocked the world... they must've taught you about it in school.'

'They did. They took us all to see Picasso's Guernica painting as part of our history lesson.'

Sebastián suddenly wondered whose side Emilio's family had been on during the civil war. He didn't seem to be a big fan of General Franco but, then again, nowadays many Spaniards would be wary of admitting their families had supported a military dictator who was friendly with Hitler.

'Amaya Arismendi was there the very day the Germans, in collaboration with Franco, bombed Guernica. Deliberately targeting civilians. Many people were there, as it was market day and there were food shortages. They knew that, of course. Amaya was warned to take shelter by a man who'd been out watching the planes circling the town, so she went and hid in a church. It's probably what saved her that day.'

'What happened at Guernica was truly horrific, Emilio, no one can deny that. However, I still don't understand how Diego met Amaya. You said she was from the Basque Country but Diego was brought up here in Las Nevadas and then went on to study in Madrid,' Sebastián said, trying to steer Emilio back to the start of Diego and Amaya's relationship.

'How did Diego and Amaya meet? They met up north, in the Basque Country, of course. He was posted up to the north with his battalion... He was on Franco's side. You'll know all about Franco and the Nationalists; they had trouble subduing the north of Spain. Lots of these young men were posted up north to keep it under control.'

Emilio fell silent again, chewing his upper lip as he let his mind wander back to those days.

'After the civil war Franco tried to appease things by establishing the industrial heart of Spain in Catalonia,' Emilio said forlornly, digressing once more. 'That's come back to bite us these days... It's rich and prosperous up there and now they want independence. Meanwhile here in the south agriculture's changed. There are no jobs any more. They've machines to do all the work now.'

Emilio was looking sad again but Sebastián couldn't help probing for more information.

'What on earth made the pair of them get together, given their sympathies were with the opposing sides in the war?'

Emilio looked at Sebastián for a moment, his black inscrutable eyes piercing him with their intelligence.

'They'd more in common than you'd think. Amaya had been living in Madrid with her family before the civil war happened.'

Emilio looked down at the black and white photo of Amaya.

'The problem was her family had gone on holiday up to Mundaka, her home village in the Basque Country, to visit relatives. It was unfortunate. When the civil war broke out, they found themselves trapped up north and unable to return to Madrid.'

Emilio chuckled.

'Amaya wasn't a country girl at all. She liked the big city. Diego was her chance to return to Madrid, really. He was on the winning side, he'd trained to be a lawyer, he'd everything going for him...'

Emilio rubbed his face.

'I can't blame her for wanting a better life. You're too young to know what we went through as a country during the civil war. The civil war brutalised a lot of people, it left a lot of scars and it destroyed families. Civil war's the worst kind of war, pitting neighbours, friends and family members against each other. Diego and Amaya carried their own scars from that time.'

He looked across to Sebastián to see if he was still following him.

Sebastián nodded sympathetically at Emilio, not wanting to stem the flow of his memories. Emilio smiled to himself and delved back into the past once more.

'Diego was the son of a wealthy Andalucían landowner, Pablo Casales. This farm was originally bought by Pablo in 1906 as a gift for his wife.'

A romantic gesture, thought Sebastián. Not on the scale of the Taj Mahal, but sweet nonetheless.

'However, tragically, Diego's mother died when Diego was barely three years old and then, much later during the civil war, the Reds or Republicans (as they called themselves) assassinated Diego's father and brother, right here in the farmhouse...'

Emilio looked out of the window for a moment as though in silent acknowledgement of the crimes that had been committed there.

The clock on the mantelpiece ticked away steadily in the stillness, in direct contrast to the melodrama of Emilio's memories. It brought a sense of unreality to his words, just as any wartime memories would to a younger generation used to peace and their creature comforts.

'The summer of 1938 was when it happened... They were

both poisoned. It could've been one of the servants who did it. As with so many stories from the civil war, nobody knows. They said a red carnation was found next to each body...'

Emilio sighed.

'There was a lot of hatred, here in the south of Spain, towards wealthy landowners in those days.'

Emilio paused again as if unsure of how to proceed.

'Because of the way his father and brother were assassinated, I think, Diego was a hard, bitter man. He frightened his own children at times, and he frightened those of us that worked for him.'

Emilio leant back in his seat. His face looked ashen.

'I'm sorry, Sebastián, I'm afraid I'm done for today. I'm drained. Too many memories. They cloud the brain. They're dug out of the depths of my soul and it's wearing me out.'

Sebastián stood up immediately, putting a hand on Emilio's shoulder.

'Please don't apologise. It's really my fault for prying so much. Nuria's going to kill me. Is there anything I can do for you?'

Emilio smiled and shook his head.

'There's nothing a siesta won't mend.'

Sebastián nodded and bent to put the photos back into their box.

He wondered how Emilio had accumulated so many photos of the farmhouse, including so many of the owners. He wondered to himself if Emilio had pilfered them before the farmhouse was cleared out. Maybe one day he'd be brave enough to ask, but he'd asked Emilio enough questions for today.

By the time he looked up again, Emilio had already fallen

asleep with enviable rapidity, with his mouth open and his head tilted slightly to one side. The expression on his face was tranquil, that of a man at peace with himself.

14

Sebastián was sitting with his feet up on the desk, going through the pile of bills on his lap, when he heard the squabbling in the courtyard.

It was a cold day, with a layer of frost on the ground that morning, so Sebastián had switched on the freestanding gas fire in his office. The fire was hissing noisily, but it still didn't drown out the voices outside, which were getting increasingly irate and loud.

Sebastián recognised them.

One was Piedra's and the other belonged to Mateo, his security guard. Mateo wasn't usually up at this time of the day as he patrolled the farm during the night, keeping an eye on the building supplies piled up in the back yard.

With an irritated sigh, Sebastián dumped the bills on the table and went to see what was going on.

It was twelve o'clock.

In the summer you wouldn't see a single workman out at this hour of the day. They would arrive at five o'clock in the morning and work until eleven, disappearing for lunch and then only reappearing at five o'clock in the afternoon when it was cooler.

But now, in the winter, it was different. The workmen arrived later in the morning and then headed off after two for lunch. So several of the workmen were gathered around Piedra and Mateo in the courtyard, interested bystanders to their argument.

'Are you accusing me of being a thief?' yelled Mateo.

'No, Mateo, *hijo de puta*, I didn't say that. Stop putting words in my mouth. I'm just saying you're not doing your job. Stuff's going missing. That's your job, not mine,' said Piedra, jabbing Mateo in the chest with his thick forefinger.

Sebastián decided to intervene before this became a physical fight.

'Mateo, Piedra, do you want to come into my office to discuss this?'

Sebastián's calm, refined tone seemed to break through the heat of the argument like a bucket of water. Both men turned to face him and, as if suddenly aware of their audience, had the grace to look contrite.

'Get back to your work!' Piedra barked at his men.

As the other men dispersed, Piedra and Mateo turned and followed Sebastián into his office.

Sebastián indicated the chairs in front of his desk and seated himself on his office chair.

'What's going on?'

'Supplies are missing. No one knows where they've gone,' Piedra said bluntly.

Sebastián felt a knot tie itself like a lead balloon in the pit of his stomach.

This was literally the last thing he needed. Even though the renovation project was nearly finished, money was running tight. As with every ambitious building project the costs had surpassed all the estimates.

He was expecting any day now for the bank to call and arrange to see him. His bank balance wasn't looking healthy.

Without saying anything, Sebastián turned and looked at Mateo.

Mateo looked steadily back at him.

'Nothing's gone missing on my watch. You saw my references. I'm a hundred per cent trustworthy. No one could get at the building supplies at night without me knowing about it.'

'What's gone missing?'

'Some of the cabinet doors for the kitchen. They're made of cherry wood and they're extremely expensive to replace,' said Piedra angrily, as though the cost of them was coming from his own pocket.

Sebastián looked at them in bemusement.

'Why would someone steal some kitchen cabinet doors?'

Both men shrugged, bemused.

'I don't understand it at all,' said Piedra, rubbing his eyes wearily. 'I mean, I understand if someone pinched a microwave or a cooker, but some kitchen cabinet doors? I don't get it. But they're gone and the inventory shows them arriving here. So the question is, where the hell are they?'

'And you've looked everywhere?'

'Yes, we've looked everywhere. Of course we have. My men have wasted the entire morning looking for them, in every conceivable place. We can't find them anywhere.'

Sebastián looked at them.

'Well, I suggest we get everyone working here in the dining hall tomorrow, at ten o'clock, and have a talk to them about it. See if anyone has any idea where those cabinet doors have gone. If we have no joy, we'll have to get the police involved.

But that's the last resort. I can't have anyone untrustworthy working here.'

Mateo and Piedra nodded in agreement. They both stood up and left the office quickly, not wanting to disturb Sebastián any more than was necessary.

He wasn't sure how, but everyone seemed to sense he was under pressure. Maybe he'd asked them one too many times how much longer the project was going to take to complete.

15

At ten o'clock the next morning, thirty-one men and one woman gathered in the upstairs dining hall of the farmhouse. All of them were politely silent as Sebastián made his way up the stairs, accompanied by Piedra and Mateo.

Sebastián looked round at them all with a heavy heart.

'Right. I guess you already know why you're here. For the first time since this project started, we've items missing. Several cherry wood kitchen cabinet doors, to be precise. It's going to delay finishing the kitchen and, quite apart from the value of those doors, it's going to be an expensive and unnecessary inconvenience. I want all of you to try your best to see if you can remember anything suspicious, or if you can figure out why someone would want to steal six cherry wood cabinet doors, of all things.'

He looked at everyone standing in front of him and scanned their faces. Many of them looked genuinely perplexed. Other faces were expressionless. Nuria's face, interestingly enough, looked strangely pensive.

Sebastián made a mental note to speak to her later.

'If anyone knows anything or has anything of interest to say, please speak to me or Mateo,' said Piedra. 'Needless to say, if we don't get any information soon, we'll have to get the police involved.'

An uncomfortable murmur rose and echoed in the large room. People shifted uneasily on the balls of their feet. Sebastián could tell contacting the police would be a big mistake. Nobody liked to get involved with the *Guardia Civil*. Still, it would have to be done, for the sake of warning off any further thieving, if anything.

Sebastián watched the men disperse to various parts of the house and within minutes the noise of drilling and banging resounded around him.

He walked quickly down the stairway to his office. He'd received an interesting email this morning. One of the local olive farmers, a man highly respected in the industry, who owned ten times the land Sebastián had, had written to him inviting him to come and visit his farm.

Clearly, the news there was a new kid on the block had got around.

Farmers the world over are used to sticking together, thought Sebastián. He reckoned it had to do with them having the heroic challenge of dealing with what nature threw at them on a daily basis, the unfair market forces constantly cutting the bottom line and the fact that most of the population hasn't a clue what's involved in getting food on to the supermarket shelf.

He was in the process of typing up a polite acceptance to this farmer's invitation when there was a tentative knock at the office door.

Nuria poked her head around the door.

'Hi Seb. Do you have a moment?'

Sebastián nodded and pushed his laptop away. He put his elbows on the table and clasped his hands defensively, wondering what was coming at him now.

Nuria came into the office and stood awkwardly in front of him. In the face of Sebastián's uncompromising silence she shuffled uncomfortably in her thick black gardening boots.

'Take a seat,' Sebastián volunteered, softening when he saw how nervous she was. He wasn't sure what had upset Nuria but it was clear something was gnawing away at her.

Nuria sat down on the edge of the chair in front of him but didn't say anything. Sebastián frowned. He wasn't used to seeing Nuria like this and suddenly, irrationally, hoped none of the men were causing her any grief. It couldn't be easy being the only girl on the farm.

Nuria took a deep breath and looked directly at him.

'I know where the cherry wood cabinet doors are.'

'You do? Why, that's wonderful! Where did you find them?'

'Don't get too excited, Seb. You won't be able to make use of them. I'm afraid you'll have to order new ones in.'

Sebastián leant back in his seat, frowning at Nuria.

'What on earth do you mean? Could you be a little clearer? For the record, I'm not understanding any of this.'

'It's pretty hard to explain. Impossible, actually. It'll be easier if I can just show you. It's José Luis, you see. He's the one who's taken the doors.'

Sebastián opened his mouth and shut it again.

'Please, please don't get too mad at him. He doesn't really understand he did something wrong and if you shout it'll only scare him.'

Nuria stood up. Sebastián looked blankly at her for a minute and then got up to follow her. They made their way with grim certainty to José Luis's workshop.

Once through the door, Nuria led Sebastián straight to one

73

of the tables where some flat pieces of wood were laid out.

He looked curiously at them.

The carving on them was amazing. There were different scenes carved into each piece of wood. In one there was a complicated depiction of the Last Supper. In another there was a bullring with a bull and a toreador. In another there was what looked like the Cathedral in Ronda. In total there were around twenty carvings of various shapes and sizes.

'These are your kitchen doors, Seb.'

He felt the shock and surprise go through him and then a hot wave of anger hit him.

He picked up one of the pieces up and turned it over. Sure enough, there on the back were the markings of a cabinet door. José Luis had simply sliced the doors into smaller, more workable pieces.

He looked across to José Luis, who was sitting quietly at another workstation. Was it his imagination or did he look slightly apprehensive, wondered Sebastián?

Nuria put a hand on his arm, as if to restrain him.

'He won't do it again. I've told him he mustn't take any materials other than the dead olive wood. He'll help pay for the replacement doors with what savings he has.'

Sebastián continued to look at José Luis, speechless.

Then suddenly he felt a bubble of insane laughter welling up and finally he could hold it in no longer. He doubled over as he laughed hysterically, losing complete control of himself.

Both José Luis and Nuria watched him, mystified. He clutched at the table edge as tears streamed down his face.

After a minute or two his laughter reached its peak and he proceeded to wipe away the tears with his shirtsleeve.

'Oh, God! What a complete and utter mess. José Luis, what on earth made you take these doors?'

José Luis looked down at the floor between his feet.

'I wanted to see what the wood felt like. Olive wood's so hard and tough. This wood's like butter compared to it. It's lovely to carve. I'm sorry for upsetting everyone.'

Sebastián tried to make the best of it.

'Look, I guess at least I know now I don't have anyone dishonest working for me. That would've been a real concern to me. José Luis, if you want to carve wood I'll provide you with something other than olive wood but you cannot use these supplies. They're expensive.'

'Would you really get me some other wood?' asked José Luis, ignoring his last comment as irrelevant.

'Yes. You've some kind of addiction to this kind of work and I don't want to find any more things going missing now you've had a taste of working on cherry wood. Find me a supplier and wood that's reasonable in cost and I'll get it for you, on condition that you'll take nothing more and when we open this bloody place to tourists you'll let us market your carvings.'

José Luis nodded silently in agreement.

Sebastián decided that was as much of a commitment as he was going to get from him and turned to head back to the office. Goodness knows how he was going to explain this insanity to Piedra, but Nuria's face was now lit up with a huge, relieved smile and that had to be worth something.

16

Two weeks later, Sebastián indicated left, after half an hour's drive from Las Nevadas, and turned into the estate of Manuel Cervantes, the hospitable farmer who'd invited Sebastián to visit him.

On the way to Manuel's farm, Sebastián had admired the surrounding countryside. The ochre earth was in evidence everywhere but the monotony of it was broken up by the spectacular pale grey hills that burst out of the landscape, like some prehistoric remnant from another age. Dark holes appeared on these hillsides from time to time, indicating that behind these limestone cliffs there lurked a voracious cave system.

Sebastián wondered how many of them had been explored.

Given how parched the landscape was you could be forgiven for assuming this part of Spain was waterless, but nothing could be further from the truth. There were no hosepipe bans here. Huge rivers lurked beneath the ground. It was these subterranean rivers that had worn away the complicated cave system in the hills.

A few kilometres south of Ronda, just outside of the village of Benaoján, was one of the most spectacular cave systems in Spain, the Cueva de la Pileta (Cave of the Pool). Emilio and Nuria had told Sebastián about it; both of them had been to see it. This cave was only discovered in 1905 so, archaeologically speaking, it was a recent find.

Deep inside the cave there were several galleries with cave paintings estimated to be 30,000 years old, created by the Palaeolithic people of Ronda before the last Ice Age.

The most intriguing thing, apparently, about the early art discovered in the Cueva de la Pileta was that there were paintings of marine animals on the cave walls. Given that Ronda was situated 2,460 feet above sea level it seemed to be an unexplained mystery.

Incredible as the cave might be, Sebastián had no desire to visit it; enclosed spaces made him feel claustrophobic. If the tourists staying at Las Nevadas wanted to visit the cave they'd have to go with someone else as a guide. Besides, he wasn't keen on bats and the caves around here were full of them. Often in the twilight at Las Nevadas they would skim across the swimming pool, hunting for insects, and if you travelled by car at night you could often spot them flying past.

Nuria had also told him how her mother used to scare her with stories of people dying when visiting the Cueva del Gato (the Cat's Cave). People were often caught out by the unpredictable flash floods that inundated its limestone galleries from time to time.

The Cueva del Gato could be seen on the way to the Cueva de la Pileta. Its entrance was said to look a little like a cat's head, but having seen this cave for himself, from the outside, Sebastián couldn't see the resemblance.

He decided as he drove towards Manuel's farm he preferred the surrounding countryside in the summer when the colours were starker and more clearly defined.

Fields of sunflowers, their heads all pointing in the same

direction, provided a splash of bright yellow in contrast to the straw colours of the grass and undergrowth. The ochre red earth contrasted with the khaki green of the olive trees and the pale grey of the surrounding hills. With a clear blue sky, this was a palette no one could really complain about...

Now it was February and the emerald green of grass grown fat on winter rain poked out of the earth, giving the farmers more work to do when it came to tilling the fields. Despite the threat of frost, clumps of wild asparagus were starting to poke through the earth, as well as wild garlic. According to Emilio, Nuria could cook a delicious Spanish omelette with asparagus picked from the farmland. Sebastián hoped he'd get a chance to try it some day.

Sebastián drove up a long road lined with cypress trees. He looked around with interest, trying to repress his envy at the healthy state of the farmland around him.

Ten minutes later he saw the house where he was expected. In contrast to the Las Nevadas farmhouse, it was a large modern hacienda, all on one level but sprawling across a large area. Like most other farmhouses around there now, it was gated.

He rang the buzzer and answered the intercom and the gates opened slowly and smoothly to let him in. So much for Las Nevadas and its thick wooden doors, thought Sebastián forlornly, which still only opened by key and brute force.

A sturdy, battered Land Rover was parked in the driveway. Sebastián parked behind it and looked around as he got out of the car. The gardens were all immaculately kept and a lively fountain trickled musically, accompanying the frenzied barking of a dog from inside the house.

The door opened and the man Sebastián took to be Manuel

Cervantes jogged down the steps towards him with his hands outstretched. Manuel clasped Sebastián's hand and patted his back, beaming with pleasure. He was a tall man, dressed casually in jeans, a chequered shirt and a pair of dusty boots. His hair was silvered but his face was surprisingly youthful. His eyebrows were black, which oddly made him look rather distinguished.

'Come in, Sebastián, come in. I'm delighted to see you. We have so much to talk about!'

Have we? Sebastián was rather taken aback by his host's enthusiasm but he followed Manuel into the house nonetheless.

17

The inside of the house was pleasingly rustic. Manuel guided Sebastián into the sitting-room where there was a fire burning merrily in the grate. A large Alsatian dog got up quickly from the behind the sofa and came forward, his tail wagging vigorously.

'Don't mind him. He's a sap. Hey, Chico?' said Manuel, stroking the dog affectionately. Loose hairs started to shed from Chico's thick coat. 'He's probably the world's worst guard dog but at least he barks when he knows newcomers are around.'

Sebastián heard a pair of high heels tapping purposefully on the tiled floor behind him and turned around.

He saw an elegant middle-aged lady, her evidently dyed blonde hair neatly coiled up in a bun (what was it with dark-skinned Spanish women and their love of blonde hair, he thought to himself) and with a thick layer of make-up. Her expression was warm and welcoming.

'This is my wife, Sonia.'

Sebastián kissed Sonia dutifully on both cheeks.

'What would you like to drink, Sebastián?' Sonia asked. 'We have anything alcoholic you could wish for, coffee or soft drinks?'

Sebastián turned politely to his host.

'I'm going to have *carajillo*, please, Sonia,' said Manuel, before turning to Sebastián.

'The same for me, thanks,' he said.

Sonia patted her husband on the arm.

'He has so much he wants to talk to you about,' she said confidentially to Sebastián. 'Ever since he heard you'd single-handedly taken on Las Nevadas, he's been wanting to get in touch with you. He can help you a lot, you know, there's not much he doesn't know about cultivating olives.'

'Sonia, *¡basta ya!*' said Manuel, with good humour but impatiently.

He turned and took a seat. Sebastián sat near the fire, enjoying the warmth.

'I'm sorry about my wife. We both love the olive business, always have and always will do, but we forget others don't necessarily share our enthusiasm.'

'That's OK. I'm going to need all the help I can get when it comes to getting the farmland back on its feet, but at the moment most of my efforts have been focused on getting the house up and running to attract paying guests through the door. I'm not sure I'm there with the farm yet. I'd really appreciate it if in a month or two you could come and have a look at it. I'm not sure much of it can be saved, actually...'

Manuel shook his head sadly.

'No, it's looking pretty bad. A travesty. The original owner, Pablo Casales, would be horrified.'

Sebastián winced. It didn't sit well with him either, having a derelict farm, but there's only so much one could do with limited resources.

'Never mind, don't despair. There's much I can do to help

you. I can give you advice but we also have an olive nursery here on our land too. We'd be happy to supply you with new olive trees, all of them disease-free and grown in controlled conditions. These are strong saplings because we sell nothing but the very best. We only offer the Jaén variety.'

Manuel leaned back on his seat and crossed his legs. When Sebastián nodded politely, he carried on talking about the olive trees.

'I can advise you on the best fertilisers, the best pesticides against the Mediterranean fly, and fungicides, of course, as well... There are many types of fertiliser available too, but if you're planting the olive trees after mid-August and before March don't fertilise them until spring.'

Sebastián nodded as Sonia brought in two mugs of steaming *carajillo* and put down a plate of sliced chorizo and Manchego cheese.

'Thank you.'

'*De nada*,' said Sonia, with a smile, before retreating again.

Sebastián munched on a slice of chorizo thoughtfully. By now Chico was sitting on his foot, salivating at the food he was eating. Surely dogs don't eat spicy chorizo, he wondered to himself? He tried to ignore the pleading face in front of him.

'Chico! Come over here!'

Chico, with his head and tail bent down mournfully, obediently went and sat next to Manuel's sofa, much to Sebastián's relief.

'Nowadays we grow olive trees closer together and therefore they tend to be smaller, but still robust. They maybe give only 10 kilos of olive per tree, not 20 or 30, but the overall production is higher per acre. They don't grow to more than two-and-a-half metres in height.'

Manuel took a sip of his *carajillo*.

'The saplings in our nursery get given growth hormones once a year, in spring, until they're ready to be planted.'

'How are the growth hormones applied?'

'It's very simple. Any gardener would be able to do it. They're mixed in with water and sprayed on to the trees in spring. They're very expensive so most farmers just rely on good fertilisers once the saplings are planted on their farm. The soil around here is very poor in nutrients. Olive tree fertilisers usually have potassium, nitrogen and phosphorous in large quantities, as well as copper, iron, sulphur and molybdenum in very small quantities.'

Manuel leaned forward and grabbed a piece of chorizo. He chewed it slowly while Sebastián looked at the fire, wondering if the wood burning in it was olive wood. Manuel waited until he had Sebastián's attention again before he carried on.

'The trees need to be pruned every year. It's very important because it will affect the quantity and quality of the olives you get. If you prune too early, before the rains of winter are done, you could be opening entry points for waterborne diseases to enter the trees. Pruning happens between winter's end and flowering but any gardener around these parts should know that. Here that's February time.'

Manuel paused for a moment to take a drink of *carajillo*.

'However, you cannot prune an olive tree before it's four years old. It usually takes around five years, with the help of growth hormones, for them to grow to almost full height.'

Sebastián nodded. He would have to start thinking about all of this soon but not yet, thankfully. He took a hot mouthful of *carajillo*, feeling the sweetness of the alcohol warm his veins as he swallowed it. Sonia had been very liberal with the brandy.

'Did you get any farm equipment with the purchase?'

'Only an old tractor and plough, but it's not in good shape. I'm going to need to buy a better one.'

'I can see if I can source a second-hand one that's in good shape, or else get you a good deal on a new one. Farmers don't make a lot of money these days so they're unlikely to be renewing their equipment regularly but I'll have a look around for you.'

'Thank you, you're very kind.'

'It's not a problem at all, Sebastián. By coming here you've become part of the community. There's been a few foreigners taking over farms round about here and so it's nice to see one of our own come back into the fold.'

'I know, they've told me there's an Englishman who's bought a vineyard in this area and is labelling his wine "*El Inglés*".'

'Yes, that's true. Wine from around here doesn't have a great reputation. The soil isn't rich enough, really, but it sells to the cheap wine merchants... Speaking of foreigners, I've heard you're opening Las Nevadas up to tourists?'

'Yes, I hope so. Very soon, in fact. I'm estimating we should be ready to open up by end of April. I really need to get feet in the door as I've taken out massive loans for this project.'

'Ronda's had a mixed bag of tourists, really. For a few years the tourists who came here from the Costa del Sol were very wealthy and money poured into the region, but since the financial crash in 2007 we haven't been able to attract the same calibre of visitors.'

Manuel reached for a Manchego slice, munching on it thoughtfully.

'I rent a few houses to tourists here and I've ended up with more than a few issues with the tenants in recent years, disputes over bills and rent that end up in court and costing me more than it's worth in rent money.'

Manuel shook his head in disapproval.

'The taxi drivers in Ronda have been hit the worst. Some are barely above the poverty line,' he continued to explain. 'The tourists that come from the Costa del Sol now take the train from the coast. They don't spend money on taxis.'

'That's certainly worrying. Yet there's so much to do here, in the winter as well as in the summer,' said Sebastián. 'It's all about attracting the right sort of client. Nature lovers and hikers would love this area. I'm hoping, with suitable advertising, to attract the right people to Las Nevadas. I own a marketing company in Madrid so that's one thing I should be able to achieve. I've a lot to do before then...' Sebastián rubbed his face. 'I need to recruit a couple of good cooks, for a start.'

'There's a cookery school in Ronda run by a man called Álvaro Gutiérrez. He also owns an expensive restaurant by the Old Bridge. He's the man to ask.'

'Perfect, thanks. I'll look him up next time I'm in Ronda.'

Sebastián leant back on the sofa and looked up at the shelves on either side of the fireplace.

'By the way, if you don't mind me asking, what on earth are all those white stones on your shelves?'

'Ha! They're not stones, they're fossils!' said Manuel, getting up.

He reached up and selected a couple carefully before passing them across for Sebastián to look at. Sebastián looked at the fossils in surprise. One was clearly a sea urchin, with the five star-shaped markings across its circular form. The other fossil was of a large oyster.

'Are these from around here?'

'Yes, in the farmland around here you can still find these. Not so long ago, when the tractors tilled the farmland they broke up rocks, many of them containing marine fossils. However, modern-day farming techniques clear the earth of all the stones when it's tilled, so these will soon be a rarity I imagine. The farmers tend to dump the excess rocks in the pit near the old quarry. That's where to go and have a look if you're interested.'

'Wow. It's astonishing. To be so high up, in the middle of a mountain range, and to find all these marine fossils, it's incredible.'

'I know. This land was under the sea once. I believe so. I don't think the marine cave paintings at the Cueva de la Pileta are a coincidence either. There was definitely sea life here once upon a time.'

Manuel took the fossils from Sebastián and placed them tenderly back on the shelf.

'There's quite a lot of work involved in cleaning them. You have to love fossils to do it. It's a hobby for me. No one else I know around here is remotely interested in them.'

Sebastián looked at the fossils and wondered if he could include fossil hunting in the list of excursions he could provide his guests with. He could see that appealing to some of the Brits or Germans. He remembered visiting Dorset many years ago as a tourist and being stunned by the number of people fossil hunting on the beach at Lyme Regis. Collecting objects seemed to him to be a uniquely and quintessentially British interest.

What an intriguing idea...

18

March 2018

10th March was a beautiful sunny day, comfortably warm, with all the promise of spring in the air.

It was Sebastián's birthday and he was just returning from lunchtime tapas at his favourite bar in Ronda, El Hornigo, where he'd been celebrating with Piedra, Nuria, Emilio and a few of the other men working on the estate. Having downed a few beers he was being driven back to Las Nevadas by Nuria, who'd remained sober, refusing drinks steadfastly like a teetotaller.

Like a bee sated with nectar, he was comfortably drowsy as they drove up the road to the farmhouse. This came to an abrupt end when he saw a familiar dark blue Mercedes car parked in the driveway. He sat up with a jerk, feeling the seat belt of the car cutting into him.

'Seb, what are you doing?'

'Why?' asked Sebastián agitatedly, completely oblivious to Nuria's question.

Nuria looked at him briefly in confusion as she drove them into the courtyard, expertly squeezing the car between the giant green farm doors. Nuria stayed silent, waiting patiently for Sebastián to explain his sudden panic.

'Hell! This is the last thing I needed...'

As soon as the car was parked, Sebastián leapt out of the car and disappeared at a running pace into the farmhouse, leaving Nuria and Emilio looking at each other in total perturbation.

Nuria shrugged and went to retrieve her shopping. Five minutes later Sebastián burst out of the farmhouse entrance, the doors banging shut behind him, and walked into the courtyard.

'Have you seen them?' he asked Nuria.

'Seen who?'

'My family.'

'Your family, Seb? No, I haven't, I'm afraid. But before you rush off again, make yourself useful and carry some of my shopping into the apartment, please. After all, you benefit from my food as much as anyone else.'

Before he could reply, Nuria dumped a heavy bag of shopping into his arms, the weight of which left him breathless for a moment. He turned and obediently followed her into the apartment, his heart and mind racing in shock.

Somewhere on his farm, members of his family were running wild.

Sebastián dreaded the thought.

The farm was still far from finished and he desperately prayed his ever-critical father wouldn't be there with them.

After dumping the shopping in Nuria's apartment he proceeded to pace the wooden floor upstairs in the farmhouse, trying desperately to figure out where his family could've gone.

An hour later he heard voices in the courtyard and poked his head out of the dining room balcony window. Sure enough, right below him he could see his father, his mother, his sister Andrea and, of course, Felipe, looking, as usual, despicably cheery and relaxed.

They were all talking to Nuria and, as far as Sebastián could see, pounding her with questions. Nuria looked faintly amused by the attention his family were giving her, at one point looking up at him as though feeling his eyes on her, and then looking away again quickly.

Sebastián took a deep breath and walked slowly down the wooden stairwell to the courtyard.

'Sebastián!' his mother yelled in glee when she caught sight of him, throwing herself at him like the sole survivor of a shipwreck. He caught her before she knocked him down with her embrace, and smelt the lingering scent of Coco Chanel that she always wore. Bizarrely, the smell of her perfume made him suddenly feel intensely homesick.

'Mum! What are you all doing here? You didn't let me know you were coming.'

'*¡Hijo!* As though we wouldn't want to be here for your birthday! With you all alone, out here in the middle of nowhere!' said his mother, infantilising him by kissing him repeatedly on the cheek.

He detached himself gently and turned to the rest of his family.

His father seemed much greyer than when he saw him last but maybe that was his imagination. The last time they saw each other, at Christmas, they had ended up exchanging insults, eventually shouting loudly at one another on opposite sides of the front door which Sebastián had just slammed in his father's face.

Wearing the proverbial white shirt under a yellow lambswool jumper and new-looking blue jeans, his father looked neat and dapper as always. He smiled at Sebastián, a genuine smile that

89

creased at the corners of his eyes.

Reassured, Sebastián went up to greet him.

His father enveloped him in a bear hug, which wasn't hard as Sebastián only measured five foot seven to his father's six foot three. The hug suddenly took Sebastián back to his childhood, when life was so much simpler and his father took care of everything. He could have held on to that feeling for an eternity but it didn't last long because Sebastián felt a sharp tug on his jacket and turned to welcome his sister.

Felipe, standing to one side, was grinning inanely at this bizarre family reunion. Nuria had discreetly disappeared, no doubt to the apartment.

Felipe and Sebastián didn't bother exchanging greetings; they were used to picking up where they'd left off.

'Well, Son, are you going to show us what you've done with the place?' asked Pedro, Sebastián's father.

'What about the presents?' asked his mother, Rosana.

Sebastián sighed. Sometimes being with his family was like facing a firing squad. Too many questions to answer all at once, shot out randomly. He hoped Nuria had survived the encounter.

'I suggest we have coffee first. You can come and see the house at the entrance of the farm. I'm staying there while the renovations are getting done on the farmhouse. We're very nearly finished. I'm hoping to be open for business at the end of April. Dad, can you drive us down?'

19

Within a few minutes they were all sitting at Sebastián's favourite spot on the terrace, looking out at the mountains of Sierra Blanquilla. The garden was looking beautifully manicured since Nuria and her small team of gardeners had got to work on it.

Honeysuckle clustered around the terrace and further down the garden a vine had been trained over several arches, out in the sunniest spot. By the clear blue pool a fig tree stood as straight as a sentinel, its trunk continually coated with black ants streaming up and down like a furry blanket. A rose bed had been placed next to the vine, the climbing roses covering the arches that extended across the bottom of the garden.

Beyond the garden there was a long span of red earth stretching to the base of the mountains in the far distance, populated only by olive trees. At times during the night you could hear a train skirting the outer perimeter of the farm, its lights creating an eerie triangle of yellow in the surrounding darkness; at others you could hear the wild hogs browsing in the moonlight. But the noise of the crickets was incessant, a constant backdrop of chirping that continued until dawn.

During the day, if you were lucky, you could sometimes spot a golden eagle hovering high up in the sky. Occasionally, they would come down from the mountains to hunt the rabbits that ate the grass and any other edible vegetation on the farmland.

'What a view, Seb,' said Felipe, stretching out his legs. 'I could almost forgive you for moving here when I see this.'

He twinkled roguishly at his brother.

Sebastián ignored him and drank his coffee quietly, trying to sober up enough to cope with the family onslaught.

'It's very beautiful, don't you think, Pedro?' said his mother, happily.

'Yes, certainly. As long as it doesn't bankrupt my son, it's worth it,' said Pedro, cautiously.

'Are you still managing to keep financially solvent, Seb?' asked Andrea, anxiously.

'For now, yes,' said Sebastián, shortly.

'I think that means not for much longer,' observed Pedro, drily.

Sebastián sighed.

'What do you want from me, Dad? Why bother coming at all if you're only here to tear me down? I don't need it, by the way. There are plenty of other things getting me down at the moment. You always need to prove a point or win an argument. Well, just take it that you've won this one, and leave me in bloody peace. That's all I ask of you.'

'By the way, what does Nuria do here?' asked Felipe, clearly trying to change the subject.

'Nuria?' Sebastián looked at Felipe suspiciously. His brother was a known Lothario.

Felipe laughed.

'Don't look at me like that, Seb! You've kept her very quiet.'

Sebastián felt himself getting thoroughly riled. How he wished they hadn't come. Seeing the anger in Sebastián's eyes

Felipe raised his hands.

'Peace, Seb. An innocent question, that's all it was.'

'Innocent!' snorted his mother, in a most unladylike manner. 'There's nothing innocent about you, Felipe. You can't be trusted with any woman.'

She turned to Sebastián.

'Your brother got himself entangled with Sñra Rosario.'

Sñra Angela Rosario was a glamorous middle-aged friend of his parents.

'Yes, that's right. He's had an affair with Angela Rosario,' said Andrea, usually the one who most enjoyed gossiping in the family. 'And now no one wants to talk to us because they blame us for allowing it to happen! As if we could have stopped him.'

The culprit of all of this sat calmly in his chair, gazing pensively out into the garden, as though he hadn't heard a word.

'Is that true, Felipe? Seriously? Angela?' Sebastián asked him.

'Yeah, it's no big deal. She's a total cougar. You could just as well say she led me astray. I don't know why everyone always assumes it's the men that err in these matters. Her husband's dull as anything.'

'Her husband happens to be a friend of mine,' said his father, bitterly.

Felipe shrugged.

'Anyway, bro, our little community in Madrid is getting too hot to handle so I thought I might stay here and give you a hand for a bit.'

'That's right, you just do your usual, Felipe,' said his mother angrily. 'Leave us to sort out your mess. There's poor Angela having to face divorce now, and you disappearing off to Andalucía and leaving her to it.'

'There's nothing poor about it, mother. Lest you forget, her husband's as rich as Croesus. She'll be laughing all the way to the bank.'

His mother pursed her lips and shook her head disgustedly.

Sebastián relaxed for the first time since they'd arrived. It was nice to know he wasn't the only disappointment in the family.

Later that afternoon he showed them around the farmhouse, starting at the mews because they were finished and looking pristinely attractive.

Normally houses in Andalucía would be painted white indoors but Sebastián was under no illusions about the cost of maintaining brilliant white walls when letting a house, so all the interior walls were painted in tasteful neutral shades of grey and beige accompanied by bright colours in the rest of the interior. All the kitchens had brilliant red units with oak surfaces and bright red kitchen stools. Wrought-iron chandeliers hung in the hallways and large windows faced out to Sierra Blanquilla, letting in as much light as possible.

Each of the mews had a little private garden, with a barbeque in it, which Sebastián had been warned was an English obsession. Any smell of meat would attract every ant, fly, hornet and wasp within a square mile so hanging wasp traps had been placed strategically in the gardens.

The family were also enthusiastic, albeit slightly forced at times, about the changes to the farmhouse. They seemed a little overwhelmed by the scale of the project Sebastián had taken on.

As they came back out into the courtyard they bumped into Nuria again, who was wheeling a wheelbarrow full of weeds towards the compost heap at the back of the farm.

Felipe rushed up to her.

'Here, let me do that for you.'

'No thanks, it's fine. I can manage,' Nuria said, smiling at him but not slowing down one iota.

Felipe gazed after her.

'What a woman! She's bloody independent. You have to watch those ones.'

Andrea grabbed his arm.

'Felipe, come on, we're going to give Seb his birthday presents and then head back to Ronda, to the hotel.'

Feeling huge relief that his vociferous family wasn't expecting to stay with him, Sebastián nevertheless felt obliged to offer them a room in his small house.

'You're all welcome to stay with me in the house, if you wish.'

'No, Sebastián,' said his mother, patting him fondly on the cheek. 'You have enough going on here. We've booked rooms and we'll head back tomorrow after lunch.'

'I think I'll take you up on that, Seb, once the rest of them have gone home,' said Felipe quickly, ignoring the arctic look his mother gave him.

Sebastián shrugged, resigned to having Felipe hang around for a while. It would be nice to have his company. He was sure one day he'd find that Felipe had suddenly disappeared off again. It's just what Felipe did. He was a free spirit, like the Roma gypsies that used to come to Las Nevadas to pick the olives in springtime.

20

April 2018

Sebastián looked as his watch as he sat in the courtyard waiting for his first guests to arrive.

His marketing firm in Madrid had done an excellent job of promoting Las Nevadas as a holiday resort and this week he already had five bookings lined up. All of them wanted to stay at the main house, so the mews houses were lying empty still, but it was a start.

They were all couples and over sixty. Sebastián wondered if they were setting the demographic that was likely to continue until the summer season or whether he would see some younger couples and families arrive in future. Two of the couples arriving were English, one of them was Dutch and the last two were French.

Sebastián had requested on the booking form that they write down what activities they were interested in. So far they had written sightseeing, walking, reading, eating and drinking. Sebastián hoped the last one was a joke as he could do without drunken hooligans causing trouble. If anyone was going to cause problems it would no doubt be the Brits, he thought to himself judgementally, as they were culturally more likely to be the hardened drinkers.

The farm's gleaming new red minibus was lodged in the

garage. Sebastián and Felipe had put together some interesting trips for the guests to choose from. Felipe, of course, had been more adventurous than Sebastián. Sebastián was wary of taking trips into the Sierra Nevada mountain range, having never been there before and well aware that frequently in these national parks there were black spots where you lost all mobile phone coverage and satellite navigation. Once he had more money in the kitty he would recruit an experienced guide; for now they would have to make do.

'Haven't they arrived yet, Seb?'

Sebastián looked up and saw Nuria standing in the doorway of the apartment, eating a sandwich and watching him with interest.

'No, not yet,' he said brusquely, feeling churlish but unable to help himself.

He was struggling to accept the camaraderie Nuria had established with his brother. Well aware Felipe was much better looking than him, and with infinitely more charm, he felt isolated and left out when the three of them were together.

Since Felipe had joined him in Las Nevadas, his meals with Nuria's family had come to an end. Instead, he was treated to the frequent sight of the pair of them flirting or giggling together. It made him feel like a black thundercloud and he was unsure why. He was pretty sure he had no romantic feelings for Nuria and that what he felt towards her was what any protective brother would feel. But he could also acknowledge to himself he wasn't the most rational or self-aware of human beings, so he could be wrong on those counts.

'What time did they say they were arriving at?'

'Four. Which was an hour ago. I haven't had a text from them either. I guess I'll have to call them and see where they are. The Dutch couple are arriving later tonight, the French tomorrow.'

'Don't worry, Seb. They'll just have been held up somewhere. Not unusual for tourists.'

'Yep.'

Sebastián tried calling the English couple but the call kicked straight onto voicemail. Fifteen minutes later, when he was about to call it a day, a car tooted outside.

Sebastián hurried out to greet the passengers and to show them where to park. He'd decided on a spot near the almond tree for their car: it provided some shade for the greater part of the day.

Behind the steering wheel of the car sat a rotund lady with a large straw hat on and long, grey pigtails tied girlishly at the ends with pink ribbons. She had a beaming smile on her face, as if this was the most exciting trip she'd ever been on. Next to her, looking a lot calmer, sat a bearded man in a Hawaiian shirt and big shades. Behind them was a white-haired couple who nodded at him politely.

The window of the car wound down, and before he could speak the lady in pigtails addressed him.

'Do you speak English?'

Sebastián nodded.

'I'm so sorry we're so late. We got a little lost on the way out of Ronda and ended up on the road to Campillos.'

'Yes, a lot of people make that mistake,' Sebastián blithely lied.

'Oh, do they? Maybe they should put up better road signs. It doesn't matter, I think we've decided it's all part of the adventure.'

Sebastián saw her partner silently raise his eyes up to heaven and smiled.

'Absolutely. I was about to direct you to a spot over there on the driveway. It should provide your car with some shade for most of the day.'

'Excellent. Right. I'll just be a minute.'

She reversed the car, with an aggressive twist of the gears that made Sebastián wince, and drove it into the space. Waiting patiently for them as they disentangled themselves from the car and pulled their cases out of the boot, Sebastián felt an almost overwhelming sense of relief they were here.

He wasn't superstitious in general but he wouldn't have felt it was an auspicious start to his venture if the first of his paying guests hadn't arrived.

'Hi everyone, welcome to Las Nevadas. My name's Sebastián and I'm the owner of the estate,' said Sebastián, once his guests were lined up in front of him.

The lady with the pigtails moved forward to shake his hand.

'I'm Leila Matthews, and this is my husband Robert. And this is Stuart and Rona McPherson.'

They all shook hands politely, English style, and he took them into the courtyard. On the left hand side of the entrance to the main house the builders had installed a lift, which had proved a godsend for food supplies and heavy items. They all managed to fit in the lift with their cases and Sebastián pressed the button to take them up to the floor above.

The lift doors opened and Sebastián had the satisfaction of hearing his guests gasp with pleasure at the sight of the high-ceilinged dining hall.

A huge chandelier with glass shades of different primary colours dominated the centre of the room.

On one side of the room a series of built-in units, square

shaped and made of dark mango wood, stretched from the floor to the ceiling. Each open unit was symmetrically filled with a motley collection of wine bottles, glassware and ornamental brightly coloured glass bowls matching the colours in the chandelier.

Dining tables of differing sizes were placed in a circular formation with high-backed grey chairs. A large dresser was placed next to the French doors and out of the open French doors, in the courtyard, the cheerful screeching of the swifts could be heard, but it was a strangely peaceful sound.

On the other side of the massive room there was a cavernous fireplace, with cut wood to the left hand side piled in a neat formation that reached up to the ceiling. Above the fireplace was an oil painting, imitating the naive style from the eighteenth century, with a pastoral scene. It depicted a sunset over the mountains of Sierra Nevada in bright luminescent colours.

Some of the yellow and blue stripes on the sofas in front of the fireplace were similar in tone to the colours depicted in the painting's sunset. This spot was Sebastián's favourite place to sit in the farmhouse, even though the sitting-rooms were far grander in scope and style.

A middle-aged lady in a suit came forward to greet the guests.

'Hello, I'm Marta, the residential manager. If you've any questions or concerns please let me know. We'll do our best to help you. Lucía and Ricardo are also my colleagues and there'll always be one of us on duty at all times. You can usually find us in the office.'

Marta showed them the office door just next to the kitchen.

'We have a small shop here in the office too, with a selection of gifts made locally. Feel free to drop in at any time to have a look around.'

Sebastián smiled to himself. They had some of José Luis's best pieces in the shop, elegantly displayed in glass cabinets. It would be wonderful if they proved popular with the guests.

The guests then followed Sebastián as he led them through to the dormitories. Due to the way the farmhouse had been built most of the bedrooms were a short distance from the dining hall. Beyond this tight cluster of en suite bedrooms you came across a door leading to two sitting-rooms, and beyond these a corridor.

The really luxurious bedrooms were on the corridor leading to the chapel. These three rooms, which were the most expensive in the place, also looked out onto the gardens at the front of the farmhouse. They had towering high ceilings and were so large the super king-size beds looked diminutive in the space.

Sebastián's guests had booked two of these rooms so Sebastián took them straight there and left them to unpack their things before they reported back to the office.

He felt absolutely ecstatic to have his first guests settled in their rooms. He walked with a spring in his step to the kitchen to check to see if Agustín, his new cook, had everything he needed for tonight. Agustín was a friendly young man, eager to please, who'd just graduated from Ronda's cookery school with glowing references. He was already pottering about the kitchen, checking on everything with an obsessive-compulsive intensity.

'Hi, Agustín. Everything OK?' asked Sebastián.

'Yes, I've got everything we need for tonight and tomorrow.

I'll need more supplies for later in the week though.'

'Just give me the list with what you need and I'll make sure it's done.'

In one corner of the kitchen, Agustín's younger sister sat on a kitchen stool, arms on the breakfast bar, flicking through a teen magazine. She had a mass of riotous black curls, neatly tied back today with a bandana, he noticed with approval. She was earning some extra money as a waitress in the evenings.

He looked around the bright, spotless kitchen. Even in the nineteenth century, when this house was built, they clearly appreciated the importance of food because the kitchen was gigantic. This had enabled Piedra to install three fridges and four freezers as well as a massive storage cupboard that stretched across the room, from wall to wall.

The gas cooker was big enough to comfortably accommodate three chefs, and the workstation could fit at least six people around it. The reddish tones of the cherry wood cabinets, the white marble work surfaces and the modern lighting all gave the place a contemporary feel. The white marble flooring was a brave choice for a busy kitchen but Sebastián felt that in the interests of hygiene it was a necessary evil. It was just as well he had two cleaners arriving at the farmhouse in the early morning and on a daily basis.

Steps to one side of the kitchen led up to the rooms in the attic space. These rooms had been spruced up to provide a bed for any staff members that wanted or needed one.

Sebastián felt it was unnecessary for the three of them to be kicking their heels while they waited for the guests to get settled in. He decided to nip downstairs and see if he could fit in a chat with Emilio. After all, the Dutch couple weren't due to arrive until after nine, and Marta could always call him if there was a problem.

He missed his chats with Emilio now he no longer had lunch at the apartment.

21

'Hello Sebastián! How lovely to see you,' said Emilio, when he opened the door. 'Come in, come in.'

Sebastián followed him into the sitting-room.

'Would you like a drink? We have coffee or soft drinks.'

'If you have some water, that would be lovely, thank you.'

Emilio reappeared a few minutes later with two glasses filled with water.

They drank companionably in silence.

'It's been a while since I last saw you. Have you had a lot to do on the farm?'

Sebastián shrugged.

'There's always a lot to do here, Emilio. And I haven't even started on the farmland yet. I have to get some money in first or the banks will give up on me. How have you been keeping?'

'So, so. The osteoarthritis isn't getting any better but the doctor's given me an injection in my left foot to try and loosen it up. Once your mobility goes as an old man, you're doomed. I'll be out walking on crutches if I have to. Nuria's got enough going on without having to take care of an invalid as well.'

'How's she doing?'

Emilio looked at Sebastián with amusement.

'I'd have thought you'd be better qualified to tell me that. Don't you see her around the farm? If she's slacking I'll have words with her!'

Sebastián had the grace to blush.

'I haven't seen as much of her as before. It's been a busy time trying to get the place open for business. I believe Felipe's been seeing more of her than I have.'

'Yes, that's true,' nodded Emilio. 'What a lovely young man he is. He's always willing to muck in when it's needed. I think the two young boys working with Nuria are appreciating the extra help.'

'I'm sure they are,' growled Sebastián.

'Will he be staying for long?'

'No one ever knows how long Felipe will stay. He's capable of disappearing at very short notice.'

'Ah. Yes. One of those. A *gitano*, in fact.'

'Yes, exactly.'

'I miss the *gitanos* we used to get here in the *finca*. There was always some sort of trouble when they were around but the majority caused no bother, it was always only a few. They're a fascinating people. They're the ones that make flamenco what it is today and who carry on its traditions.'

Sebastián nodded in agreement.

He loved listening to Emilio's memories. It was utterly tragic that society saw the elderly more and more as a burden or an inconvenience. Back in time, in the age of storytelling and bards, the elderly were valued for their wisdom and experience. After all, so few people made it to old age in those days.

Now an ageing population seemed to be surplus to requirements.

Sebastián looked back to his student days at Madrid University and remembered when he'd studied that Old English epic poem, *Beowulf*. A poem clearly written for entertainment, with many legends incorporated in it that had been passed down by word of mouth. People in those days really listened to the stories others had to tell. But then again they didn't have the internet in those days or instant access to social media.

The Chinese still know how to venerate the elderly, he thought, remembering getting a free drink from a Chinese waiter at a restaurant once, when he'd passed the food dishes to his father before helping himself to them. A flash of guilt hit him as he thought about his current fractious relationship with his father. He really had to try and make an effort to mend it for both their sakes.

Emilio was looking at his hands, drifting off into other worlds and thoughts too.

'How long did they stay for?'

'Who? The gypsies? The harvest season around here is between November and January. We relied on the gypsies to harvest the olives, as cheap labour, though nowadays of course everything is done by machinery. Depending on the size of the farm they could spend months picking olives or just a couple of weeks. The gypsies used to get paid by the bucketful of olives at the end of each day, but the chancers would generally go where the pay or the perks were best. Like anyone else would, I guess, but it meant they were unreliable. They had no sense of loyalty.'

'Did they just camp outside?'

'Yes, of course. No one trusted them enough to let them stay in their homes. They'd no fixed address, no identification papers either, so there was no way to trace them. People were cautious. As a young man, I was absolutely fascinated by them and I used to sneak up near their camps to watch them.' Emilio took a deep breath. 'I tell you, the women ruled the roost with the gypsies. You didn't mess with their women. Some of them were stunning but wild as anything.'

Emilio chuckled to himself.

'I always tease Nuria and call her gypsy. She could just as well be a gypsy, except for her love of home. There's a mother hen in there somewhere.'

Sebastián wholeheartedly agreed Nuria was like a gypsy. She was very much her own person, so independent you were scared you'd be shouted at for any old-fashioned courtesy, like opening a door for her. Still, out of respect for Emilio he decided not to say anything, in case the long list of things that irritated him about her slipped out. Emilio was her dad, after all.

22

Sebastián leant his head against the back of the armchair in Emilio's apartment and felt his muscles loosen as he relaxed. For some reason, in this room he was able to totally switch off from everything else going on around him.

Here, he wasn't tempted to think about the bills on the office desk, waiting to be paid, or the fact that he needed to check to see if any more reservations had been made for Las Nevadas, or indeed that he needed to place a call to an engineer to fix his broken washing machine, which thankfully was still under warranty.

All his to-do list vanished into the nether world when he was seated here with Emilio. Looking back in time, as they tended to do when they were conversing, the past seemed substantially more real than the present.

'I wasn't the only one who liked the gypsies.'

Sebastián lifted his head and looked at Emilio enquiringly.

'One of Diego's sons fell in love with one of the gypsy women, much to the disapproval of his father and the gypsy community. For two years he was always with her at harvest time, inseparably so. She was called Rebekka, if I remember rightly. Then suddenly, one day, both of them vanished.'

'Vanished?' asked Sebastián, startled and beginning to wonder for the first time if Emilio was making all this up.

'Yes. No one had a clue where they went or what happened to them. Rebekka's family never set foot on this land again and Diego was like a broken man. The police were called in, of course, but they found nothing. Absolutely nothing. To this day it's an unresolved mystery.'

Emilio paused for a moment. The little mantel clock pulsed away in the silence, as though taking them back in time to another age.

'There were rumours and gossip, of course. Some of the workers on the farm were muttering blackly that Diego Casales had done away with them. Which was ridiculous, of course, absolutely crazy. That man loved his son with a passion...' Emilio paused for a moment and coughed. Sebastián didn't say anything, intrigued to hear what he had to say next.

'One of the maids working in the house reported hearing Diego and his son arguing loudly the night before they disappeared. That's what caused the rumours to begin.' Emilio shrugged his shoulders dismissively. 'However, Diego had a quick temper, as I've said before. It wasn't unusual for him to be fighting with one of his children, quite the reverse in fact.'

'My goodness, I hope we're not going to end up finding a couple of dead bodies on the farm!'

'No, no,' chuckled Emilio. 'The most likely thing is that they took off to start a new life together. Pity they never came back. Diego was a harsh man but he wasn't unforgiving. He would have welcomed them back into the fold eventually.'

'What about the rest of the children? How did they all feel?'

'They were all upset, of course they were. They'd come to celebrate the Christmas holidays here and it ended up in disaster. It was horrible for all of them.'

109

Emilio sighed.

Outside in the courtyard, from a cage hanging by the window, a couple of José Luis's yellow canaries burst into song, trying to compete unsuccessfully with the racket the swifts were making in the palm tree.

'However, it wasn't the only scandal they lived through as a family. Another of Diego's sons had become a priest, much to the delight of his parents. But when he impregnated one of his parishioners – a huge scandal in those days – all hell broke loose. His father cut off all contact with him for a long time but eventually relented. Diego was fierce but he wasn't inhuman, by any measure.'

'Yes, I do wonder how long it'll be before the Catholic Church allows priests to marry and have families, like they do in the Protestant faith,' Sebastián said. 'It's absurd. My view is men aren't infallible and it's unnatural for them to have their natural instincts curbed in priesthood. It should be a matter of choice for all priests.'

'Ha, you must be joking. You've seen them all on TV. All the highest-ranking priests are old men and no one changes the status quo at that age. And I don't think they will ever trust a younger man to change things either.'

Emilio looked pensively across at an engraving of the Virgin Mary above the fireplace carved by José Luis.

'The Church will always be hundreds of years behind the rest of civilisation. Look at contraception. When I was a young man you didn't use contraception because it was a sin. Nowadays you'd have to be a fool not to see most Catholics, devout or otherwise, are using contraception in the face of the Church's teaching against it.'

Sebastián decided he'd better leave before they tied themselves down in a theological discussion which he didn't feel he was qualified to argue.

'Emilio, I'd better get moving and see how our new guests are getting on. Don't get up, I can let myself out,' he said quickly, standing and picking up the two empty glasses to take through to the kitchen.

'It's been good to see you, Sebastián. You should drop by more often,' Emilio said.

'I will do. The same goes for you, Emilio. Any time you see the downstairs office door open, I'll be at my desk.'

'I'll tell Nuria you came by. She was complaining she never sees you these days.'

Sebastián waved at Emilio and left, hiding the sudden elation he'd felt at knowing Nuria was missing seeing him.

23

As Sebastián stepped out of the apartment, Leila Matthews suddenly accosted him.

'There you are! We've been looking all over for you. We're wondering if we could have a quick look at the chapel. When you look at it from the upstairs corridor you can't see it clearly through the wooden lattice work.'

Sebastián looked down at her flushed, shiny face and noted the enthusiasm in her eyes. He couldn't help but be gratified at her obvious interest in the building.

'Oh. Yes, of course. I have a key in my office. I'll go and get it. We're hoping to be able to host small weddings in it in the near future. It's been left pretty much intact from when it was built in 1856.'

Sebastián nipped to his office and came out with the key, by which time Leila's husband and the McPhersons were also congregated in the courtyard. They followed Sebastián as he walked across the courtyard to a large wooden door that fitted neatly into the arch in the wall.

He put the key in the lock and after turning it a few times he gave the door a vigorous tug. Nothing opened. Cursing the old door, he tried turning the key again and pulling on the door handle. Just as he was wondering what he could do to get the wretched door open, he heard a familiar voice behind him.

'You have to pull the handle down, Seb, otherwise it won't open. Here, let me have a go.'

Nuria gave him a gentle shove and placed herself in front of the lock. Putting one boot firmly against the wall, she pushed down on the door lever with both hands and pulled back. The door opened with a complaining squeal, suggesting the hinges needed to be oiled.

Dank, cool air seemed to envelope them like fog. Sebastián hung back for a moment, feeling the stillness and sacredness of the place affect him. It felt sacrilegious to be entering solely out of inquisitiveness; the chapel belonged to people who genuinely worshipped God.

Meanwhile, his English guests had walked in with a gasp as soon as Nuria had switched the lights on.

Whoever had designed the old farmhouse had kept to spartan simplicity in the design of its outer formation, yet seemed to have reserved all their creative flair for the inside of the chapel. The same kind of idea as used in Russian Orthodox churches, thought Sebastián, like the Cathedral of Christ the Saviour in Moscow.

Black marble pillars behind the altar stretched to the top of the ceiling. A large, badly damaged oil painting of the Virgin Mary hung between the pillars, her flowing gown dark blue with a pattern of gilt stars shining through the material. The Virgin in this painting was dark skinned with black hair and looked like a gypsy. A refreshing change to the sanitised white-skinned versions of the Virgin you'd see in any gallery in Europe.

Underneath this painting there was a classical statue of the Virgin and Child with gilt halos covering their heads. The altar table was intricately carved with floral motifs: lilies, roses and irises. Two ornate antique bronze candelabra stood at either end of the altar.

Around the edges of the ceiling were painted fleur-de-lis in brilliant blue and gilt. At the top of the ceiling a colossal circular wrought-iron chandelier hung, clearly meant to be lit with candles. Now, however, modern electric cove lighting had been installed on either side of the room, above oil paintings of the disciples that were symmetrically placed on the walls. Sebastián didn't know enough to be able to decipher who the individual disciples were in the paintings.

The floor was a complicated mosaic of blue and white tiles, a pattern that led the eye cleverly to the altar. Each wooden pew was carved with various symbols, lilies, doves, pears, anchors and crucifixes. It was an almost Gaudiesque orgy of symbolic imagery.

Sebastián was always amazed at the amount of work that had been put into this small chapel.

His guests (or maybe, Sebastián ruminated, they should be more accurately called clients) were looking around with great delight. Hopefully the novelty of seeing the chapel wouldn't be the only highlight of their stay.

Felipe was meeting with all of them tomorrow to discuss which trips they'd be interested in doing while at Las Nevadas.

Sebastián turned to thank Nuria for opening the door but he soon realised she'd disappeared out of the chapel. Disappointed, he waited patiently for his guests to finish looking at the chapel and then locked up.

'Thank you so much,' said Rona McPherson, softly. 'It's been absolutely wonderful to see it. We could only see tantalising glimpses of it from upstairs.'

'It's a pleasure. I hadn't considered it would be of so much interest to guests staying here but I might have to rethink that.'

'Oh, definitely. I can't imagine anything more amazing than getting married in that chapel. It's so gorgeously unique,' said Leila enthusiastically.

'Yes, very unusual,' agreed Robert.

'Although I have to say, I'm ready for my dinner,' said Stuart, looking pointedly at his watch.

Sebastián looked at his watch. It was only half past eight, a ridiculously early time for dinner. Agustín would have a fit if Sebastián asked him to give them dinner at this hour. Clearly they hadn't taken into account that the English were used to eating so much earlier.

'I suggest, if you're hungry, we can get Agustín, our chef, to put out some tapas and some wine. It'll still be a little longer for dinner orders to be taken but tapas should keep you going.'

'Sounds good to me,' said Stuart eagerly.

They all traipsed up the main staircase to the first floor and Sebastián disappeared into the kitchen to help get some tapas together, enjoying listening to the background sound of chatter and laughter in the dining room. This farmhouse had lain empty for far too long. It needed people to keep its heart alive and well.

24

Sebastián was having a nightmare in which he was watching helplessly as Las Nevadas caught fire. The fire had started out in the kitchen and was slowly making its way to the bedrooms. In the distance he could hear the fire alarm ringing persistently and loudly.

Then he suddenly woke up, realising the fire alarm in his dream was actually his mobile phone ringing loudly on his bedside table.

He groaned and put his bedside table light on.

The clock said 3 a.m.

Then he looked at his mobile, which by now had jumped to voicemail. Five missed calls from Ricardo, the manager on duty that night. He quickly dialled Ricardo's number, which was now showing he was on another call.

He decided to get dressed quickly and head up to the main house as soon as possible.

By the time he'd thrown some clothes on and found his car keys, he saw Ricardo was calling him again.

'Ricardo, what the hell's going on? Are you all OK?'

'We've got a problem with the visitors. They're saying there's someone pacing in the attic above their rooms.'

'What?'

'They're saying they can't sleep because someone's walking

on the floor above their bedrooms,' Ricardo repeated patiently.

'Don't be ridiculous. There's nobody up there. Piedra's fixed the roof and there's absolutely nothing there.'

'Well, they're adamant they can hear someone.'

'OK. Try and keep them calm. I'm heading up there right now.'

'Sure.'

Sebastián walked out of his bedroom and realised Felipe was still asleep. He grinned maliciously to himself as he decided to wake Felipe up. Most mornings when Sebastián left the house Felipe would be lying ensconced in his bed, only turning up at the farmhouse in the late morning looking sickeningly refreshed. It was about time he got to share in the responsibilities of running the farm.

Sebastián walked into Felipe's room and put the light on.

'Seb, what the hell are you doing?' asked Felipe groggily, sitting up abruptly in his bed.

'Come on, wake up, sleepy head! I need you to charm our visitors, who are scared to death at the moment.'

'What?'

'We need to head up to the farmhouse.'

'What time is it?' asked Felipe, blinking blearily at his watch, trying to bring it into focus. 'But it's three o'clock!'

'Well done, Felipe. Time to get up.'

'Have you gone mad? Why?'

'Our guests are saying they've a problem sleeping because someone's walking about in the attic.'

Felipe fell back onto his pillows with a groan.

'I know, it's all a bit crazy but we need to resolve this or we'll get bad reviews, and that could kill my business.'

'OK. OK. Give me five minutes.'

Sebastián waited in the car, hoping Felipe wouldn't take too long, but his brother surprised him. In less than five minutes Felipe appeared at a run, slamming the front door shut behind him and flinging himself into the seat of the car.

When they arrived at the farmhouse they could see all the lights were on. Mateo, the security guard, was waiting for them downstairs.

'Hi Mateo. Did Ricardo call on you too?'

'Yes, when he couldn't get hold of you, he called me. Sounds like the tourists have gone a bit crazy.'

'Yes, but careful what you say in front of them. I don't know how good their Spanish is and I don't want to offend them. Right, I'd better get up there. Tell me, Mateo, do you have a torch I could borrow?'

Mateo held up the torch he was holding.

'Fantastic. We'll also need the stepladder. There's one in the kitchen if I remember rightly.'

They turned and walked up the stairs. They blinked when they got to the top of the stairs from all the bright lights.

After a moment, Sebastián could make out the guests, dressed in their colourful nightwear and looking slightly bedraggled, sitting in front of the crackling fire that Ricardo had wisely lit for them. They had cups of steaming hot coffee in their hands.

The tall Dutch couple were also sitting there, statuesque, on a sofa with the English guests. Mr and Mrs Pleiter had arrived very late last night and would not be best pleased with this interruption to their slumber.

Sebastián sighed. What a disastrous first night. It had all been going so well up to this point.

'Hi, everyone,' he said, trying to sound authoritative. 'I do apologise for your disturbed sleep. We're going to get the stepladder and have a good look around in the attic. Hopefully we'll get this problem resolved as soon as possible and you can get back to bed.'

'There's definitely someone up there, walking around. It's terrifying to hear it,' said Rona, looking out of her mind with terror.

'It does sound like someone's pacing up there,' added her husband.

'Well, it's easy to have a look and see what's happening if you'll just excuse us for a few moments. Our builder has redone the entire attic space so I'll be very surprised to find someone up there.'

'It could be a ghost,' said Leila, looking shaky and absolutely terrified.

'Let's not get carried away too soon,' said Felipe reassuringly, keeping a straight face.

They went to get the stepladder and trooped along to the corridor in front of the chapel. Sebastián had left Ricardo behind to attend to the guests so it was just Mateo, Felipe and him.

'These people,' said Felipe disgustedly under his breath. 'Ghosts, indeed! They've clearly been reading too many romantic novels. Crazy bastards.'

'Shhh,' Sebastián said sternly, quelling his brother with a fiery look.

They got the trapdoor open and then Sebastián took the torch in his mouth and climbed up the ladder, Mateo holding on to it from below. He heaved himself up on to the dusty attic floor and then moved to one side. Felipe appeared two minutes later, looking like he was having fun with this latest adventure, and not in the least bit afraid of what they might find.

Sebastián stood up, gripping the torch in his right hand. The attic reminded him of a catacomb or one of the sherry cellars in Jerez. It seemed to stretch on forever and had the atmosphere of somewhere that was totally detached from the outside world. Wooden beams stretched across the roof space, criss-crossing neatly into the far distance. Now and again the torch hit the glint of a steel girder, placed by the latest builders to give added support to the old building. The floor space was covered in rough-hewn planks of wood.

Sebastián shone his torch and moved slowly round in a circle. In an instant his heart stopped as he caught sight of a pair of red eyes gleaming at him from the far corner.

Unthinkingly he reversed into Felipe and trod on his foot.

'Ow! Watch what you're doing, Seb!'

Felipe suddenly seemed to notice Sebastián wasn't paying him any attention. He peered over his shoulder. 'Have you seen something?'

Sebastián didn't answer. He started to move slowly towards the glinting eyes staring unflinchingly at him from other end of the attic. He could hear and feel Felipe breathing heavily down his neck, as he tried to catch sight of what had caught Sebastián's interest.

'I see it, Seb! What the hell is it?' whispered Felipe excitedly.

Sebastián lifted his hand in irritation, trying to keep Felipe quiet as he walked slowly towards the strangely intelligent-looking eyes. He was fairly sure by now he knew what he was dealing with but wanted a closer look to make sure.

Step by step they moved closer and still those strange eyes remained in place, determinedly unmoved by the two men inching towards them. Once they were within five feet, Sebastián moved to one side to allow Felipe a chance to have a look.

His brother suddenly convulsed with silent laughter. Sebastián grinned at him.

'Hell! It's an owl of all things.'

The owl blinked at them and ruffled out its handsome brown and black plumage, clearly undaunted by their presence. Its curious orange eyes stayed on them, though, watching their every move with interest.

'If I'm not mistaken, it's a *Bubo bubo hispanus*. An eagle-owl. Nuria told me they used to live at the farmhouse many years ago. I guess the workmen haven't scared them away. I wonder how they got in, though?'

'I'd have a look to see if we can find out, if I were you. You can't have your guests, who've paid a fortune for their rooms, complaining they can't sleep at night.'

'I know, although it might be easier to get Piedra up here in the morning. He knows this roof space better than I do.'

'Let's have a quick look just now and then I agree, leave it to Piedra to sort out in the morning. Eagle-owls are big birds. There must be a massive hole somewhere around here.'

They both turned slowly in a circle, letting the torch arch its way from side to side of the attic space. Sebastián paused for a moment when the torch glinted on something in the right hand corner. He walked slowly up the attic to see what was there.

It revealed itself as a metallic box, approximately 40 cms by 20 cms. It was rusty and sitting in the recess between two beams. Sebastián moved it cautiously with his foot. He'd seen some large hairy spiders drowned in the pool outside and he didn't fancy coming across one unexpectedly, especially not in a dark gloomy attic.

The box scraped across the floor.

Sebastián bent down and lifted the lid off it. Inside was a mass of old papers. He was intrigued.

He replaced the lid and picked it up. Felipe had been watching him with interest.

'This place has more and more surprises. We should really bring up more torches and see what else we can find.'

'Tomorrow, maybe. When Piedra's here with us. I'm hoping if the guests are told it's an owl they'll calm down enough to get some sleep. We're not going to find anything when it's pitch black outside. It's easier to spot large holes in the daylight.'

Felipe turned back to the owl.

'Sorry, old fellow, looks like your days here are numbered.'

'I wish we could find somewhere else for him, or her, to stay. I might call Manuel in the morning, to see if he has any ideas on what to do with an eagle-owl. For all we know, they might be endangered.'

'Your farmer friend?'

Sebastián nodded. Felipe shrugged.

'Yeah, he might know what to do. I can't believe it's the first time an owl's made its home inside someone's attic. After all, we're out on the edge of the wilderness here.'

The pair of them turned and walked back to the trapdoor at the far end of the attic. Sebastián slid onto his stomach when he reached it and handed down the metallic box to Mateo, who looked bemused but took it obediently without asking any questions about its contents.

Then Sebastián let himself down the ladder and held it for his brother.

'I suggest we keep the ladder up in case the guests don't accept our explanation or want something done about the owl tonight. I wouldn't like to frighten it off but we can do that if it's really going to bother them.'

They walked along to the dining hall. Six expectant faces looked at them as they entered and Sebastián found himself clearing his throat nervously.

'We've found the culprit. There's an eagle-owl who's made its home in the attic.'

There was a united cry of surprise and delight from his guests.

'So the main question is, can you wait until the morning to get this problem sorted? If you can deal with the owl staying here for tonight, I'll get my builder here in the morning to see if he can seal up any entrance, so once it's out the owl can't get back into the attic.'

Sebastián paused to look at his guests. All of them were looking at him impassively.

'If, on the other hand, you'd prefer him gone tonight I could try to frighten him off but to be honest it'll be easier to do it in the morning. I'd also rather speak to some locals about the best way to get the owl to move on to new pastures.'

Mr Pleiter nodded.

'It's fine by me to wait until tomorrow.'

'Yes, but it's not you that has to deal with the noise of the owl walking up and down. It's only our end of the building that's affected,' complained Stuart.

Mr Pleiter shrugged dismissively at him.

'What do you think, ladies?' asked Robert.

'It's fine by me. I'm so relieved it's nothing sinister,' said Rona.

Leila nodded. In spite of the coffee, she was struggling to keep her eyes open and looked as though she was ready to fall asleep on the sofa.

'OK, Mateo, can you shut the trapdoor again?' asked Sebastián decisively, turning to the security guard, who nodded. 'Right, we'll let everyone get back to bed. Thank you for your understanding. I'll see you in the morning.'

Within a short space of time Sebastián and Felipe were driving down to their house, watching carefully so they didn't unexpectedly hit any rabbits or hares on the road. There were no streetlights here in the countryside. Despite the starry sky and the pale circle of the moon it was very dark. Sebastián made a mental note to get a telescope; he was itching to see this beautiful night sky in more detail.

The crickets, reassuringly, were out in full chorus that night.

'I do like it when you're bossy, bro. It's a new side to you. Telling your minions where to go.'

'Oh, shut up, Felipe.'

'There you go again.'

'By the way, don't forget you told them you'd take them up to Sierra Nevada in the van tomorrow.'

Felipe groaned.

'Hopefully they'll give up on the idea. I don't think after tonight we'll see any of them before lunchtime anyway.'

'I'll make sure you're reporting for duty at twelve.'

Felipe slouched despondently in his seat. Sebastián grimaced to himself. Tomorrow was going to be a long day for the both of them.

The metal box they'd found in the attic lay forgotten, for now, in the boot of the car.

25

It was six o'clock in the evening when Sebastián started to wonder where his guests were. They'd set off from the farmhouse at half past twelve, in the red minivan, to visit a small area of Sierra Nevada, with Felipe deputising as tour guide.

The trip marked out by Felipe was only supposed to take four hours. Where the hell were they? Sebastián tried calling Felipe at ten-minute intervals but his phone stubbornly wouldn't connect with Felipe's. There were many black spots around Spain where there was no possibility of establishing mobile phone reception and clearly Sierra Nevada had plenty of them. Eventually he put the phone down on his desk, feeling pathetically helpless.

He scrolled aimlessly down the photos Felipe had sent to his mobile phone a couple of hours ago.

In one of them there was a blurred picture of a wild Mouflon sheep, its horns curled magnificently on either side of its head. It was standing against a rocky outcrop. Its horns looked almost too heavy for the strangely elongated head with its gleaming white snout.

In another photograph a large green ocellated lizard basked in the sunlight.

Sebastián sighed. Maybe they'd just got distracted on the journey. After all, the guests were all keen wildlife geeks. Their apparatus had taken up most of the space in the boot; an assortment of cameras and binoculars, notebooks and even folding stools.

Still he couldn't shake off a feeling of misgiving and anxiety. The last thing he wanted was for his guests to be stranded in the middle of Sierra Nevada at night. How long did he leave it before he called the police, for example?

One of the photos Felipe had sent him had shown a mountain road sagging downwards on the edge of a ravine, where part of it had been washed away by winter storms. He couldn't help but think of the rough terrain the van was driving through.

He shook his head resolutely and, turning to his computer, he started to look at his emails to distract himself.

At least they'd now resolved their problem with the eagle-owl.

One of the farm workers who worked for Manuel, Nicolás, had come down mid-morning to help remove the owl from the attic. Nicolás apparently liked birds of prey and had already had some experience with them, having removed a couple of owls from a barn on Manuel's property a few years previously.

According to what Manuel had told Sebastián, Nicolás had apparently at one time even kept an injured golden eagle in the bathroom of his own home until the eagle's wing healed sufficiently for it to be released into the wild again.

At the end of the day Nicolás wasn't really needed, for as soon as they came within a foot of the squawking owl, it launched itself into the air and then swiftly disappeared through a hole in the corner of the attic. Nicolás and Sebastián had then studied with interest the hole the owl had escaped through.

It was a surprisingly tight hole for such a big owl to squeeze through, barely 30 cms across, and placed where the rafters of the roof coincided with the wooden planks of the attic floor. Later, Piedra had cut up some pieces of wood and nailed them into place over the gaping hole. Sebastián devoutly hoped that would be the end of any owls creaking up and down the attic floors at night.

Sebastián's phone started ringing at seven o'clock. Seeing it was a call from Felipe he rapidly reached across the table to answer it.

'Felipe, *hombre*, where are you?'

'We're at a small village called Yegen. I'm afraid we got a little lost. I was panicking at one point because we were going to run out of fuel but thankfully we've reached Yegen. We're going to be back late because it's going to take at least three hours for us to get home. We're going to get something to eat here. I think you're going to have to recruit someone who knows this mountain range well enough to take the next trip.'

'Yes, you're absolutely right. We can't have groups of tourists lost in the mountains. Is everyone OK with the trip so far?'

'Oh yes. They're delighted with the trip. You've seen the photos I've sent you? They've spotted wild goat, wild hogs, birds and lizards (no doubt they'll tell you which ones). At one pit stop we disturbed a number of golden eagles that were perched on the other side of the hill we were on. They took off when they saw us. It really was an amazing sight. The scenery's absolutely stunning.'

Felipe paused for a moment and Sebastián smiled to himself. It wasn't like Felipe to wax lyrical about nature.

'I don't think they remotely regret coming but we'll be back late. I'm coming back on the main road to Ronda, going past Granada. The mountain roads are just a maze and I'm not travelling on them in the dark.'

'No absolutely not, that would be a disaster, Felipe. OK, best of luck for the trip back home. Well done for making it to Yegen. I wasn't sure at what time to contact the police or mountain rescue.'

'I'm glad you didn't. That would've looked totally unprofessional. At least I can pretend, for now, that I know what I'm doing.'

'OK. Well give me a call if any problems arise, but if not I'll expect you back around elevenish.'

'Yes, see you then, Seb.'

Sebastián hung up feeling slightly guilty. It couldn't have been easy for Felipe when he found himself with a low petrol tank and absolutely no idea of where he was. It was obvious Sebastián was now going to have to pay an experienced driver to navigate the mountain trails.

They were learning as they went along but nothing seemed to run smoothly. He sighed. He would ask Nuria and her gardeners if they knew of anyone who'd like to help out with trips to Sierra Nevada. This might prove to be harder than they realised. Most of the locals he'd met with in Ronda didn't seem terribly interested in exploring the wilderness of the mountains around here and as a consequence had minimal knowledge of Sierra Nevada and its mountainous roads.

Still, on a positive note he had several bookings for the mews houses and the farmhouse over the next few months. Slowly but surely there was a steady trickle of guests arriving and this would then spill over to his sorely tried bank account.

He called Agustín, the cook, to let him know the guests wouldn't be eating at the farmhouse tonight and then he leant back in his chair trying to decide what to do for the next few hours while he waited for them to arrive.

He suddenly remembered the rusty old box he'd left in the boot of his car. The box they'd found in the attic yesterday. Now was as good a time as any to explore its contents.

26

Sebastián lifted the lid off the box and peered inside.

The box was half empty apart from a large bundle of papers tied with a red ribbon. All the papers were handwritten. It seemed strange they had been left to moulder in the attic. The farmhouse was so big there was ample space to store a box of letters in any of the downstairs rooms. Clearly, whoever had left the box in the attic hadn't been able to throw the letters away, but equally didn't want anyone else looking at them either.

He cut through the red ribbon and lifted the first letter out of the box, spreading it out and positioning his desk light on it so he could see it clearly. The writing was neat, the letters tightly fitted together so that their loops merged into the words on the page:

13th December 1977

Dear Father

I'm sorry we left without saying goodbye and I am sorry for the pain I'll have caused you.

You will never, ever, understand but Rebekka is my soul mate and I cannot live any longer without her.

I have pleaded and begged with you but you never accepted the seriousness of my feelings for her. Her family were just as unhappy as you were about our relationship. Why you all objected so strongly I'll never know.

The world has moved on, nobody has arranged marriages any more. We no longer live under a dictatorship. Now we have our political freedom we shouldn't be living with a dictatorship within our own families.

I know you cursed Rebekka and her family for being illiterate. Being illiterate does not equate to stupidity. Theirs is a different culture to ours and, of course, a different way of living. They might be poor but they are rich in ways our family never was. The bonds they have with each other are far stronger than the ones we have with each other.

I would hate to lose contact with you forever.

Please, if you ever feel able to, write to me leaving your letters with my friend Pedro Lantro who lives in 71 Avenida de la Serranía, Apartamento 2, Ronda, Málaga 29010.

Yours dutifully
Gabriel Casales

Sebastián, who was leaning across the desk with interest as he read, sat back in his chair. His heart was beating uncomfortably rapidly as the full implications of the letter sank into him. This was clearly a letter from a son of Diego Casales, the previous owner of Las Nevadas. He remembered Emilio telling him about the gypsy girl Rebekka and how Diego's son had disappeared with her.

He reached across and pulled out another letter, casting a quick glance at the others in the box. All of them were written in the same handwriting.

The second letter was in much the same vein as the first:

25th January 1977

Dear Father

I know you'll still be angry at my leaving with Rebekka. I'll just keep on writing to you because I would like to think you'll be pleased to know we are well and safe. As long as I can do so I will send these letters in the hope that one day you'll soften enough to reply and we can establish communication once more.

I have found work here on a fishing trawler. It is a new life for me but one that suits me. A family, who've lived off the sea for generations, own the fishing trawler. I work with the father and two of his sons. When we are out at sea I find I can leave all my troubles behind. It's hard, backbreaking work but there are moments that are very special. Sometimes in the evenings we see dolphins leaping in the sea around us. Other times we have orcas following us when we have filleted some of the fish.

We spend long nights playing cards and drinking wine. Many nights I lie on my bunk and feel very alone but when I come back to shore Rebekka's always waiting for me, with a lovely smile on her face. Rebekka has found work as a waitress at a café in town. On my days off I go and sit in the café and help her clear up at the end of the day. We are happy.

And you, Father? How are you? Is your leg still giving you some bother? How are my brothers and sisters? I hope you are all doing well. I think of you all in Madrid now. Carlos will be back at college, Silvia will be starting senior school and Miriam will be busy with her children. Alvaro will still be working at his new job at the Ministry of Agriculture, I guess. I think of them all the time.

133

Take care of yourself, Father,
  Gabriel Casales

Sebastián put it down and rummaged in the box, looking at the dates on the letters. They were in chronological order. 5th February 1977, 13th March 1977, 8th April 1977, 20th May 1977, 2nd June 1977, 6th July 1977. Then he found there was a big time lapse. The next one was dated 22nd March 1983:

Dear Father,

I have been thinking of you often recently. I had vowed not to write any more, after not hearing from you for so many years, but this year my first child was born. A boy. We have named him Andrés Daniel Casales. I feel so sad that you aren't here to share in our joy. I wish you would write to us because I would love to be able to come down and see you once more, to show you your grandson.

He has ink black eyes and dark brown hair. He has the Casales nose and mouth. He is a placid boy, content to play with his toys, and he sleeps well. The local community here have given us a lot of support and love. They brought us meals for many days after Andrés arrived. They have shared in our sorrows and our joys over the last few years and have become a sort of family to us. But still I cannot stop thinking of you and wondering how you all are. I cannot cut all my childhood memories from my mind and whenever I look at Andrés I feel great sadness that he does not know his grandfather or his uncles and aunts.

I know I hurt you, Father, but please could you find it in your heart to forgive us and receive us once more into your home? I would love to show Andrés where I grew up and for him to meet his extended family.

With sincere wishes for your forgiveness,
Gabriel Casales

Sebastián put the letter down. He suddenly felt as though he was intruding on someone's private life, ogling at someone else's tragic story.

Again he thought of his own difficult relationship with his father. There was really no comparison. His father would never disown him, let alone refuse to meet any grandchild of his. Even in all their most intense arguments, Sebastián knew his father loved him and cared about what happened to him.

There was no sign that Diego Casales had made any effort to contact his son. Gabriel's sadness seemed to permeate all his letters to his father despite his assertions that he was happy and well.

Sebastián decided he needed to speak to Emilio in the morning. There had to be a way of tracking down Gabriel or his descendants. These letters had to be returned to them. They didn't belong here any more.

Surely Emilio would know of a Casales family member or someone who could trace the whereabouts of Gabriel Casales.

Maybe he should also ask Adolfo, the solicitor who seemed to know so much about everyone in Ronda, whether he had any leads as to where Gabriel Casales might be living. He also had the address of Gabriel's friend in Ronda on one of the letters: Pedro Lantro. That was another lead he could follow up on.

As he sat musing he heard the van bumping over the cobbles on the driveway outside the farmhouse. He hastily dumped the letters into the metal box, switched off the lights and locked the office door before going out into the dark courtyard to greet his tired brother and guests after their day's travel.

27

May 2018

Sebastián slouched in the chair of the waiting room at Casa Valiente, the estate agent and solicitors' office where Adolfo worked. He felt uncomfortable sitting in this office again. The last time he was here he'd had a panic attack. Like anyone who's ever had a panic attack he couldn't dissociate himself from his surroundings or the memory of the anxiety that had engulfed him.

Still, he was here with an important motive. He wanted to see if Adolfo, a huge fount of local knowledge, could tell him how to contact the Casales family, or if he'd know where Gabriel Casales might be living these days.

The Casales letters were keeping his mind occupied, a useful distraction from his brother's latest romance, with Nuria. Earlier that morning he'd arrived at his office only to see Felipe sheepishly making an appearance out of Nuria's apartment. Neither of them pretended they didn't know what that signified. Sebastián hoped Felipe wasn't going to cause a ruckus with his latest fling (and with Felipe it always was a fling).

'Sebastián?'

Sebastián recognised the prim tone and looked up with a smile to see Adolfo in the doorway beckoning him to his office. They shook hands amicably.

'How are things going? It's been a while since I last saw you.'

Sebastián grimaced.

'Yes, as you know there's a lot of work to be done at Las Nevadas. It never seems to end.'

Adolfo nodded as they sat down in his office.

'How may I help you?'

'I wondered if you would be able to advise me. I discovered in the attic of the farmhouse a box of letters from Gabriel Casales to his father and I feel duty bound to return them to him or to a member of his family. It doesn't look as if Diego Casales ever replied to his letters – I wondered if you would have any information that might help in this respect. Emilio said this firm dealt with Diego Casales's will.'

Adolfo put his fingers together pensively.

'It's very interesting that these letters have been discovered. I cannot think of a reason why Diego Casales wouldn't have written back to his son.'

'Well, he ran off with the gypsy girl, Rebekka, didn't he? In the face of Diego's opposition to the relationship.'

'Yes but Diego Casales had forgiven Gabriel.'

'How do you know that?'

'Because he left Gabriel as one of the largest beneficiaries of his will when he died in 1989.'

'By Spanish law you can't disinherit your children.'

'No, you can't. But only a third part goes to the children, another third goes to your preferred child or children, and the final third is at your discretion. Diego Casales fully included Gabriel in his testament; in fact the final third of his estate was to go to Gabriel in its entirety. He wouldn't have done that if he still felt angry with him. The problem was, no one knew where Gabriel was at the time the will was read and no one had been in contact with him. We did a search for him but we never had any joy. The money went to the remaining children.'

'But what about these letters? They're heart-rending. It's clear he never heard from his father.'

'It's a mystery to me. I know if Diego Casales had received them he would have replied.'

'So you think someone kept the letters from him? Hid them from him?'

'It's the only conclusion to draw. Diego had forgiven his son. He would have reached out to him if he could've done so.'

Sebastián pondered this. The implications were quite startling. Who could have intercepted the letters and kept them all these years?

'In the first letter he asks his father to leave letters with a friend of his in Ronda. Is that a lead worth pursuing?'

'Let me see it,' Adolfo said imperatively, holding out his hand.

Sebastián passed him the letter and watched as Adolfo read it carefully.

'Pedro Lantro... I don't know anyone of that name. Your only option, I guess, is to see who lives there now and if they know anything about this Pedro Lantro. Other than that, I think you'll find yourself facing a brick wall in terms of finding Gabriel's whereabouts. We tried with all our resources to find him and we got nowhere.'

'Before I head back to Las Nevadas I think I'll stop by this address.'

'Good luck with your quest,' said Adolfo. 'If you ever do, by some miracle, find Gabriel Casales, you should tell him he's entitled to reclaim his share of the money. It was handed out to his siblings. By law they had to wait for five years while we searched for Gabriel but at the end of that period the money was divided up between them. He still has a right to reclaim it. It would be a fairly arduous legal process, though.'

Sebastián nodded and stood up to shake hands once more with Adolfo. As he left the office he felt the satisfaction of gleaning another piece of valuable information that might one day unlock the mystery around these letters.

28

It was early on Wednesday morning and Ronda was already bustling with activity. Sebastián took his phone out and typed Pedro Lantro's address into Google Maps: 71 Avenida de la Serranía.

He decided to walk there, leaving his car at Casa Valiente, as he felt the need of some exercise. He followed the directions on his phone meticulously until he arrived at Avenida de la Serranía forty minutes later. It was a relatively nondescript, quiet and leafy street with neat, bleach-white, two-storey houses and tidy, well-kept pathways. There were red tiles on the roofs and around the lower half of the houses. Trees were planted at regular intervals, mostly orange trees but also the odd palm tree.

Right at the end of the street, at a dead end, there were two significantly larger buildings, each five storeys high and on opposite sides of the road. Sebastián headed towards these buildings, guessing Pedro's flat must be in one of them. He eventually found door number 71 and looked at the various names listed next to it. Gabriel's letter had stated Pedro's flat as Apartamento 2 (Flat 2). There was no name next to the doorbell for Flat 2 but Sebastián decided to push on it anyway.

A woman's voice answered abruptly through the intercom. She sounded very young.

'*Quién es?*'

'*Hola*. I'm looking for Pedro Lantro? I'm from *la finca* Las Nevadas.'

The door buzzed open. Sebastián left the sunshine outside and entered a dimly lit stairwell with a lift to one side. He walked up to the first landing where he saw a door was open. A girl in her late teens, dressed fashionably with big circular earrings and a thick layer of make-up, greeted him.

'*Hola*. I'm Carmen Lantro. Come in. My grandfather is in the sitting-room.'

He walked into the flat and immediately could hear the television blaring away at high volume. Carmen led him directly along the hallway to the sitting-room. On a comfortable armchair sat an elderly man avidly watching the television. He had snow-white hair against his tanned skin and a back that was uncomfortably hunched over.

Carmen reached over and switched the television off, saying loudly: 'This gentleman has come to see you, Grandad. He's from Las Nevadas.'

Pedro turned awkwardly to look at Sebastián. His painfully slow movements suggested he suffered from rheumatoid arthritis, which was a rare occurrence in the dry climate of Ronda.

Sebastián shook hands with Pedro and took a seat on the sofa next to him. Carmen plonked herself on an armchair to watch them. She gave the impression she didn't have much to occupy herself with and this was a welcome diversion to her daily routine.

'Hi. I'm Sebastián Ortez, the new owner of Las Nevadas,' Sebastián said loudly, hoping Pedro could hear him. 'We were looking around in the attic there and we found a box of letters from Gabriel Casales.'

Pedro nodded but didn't say anything. His eyes were wary and watchful.

'In one of his letters Gabriel asks his father to write to him at this address. As I'm keen to return the letters to Gabriel, I was wondering if you would possibly know where he is. So we can get in touch with him.'

Pedro shook his head.

'I lost contact with Gabriel years ago. I could tell you the last address he lived in but I guarantee you he'll have moved on from there. We're talking at least twenty years ago...'

'Well, I guess it might be a start. If not, I'll have to return them to one of his brothers or sisters.'

'I would strongly advise against that. Gabriel probably wouldn't want his siblings reading over those letters, especially if they're very personal. Look, I'll make some enquiries and if you leave me your phone number I'll give you a call when I hear from him, or if I hear from someone who knows of him. I would prefer Gabriel contacted you himself, rather than handing over information he might not wish for you to know.'

'I understand that. However, it's not just me who has a reason to find him. The lawyers who looked after Diego Casales's affairs would like to speak to him too. He was left a substantial amount in Diego's will and never claimed it because they couldn't locate him.'

Pedro shook his head in disapproval.

'What a farce! Diego Casales never cared a jot for Gabriel! He never contacted him once. I should know. There were many times I wanted to go up to Las Nevadas and confront him about it but Gabriel always stopped me. He didn't want any more bad blood between him and his father.'

'We've reason to believe Diego Casales never received these letters.'

'Nonsense. Why wouldn't he have received them? You said they were put in the attic at Las Nevadas.'

'Yes, but the people who knew Diego are convinced he would've welcomed his son back to Las Nevadas and that he would've got in touch if he could've done so. Somebody obviously kept the letters away from his father.'

Pedro looked down at his hands as he pondered for a moment. He didn't seem convinced by this argument.

'It seems unlikely to me. I don't know who would have done that. The only ones I can think of, who would've had the authority to take those letters before they reached Diego, would be one of his children. But I can't think which one of them would be so against Diego getting in touch with his own son. As far as I was aware, Gabriel's siblings loved him. The only one that possibly comes to mind is Carlos...'

'The son who was a priest?'

Pedro snorted.

'Yes, him. Gabriel said to me in confidence once that you had to watch Carlos. He didn't think his brother was trustworthy. He didn't explain further but he was always a good judge of character.'

Sebastián shrugged.

'Well, I guess the main thing is to try and find Gabriel now. These letters belong to him. Here's my business card with my name and number. Most of the time you'll find me at Las Nevadas. Feel free to get in contact any time you wish to.'

'OK. I will do. Thanks for dropping by. I'll let you know how I get on.'

Sebastián shook hands with Pedro and kissed his grand-daughter dutifully on both cheeks.

He exited the building feeling slightly disheartened by his conversation with Pedro. Even if Pedro did manage to get in touch with Gabriel, there were no guarantees Gabriel would want to make himself known. Still, he'd done all he could for now.

It was time to focus on the farm once more.

29

Sebastián arrived at the farmhouse just in time to disturb Nuria and Felipe in the middle of a kiss. They were curled up together on a bench in the front garden. They waved at Sebastián carelessly but he didn't bother waving back. He just scowled at them and drove his car into the farmhouse courtyard.

He couldn't explain to himself why it bothered him so much to see them together.

Twenty minutes later, Felipe was standing in the doorway to the office.

'Seb.'

'What?'

'What's eating at you?'

'What do you mean? Me? Nothing. I'm just feeling fed up because I've had an unsuccessful trip to Ronda. I haven't had much joy in locating Gabriel Casales, the man who wrote those letters. Now it turns out he also had money left to him in Diego Casales's will but never claimed it. It's getting more and more complicated.'

'Are you sure that's all it is?'

'Yes, why?'

'Because it's begun to occur to me you might not approve of my relationship with Nuria.'

Sebastián shrugged his shoulders nonchalantly.

'It's nothing to do with me, although I don't think it's very professional to have members of the staff snogging in the garden.'

'Fine. This whole thing bothers you, though.'

'Felipe, will you just stop? I don't need any stress from you. You're supposed to be helping me out here, remember?'

'OK, but I'll just say I think you're a dog in a manger, Seb. You don't want Nuria for yourself but you're clearly not happy about her having a relationship with me. I like her. I think she's a sweetheart and I think you should accept our relationship and get used to it.'

'Until you dump her like you've dumped every other woman in your orbit, Felipe.'

'That's harsh. A leopard can change his spots. Don't keep making assumptions about me.'

'OK. OK. I'm sorry. Was there anything else you wanted to talk to me about?'

'We're wondering if you'd like to join us at the flamenco concert at the bullring in Ronda next month.'

'To play gooseberry? No, thank you.'

'There's a few of us planning on going. A few of Nuria's friends are wanting to go too.'

'Is that so? Well, maybe, then.'

'Fine. We'll get you a ticket.'

Felipe walked out of the doorway and headed up to the farmhouse for his lunchtime coffee.

Sebastián picked up the box of letters and rammed it onto the crowded shelf behind him. Neatness wasn't one of his virtues, he thought, looking ruefully at his desk. He dreamed of the day he could afford to hire a secretary.

He decided he couldn't face sitting down at his desk today. Stacks of paperwork were a real turn off.

He'd left the office door open, so he went to the doorway and looked out. José Luis, in his thick grey work overalls, was heading back to the workshop after his lunch at the apartment.

'Hi, José Luis. How are you doing?'

'Nuria's gone to get a snake out of the swimming pool.'

'I'm sorry. Say that again? I don't think I heard you right.'

'Nuria's getting a snake out of the swimming pool,' repeated José Luis patiently. 'The little girl with the red hair, the one that's staying at the mews this week, was screaming that a snake was hissing at her in the pool. Her parents couldn't see anything when they looked, so they thought she was just making it up. But Nuria says some snakes like water so there might be one there after all and she's gone to find it.'

'Good grief! Why would a snake want to sit in a pool of chlorinated water?'

'I don't know,' said José Luis, nonplussed. Clearly deciding he'd said enough, he carried on walking towards his workshop.

Sebastián slammed the office door shut and walked over to the swimming pool, glad of the distraction of getting involved in something practical, although not convinced there was any real reason to worry. He couldn't see why a snake would decide to make its home in a swimming pool.

Sebastián loved the gardens at the front of the farmhouse. With plenty of irrigation and fertiliser they now looked a picture of health, the greenery providing plenty of speckled shade along the cobbled driveway.

He walked briskly along the pathway to the swimming pool, noticing that the little orange trees already had fruit starting to grow on them. In the distance, next to the swimming pool, the sweeping, graceful branches of a miniature willow tree could be seen. This tree would grow to be ten times bigger but it would take time, approximately fifteen years in fact.

At this time of day most people would be either having lunch or relaxing after having eaten, so nobody was out sunbathing on the sun loungers and there was no sign of Abigail, the precocious little girl who'd supposedly spotted a snake.

At one end of the pool Nuria was stretched out on top of the diving board overlapping the edge of the pool, with her head bending down, the ends of her jet-black hair trailing in the water. She seemed to be poking around in the square entrance to the pool's filter system.

'Hi, Nuria.'

Nuria looked up at him, holding on precariously to the side of the pool. She swung her legs forwards so she could sit up.

'Hi.'

'I've just heard some ridiculous story from José Luis. He says there's been a snake spotted in the pool?'

'It's not ridiculous. Come here.'

Sebastián walked around the edge of the pool to where Nuria was sitting.

'Be quiet for a minute and listen.'

She bent down and poked in the water filter with a stick.

Hissing reverberated from the filter. Sebastián jumped up hurriedly.

'*¡Madre mía!* So she was right. What's a snake doing in there?'

Nuria pushed her hair out of her eyes.

'It happens quite a lot with grass snakes or viperine snakes. When the weather's warmer they find it harder to find water and often end up lodging themselves in water tanks or swimming pools. They're pretty harmless, actually. They can bite but they're not poisonous.'

'I should hope not. I'd get sued if someone swimming in this pool ended up in hospital with a venomous snakebite. How on earth are we going to get it out of there?'

Nuria smiled cheekily and curled her lip at his use of 'we', which made Sebastián suddenly feel very small and foolish.

She shrugged.

'It's quite tightly coiled up in the filter. I think the best thing is to put the filter on and see if that gives it enough of a fright to dislodge it.'

She disappeared along the base of the pool into a small room where the filter engine was placed. Sebastián quickly moved a safe distance away from the filter but still kept it in view so he could see if and when the snake decided to move.

It didn't take long after the engine started for the snake to shoot out of the filter, swimming rapidly with its strange wriggling motion until it reached the bottom of the pool.

Sebastián looked down at it with interest. The snake was about 80 cm long and a pale brown colour, with an attractive pattern of chocolate-coloured diamonds on its body. The snake's expressionless, unblinking eyes were placed close to the top of its head. Obviously this would make hunting on the water surface easier. For now, though, it stayed motionless at the bottom, like an effigy carved into the floor of the pool.

Nadia appeared next to Sebastián carrying a pool net, and deftly scraped it across the bottom of the pool, scooping up the errant snake. Sebastián moved hurriedly out of the way as the net surfaced; he was no fan of snakes.

Nuria lifted the net, then quickly walked over to a plastic container and emptied the snake carefully into it, slamming down a plastic lid onto the container so the snake couldn't escape.

'I'll have to release this one some distance from here. Snakes can be like homing pigeons sometimes and we don't want this one coming back to pay us a visit.'

'No, definitely not. Are you going to take it away now?'

Nuria lifted up the container and nodded.

'Yes, no time like the present.'

'Do you want me to go with you?'

'No, I'll be fine, thanks,' she said brusquely. 'It's not the first time I've had to deal with viperine water snakes.'

'OK. I guess I'd better get back to my paperwork.'

'OK.'

There was a brief moment of awkward silence before they turned and walked back towards the courtyard. Sebastián was kicking himself mentally for not having more conversational flair. Unlike his brother, he'd never been any good at small talk.

30

Sebastián looked around the crowded bar and then looked at his watch again, wishing the time would go by faster. Ten minutes ago he'd decided he was going book a hearing test. Since they'd entered the bar he hadn't been able to hear what anyone was saying to him and this was annoying him hugely. He was starting to wish he could lip-read.

Loud music, the chink of ice poured into cocktail glasses, the dragging of stools across the stone floor and of course the crescendo of voices in the room all combined into a cacophonous din. The noise around him thundered in his ears but a group sitting on the other side of the room seemed to have particularly penetrating voices. He couldn't understand how they could be talking so loudly; he was able to hear *them* perfectly clearly but was struggling to hear anyone next to him.

The flamenco concert was due to start at nine o'clock and they were currently ensconced in a bar called El Pavo de Oro (The Golden Turkey), situated just five minutes from the Plaza de Toros, where the concert was taking place. In the end there were twenty of them gathered in an amicable group at the bar. Most of them were Nuria's friends and most of them were male. Unsurprising, given that most of the time Nuria behaved like a total tomboy.

Nuria's girlfriends looked relatively conventional, to Sebastián's surprise, although the biggest surprise of the night was how pretty Nuria looked when she bothered to dress up. He couldn't help staring at her at various points, as if trying to make sure it really was her.

She was wearing a floor-length, venetian red dress made of chiffon, and high-heeled black sandals. The red brought out the warm mahogany tones of her skin and her black, mascaraed eyes shone brilliantly in the dim light of the bar. Sebastián had wondered how much of her dark skin had been weathered by the sun but in her sleeveless dress he could now see she was naturally dark skinned: there were no tan lines on her at all. Silver jewellery sparkled on her neck, ears and wrists. She really did look very beautiful.

By her side Felipe looked remarkably good too. He'd clearly dressed with care tonight and he looked like he'd just come out of a hair salon. They made a handsome couple. Sebastián ruefully rubbed his unshaven cheek. He'd been caught up in some last-minute accounts and hadn't had any time to get ready. He'd hastily thrown on a jacket this evening before he'd got into the waiting car with Felipe and Nuria.

Gone were the days of carefree abandon. These days he could only think of his overdraft. He was continually trying to calculate when he might actually break even. The sooner he managed to get the olive trees planted, he'd decided, the better. It would still take five years for them to grow to full size but they would provide a steady, and welcome, income every year.

He had to sit down with Nuria and the other two gardeners to see whether they would need more manpower to do the planting across the 150 hectares of land. It was a job made all the harder because they would no doubt need to hire a small digger to uproot the old diseased trees that were currently in place on the farmland.

Sebastián realised with a shock somebody had asked him a question and everyone was turned expectantly towards him to hear his answer. He shook off all thoughts of the farm.

'I'm sorry, what did you say?'

Felipe looked amused.

'They're wondering when you get to take some holidays?' Felipe yelled at the top of his voice, his strident tone causing a momentary silence as the people sitting near Felipe turned around to stare at him.

'I don't take holidays at the moment, I'm afraid, and I won't until my financial situation stabilises.'

'You'll be more productive if you take some time off,' said one of Nuria's friends.

Sebastián smiled. In his view there were too many *fiesta* days in Spain. Not only was he expected to pay double salaries on *fiesta* days, he also inevitably ended up short-staffed. People here had to be prised away from their holidays; there was nothing they held dearer. Madrid was different. Business was the drumbeat of the city, and its inhabitants had a more committed work ethic.

'I might take some time off one of these days,' Sebastián said, nodding noncommittally to his audience. He continued to make an effort to follow the conversation once the spotlight wasn't on him.

Much to Sebastián's relief they left the bar twenty minutes later and headed to the bullring. It had been built more or less at the same time as the farmhouse at Las Nevadas. It was mostly known for its most famous bullfighter, Pedro Romero, who demonstrated art and skill, as well as exceptional courage, in the bullring. Because Ronda was a small town there were fewer bullfights compared to a city like Sevilla, but the bullring was often used for impromptu concerts like tonight's flamenco performance.

As they walked towards the bullring they crossed the new bridge spanning El Tajo Canyon. Sebastián couldn't resist stopping to look briefly down at the canyon through the metal bars that opened at intervals along the bridge.

Although the Celts or Iberians (there was much historical debate as to which) occupied this city before the Romans came, it was the Romans that gave Ronda its name. The city was named 'Arunda' by its Roman conquerors, meaning 'surrounded by mountains'. Not very original, perhaps, but apt. Apparently, as far as he understood it, the Romans used to have chariot races on the flat ground at the bottom of the canyon. Now that would've been a sight to see.

Sebastián felt a tug on his jacket and turned to find Nuria and Felipe waiting patiently for him as the others walked on ahead. He walked briskly with Nuria and Felipe to catch the others up.

Half an hour later, Sebastián decided that the whole outing was going to be torture for his poor eardrums. If the noise at the bar hadn't been bad enough, the flamenco songs were giving him a headache. This concert was no sanitised version of flamenco the tourists were taken to see; this was music for the aficionados, and Sebastián had very quickly decided he wasn't one of them.

He liked the guitar music and the hand clapping but the

main vocal seemed to him to be shrieking out the song like a banshee, with a chorus of voices echoing his words.

He looked sideways to Nuria and could see she was evidently relishing the music, sitting upright in her seat spellbound, oblivious to anything else. He then peeked around her at Felipe, who caught his eye. Both of them bent down and quickly smothered their laughter in their jacket sleeves.

This was going to be a night to remember.

After a minute Sebastián sat up again and studied the bullring. It looked beautiful tonight, its many columns lit by torches casting a magical atmosphere over the arena. Above them the stars were shining brightly in the night sky, a ceiling made of a million diamonds sparkling among the velvety blackness of the night.

In the centre of the bullring, behind a microphone, a well-built lady dressed in a white and gold spotted flamenco dress now sang her song. Behind her, three ladies acted as a Greek chorus. At intervals all of them clapped in tune to the guitar. This was flamenco stripped back to its basic origins, without the dancing accompanying it. Emilio had told Sebastián that flamenco dancing, so often expressing the emotion of the song, was a late development in flamenco's history. Back in time, no dancing accompanied flamenco singing.

Apparently many scholars now believed that flamenco originated with the Arabs firstly, and was then adapted by the Christians and Jews, with the gypsies then taking ownership of it up to the present day.

According to what Emilio had told Sebastián (Emilio had a keen interest in the history of Ronda) the Arabs conquered Ronda in 713 and then weren't evicted from the city until

1475. Many agreed to convert to the Christian religion in order to stay put and keep their possessions, but they practised their Muslim faith quite often in secret.

Emilio reckoned if you did a DNA test on a lot of Spaniards in the south you'd find plenty of traces of their Arabic past. Arabic was actually taught in Spanish schools for hundreds of years after the Arabs had left the country, as a compulsory subject.

Sebastián felt a sudden sharp tap on the back of his head and looked around. Felipe had reached across behind Nuria's chair and smacked the back of his head. He must have been visibly drifting off.

He looked at Felipe who looked back at him expressionlessly, knowing full well it wouldn't take much to set them off laughing again.

Sebastián looked away again and decided to focus on the performance.

This time he felt more hopeful as he watched two dancers move to the centre of the stage.

As he watched their curiously dramatic and powerful movements he admired how strong a role women had in the dance. This was a dance for equals. The women did not play the shrinking violet, and for such an ancient dance form it didn't show off the machismo of the male dancer, as the tango did. However, he couldn't see why the women's flamenco dress had to have such a long train, it definitely wasn't something designed with health and safety in mind; indeed, it seemed to get in the way constantly, with the women pushing it from side to side as they danced...

He decided he liked this form of flamenco better; he liked

to hear the castanets played in time to the music and to see the male dancer tapping his shoes to the beat of the clapping. From that point onwards the evening seemed to go by faster. Before he knew it he was in the car with Felipe and Nuria heading back to Las Nevadas.

31

After the flamenco concert and in the early hours of the morning, Felipe and Sebastián dropped Nuria off at the farmhouse entrance (where her father had helpfully left the small door open for her) and then drove back down to their house at the entrance of the estate. They went in blithely through the solid front door and stopped in their tracks when they saw the lights were switched on.

Someone had broken into the house while they'd been out.

The dresser in the hallway had its drawers pulled out and the contents thrown across the floor. Wordlessly, Felipe and Sebastián quickly walked from room to room to check the damage, making sure no one was still around. Sebastián then sat down heavily on a dining room chair trying to get his head together as he looked around at the mess.

They'd broken in through the metal mesh of the terrace shutter. Clearly that was the weak point in the house.

'Here Seb, have a drink of this.'

Felipe handed him a glass of whisky. Sebastián didn't like whisky but he downed it in one go.

'OK. So it's not as bad as it could've been,' Felipe said calmly. 'They've taken the televisions, the iPads and the cameras. We'll get those back on insurance. They seem to have left everything else. It could've been worse, a lot worse. Some of these thieves like to destroy and break things for the sake of it. Nothing's damaged. Once we pick everything up the place will look a lot better.'

'Yes. I suppose so.'

'Are you OK, Seb?'

'I don't know, to be honest with you.'

'Look, it's late. It's two in the morning. I suggest we get to bed. I don't think anyone's going to try and come back here tonight. We can coil the metal chain across the broken part of the shutter. We'll hear them if they try it again.'

Sebastián nodded and got up to retrieve the chain from the garage. Felipe helped him coil it around the broken part of the terrace shutter. The thieves must've had strong tools to break the metal rungs of the shutter apart.

Half an hour later Sebastián lay in his bed, staring at the ceiling.

They had to call the *Guardia Civil* first thing in the morning. He would also call Piedra and see what could be done with the terrace doors. Poor Piedra. Sebastián felt like he was calling him in on a constant basis, although Piedra didn't seem to mind.

He felt an insane rage grip him as he thought about the bastards who'd broken into his home. He'd make damn sure they wouldn't ever be able to get in again. Filled with fury, he tossed and turned for most of the night, his anger fuelling his insomnia. When the threads of light came through the bedroom shutters he decided to get up and tidy up the mess as best he could. Sleep was eluding him and he couldn't rest until he had some control over the situation.

Two hours later Felipe walked into the sitting-room, yawning.

'What on earth are you doing?' Felipe asked sleepily, surprised to see Sebastián fully dressed and active, walking from one side of the room to another.

'Putting stuff back where it belongs.'

Felipe looked around. The house was getting back to its normal self again.

'Please don't tell me you've been up all night. Actually, don't say anything. I can see it in your face. The bags around your eyes are huge. Seb, you've got to keep cool. You can't let these guys screw around with your head.'

Sebastián smiled at him sadly.

'I know. I just felt mad as hell and I knew I wasn't going to get any sleep until the house looked normal again. I'm going to call Piedra now and see if he can recommend a company to come and put in a stronger entranceway, one that has iron bars on it. Shutters are not strong enough, clearly.'

Felipe nodded and went through to the kitchen to make some coffee.

Twenty minutes later, two members of the *Guardia Civil* arrived and promptly proceeded to give Sebastián a stern telling off for tidying up and touching everything.

Sebastián apologised and shrugged his shoulders, happy for them to assume he was a dim-witted *Madrileño*, because he was almost a hundred per cent sure that whoever had broken in hadn't left any identifiable traces. These guys were clearly professionals: the chance of them leaving any fingerprints or DNA was dubious at best.

Less than three hours later a welder arrived and was soon busy at work erecting a solid metal gate at the back of the house, having removed the original shuttered entrance.

He took his time; it was the weekend and he was getting paid double for his efforts.

Sebastián spent the rest of the morning on the phone trying to arrange appointments with alarm and CCTV companies.

Felipe shook his head incredulously at Sebastián's determined efforts to make the house a fortress, and disappeared off.

Later that afternoon, Sebastián went up to his office at the farmhouse.

He'd texted Nuria earlier in the day, requesting her to meet him in the office with the other two gardeners. He wanted to discuss the planting of the olive trees with them. His single-minded focus had now zoned in on the farmland and he needed to see it working for its keep.

At four o'clock in the afternoon, on the dot, the three of them turned up at his office and sat politely down.

'OK, guys. I don't know if Nuria filled you in but I want to get cracking with the planting of the new olive tree saplings. At the moment Manuel has them sitting at his farm, waiting for our convenience. Ideally I'd like to start as soon as possible, but we'll need to hire a digger to clear the land and we'll have to lay down a new irrigation system because the old one's defunct. I think you've ordered the new irrigation system in, haven't you, Nuria?'

'Yes, all of it has arrived and it's stacked up in the stables at the moment. I gave you the receipt a month ago.'

Sebastián ignored this glaring criticism of his accounting skills and changed the subject.

'How soon do you think you could get started on the planting?'

Nuria pondered this.

'I think as soon as we've recruited six more gardeners. It'll take a week with the digger to clear just 30 hectares of the old trees. After that, three of us can work to clear trees and dig irrigation trenches, and the other six of us can start with the planting and laying down the new irrigation system. Within a week we should be able to start planting assuming nothing unforeseen happens. And with nine of us working on it we should be able to get quite a lot done.'

Sebastián nodded.

'Right, well, as soon as the three of you have found six other qualified gardeners, who'll be able to commit full time to helping you out for a couple of months, we'll get started. Hopefully very soon.'

The three of them nodded in assent.

'Felipe told me your house got broken into,' said Iván. 'Is that true?'

'Yes, it really was crap, to be honest with you. Not what I needed, but then it never is. I can't help thinking they must've been watching the house because we were both out last night at the flamenco concert. So, yes, it's not a nice feeling but the house will soon be like a fortress and I defy anyone to get past the security I'm putting in.'

'It's getting worse, the burglaries around here,' said Jorge, the other gardener. 'My uncle, who works for the *Guardia Civil*, says they're usually professionals and often dangerous. They think nothing of holding people up in their homes.' He looked sympathetically at Sebastián. 'I don't think they would've stopped even if you'd been at home. They like to steal cash and get their hands on your credit cards. Country houses that are slightly isolated are always going to be more of a risk, of course. It's good you have a security guard here in the farmhouse.'

At this point there was a sharp rap at the door and Felipe came in without waiting for permission, holding in his arms a small black dog. The surprise left the others speechless.

'Here you go, Seb. This is what you need.'

Sebastián looked blankly at his brother.

'It's a guard dog.'

The puppy licked Felipe's hand.

'Don't be absurd, Felipe. That thing? It wouldn't scare away a bird, let alone a burglar.'

'It's not absurd. This is just a puppy. It grows into a big Alsatian when it's older.'

At this point the puppy yawned and laid his head on Felipe's arm. Jorge and Iván burst out laughing.

Sebastián looked the puppy over, sceptically. It had floppy ears, so clearly it was still a long way from being an adult Alsatian with its pointed, triangular, upright ears.

'It's absolutely gorgeous,' said Nuria predictably, standing up and stroking its soft head. Felipe basked in the glow of her appreciation, listening with pleasure to her crooning over the puppy as though she was talking directly to him.

'I don't know, Felipe. I don't need any more responsibilities foisted on me at the moment.'

'Seb, this dog will be better than any alarm system. He'll be easy to look after, unlike your overdraft.'

Nuria stared fixedly at Felipe.

'You do talk a lot of rubbish sometimes, Felipe. Dogs are not easy to look after. Where did you get that idea? They need to be exercised, especially this breed. And trained...'

'It'll have the run of the garden at the house. That will give it plenty of exercise.'

'Oh no, it won't. Guard dogs around here are regularly poisoned, or burgled if they're pure breed, which that one looks like it is,' said Nuria. 'If you keep this dog, it'll have to stay indoors most of the time and it'll have to be exercised by its owner.'

'OK fine, Nuria,' said Felipe wearily. 'I'm happy to exercise it. Will you stop fretting? It makes sense for Seb to have a guard dog. Most houses around here have one.'

Nuria sighed impatiently but refrained from giving any more objections to Felipe's bright idea. They simultaneously turned to look at Sebastián.

Sebastián could feel himself weakening. It was a cute little thing. And it would be good company once Felipe moved on, which Sebastián was sure he would do sooner or later.

'Where did you get it from, Felipe?'

'I got it from a friend of mine in Ronda. His bitch had a litter of seven and this one was the last one remaining. Apparently because it's mostly black, apart from its two front paws, nobody wanted it. Most people prefer Alsatians to have all the usual markings. My friend said it has a lovely temperament.'

'How much did it cost you?' asked Sebastián, defeated.

'I paid 500 euros for it.'

'What?'

'500 euros. It's a bargain, Seb.'

'You were ripped off,' said Iván, morosely.

'Shut up,' said Felipe angrily. 'I wasn't ripped off. These dogs are hard to come by, I'll have you know.'

'Felipe, this isn't helping me financially and it'll be months before the puppy proves its worth,' said Sebastián, trying to be realistic.

Felipe held the dog out to him imperatively.

'Look at him. You can't turn him away.'

Sebastián looked again at the puppy, whose circular orange eyes seemed to be regarding him pleadingly.

'OK, fine, Felipe. I'll pay for it. But next time you decide to help me out, can you run it by me first?'

'Of course. Here you go, have a hold of him.'

Felipe handed the puppy across the table to Sebastián, who held him gingerly before putting him gently onto his lap. This was a first for Sebastián.

'What am I supposed to feed him? Milk?' he asked, pathetically. The others in the room started to giggle.

'Not milk. This puppy needs water and good quality tinned puppy food,' said Nuria firmly. Sebastián looked at her. Where did she learn to look after puppies?

As if hearing his unspoken question, Nuria added, 'I used to have a dog when I was little. I'm going shopping this afternoon so I'll get you some puppy food.'

Sebastián nodded his thanks.

He looked down at the puppy, which was now sniffing interestedly at the papers on his desk. He patted its head and was gratified to see its little tail waving in response. This puppy might end up being the easiest employee to please after all, he thought to himself.

32

Three weeks later, Sebastián was firmly regretting his impulsive purchase of Caro, his diminutive Alsatian puppy.

Sebastián had named the puppy Caro as a sarcastic commentary on the amount of money Felipe spent on purchasing him. *Caro* means 'expensive' in Spanish, which was very apt, as Sebastián was keen to point out to his spendthrift brother.

Caro had spent the first night crying his heart out in his blanketed box. Finally, after getting up five times to soothe him, Sebastián ended up carrying him into his room where the puppy settled quite happily under his chin, preventing Sebastián from moving in his sleep. He did not enjoy being woken up in the early hours of the morning with a sticky wet lick on his face, and decided that all mothers, both animal and human, deserved a medal.

Today he was out in the olive grove trying to help with the planting of the new olive tree saplings. He felt there was something profoundly satisfying in planting a new tree.

Planting a tree was to many people almost a religious ritual, symbolising new beginnings, friendship, remembrance, protection or peace.

For some cultures, trees were a very sacred entity, and he could totally understand why. A few well-known olive trees in the Mediterranean were estimated to be between 2,000 and

3,000 years old. In terms of human history, that was incredible. Trees will eventually outlive us all, he thought to himself as he looked at the new saplings, as long as we don't destroy the planet first.

They were all wearing caps in a bid to fend off the fierce summer sun, sweat was glistening on their arms and their shirts were soaked with it. Bottles of water were stacked up in an icebox. Every day they worked the farmland, Nuria would put the water bottles in the freezer the night before and then let them defrost slowly in the icebox as they dug holes and planted the olive trees. Sebastián thought nothing tasted better than that ice-cold water after a hard shift in the harsh sun.

The gardeners were measuring out meticulously the placement of the new olives, so they would all be planted in neat lines across the farmland.

All the farmland they'd already worked on had been cleared of rogue grass and vegetation, the newly groomed earth now gleaming a bright oxidised red. The saplings, barely reaching Sebastián's shoulder in height, were slowly getting planted in precise rows and Sebastián imagined their roots, originally confined to a plastic pot, now enjoying stretching out into the space around them.

Gardening was a curiously silent job. A couple of the gardeners had headphones on but the rest just worked in the quiet, with totally absorbed concentration.

As Sebastián dug away at the soil, creating an adequately sized hole for a sapling to be interred, he reflected on how much had been achieved the last few months.

The mews were now fully booked up until December and the farmhouse rooms were booked until the end of September.

He'd upped the prices for the *Feria de Pedro Romero* held in Ronda in September.

Alongside the increase in bookings, his staff had also increased. He had a dedicated team of three sports aficionados to take his guests mountain biking, hiking along country trails in and out of olive groves, vineyards and rough mountain terrain, and, for the wildlife enthusiasts, on day trips to the more remote and beautiful corners of Sierra Nevada.

He also had two talented chefs in the kitchen at the farmhouse, as well as a group of young students who worked on a rota as waiters. In addition he also now had a bank, or waiting list, of vetted employees who could be called on if he needed anyone to stand in for an existing member of staff.

There were definite advantages to starting a business in an area of Spain that had such high unemployment. It meant there was a decent pool of talent to draw from and the wages were never extortionately high (though not for want of trying, thought Sebastián, grimly, remembering the few who had tried to cajole him into paying them a higher salary).

He was starting to break even.

He had the business consultant at Ronda's Unicaja Bank coming out to advise him on other projects that might increase his cash flow. However, remembering those scary days when his overdraft was growing at a frightening rate, he was glad to be breaking even.

Eventually stamping down firmly on the oxidised earth around the sapling he'd just planted, Sebastián looked up to see what the others were up to. All of them were busy with their tasks. No instructions were given but they each silently understood their role in the planting and were efficiently spreading themselves out as they worked. In fact, Sebastián sometimes felt he was a hindrance to this intricate dance the gardeners were weaving across the landscape as they worked.

Nuria was wearing a dirty sleeveless vest and a pair of shorts that barely covered her backside, as well as her thick gardening socks and boots. Her sinewy arms showed their firm muscles as she dug into the earth.

She never seemed to tire, whereas Sebastián felt the pain of digging along his back and shoulders. In fact, the morning after the first day of planting he'd barely been able to get out of bed. He'd definitely become a bit of a slob since moving here and abandoning his swanky gym in Madrid.

His mobile phone rang, startling the others.

'*¿Si?*'

'Sebastián, a man called Pedro Lantro called the farmhouse wanting to speak to you. He said it was important so I thought I should give you a call.'

'Yes, thank you Emilio. Did you get his number?'

'Yes, of course.'

'I'll be there in fifteen minutes.'

Sebastián hung up and walked for five minutes to the farm track where he had left his agricultural quad bike parked next to the van the other gardeners had used. The bike was noisy and seemed to desecrate the peacefulness of the countryside but it enabled him to keep tabs on what was going on around the farm.

Once he had parked the quad bike in the rear garage, he walked through to the farmhouse courtyard only to see Felipe, with Caro on a leash, chatting avidly to a glamorous young girl with long blonde hair.

Sebastián frowned. In his view a puppy was a dangerous magnet for the ladies and this could only spell trouble as far as Felipe was concerned. Still, whoever Felipe decided to talk to, it wasn't really any of his business.

He picked up Pedro Lantro's phone number from Emilio and went into his office to make the call, remembering to keep his voice as loud as possible so Pedro would be able to hear him.

'Pedro? It's Sebastián here. I was told you had something important to tell me?'

'Ah yes. I've managed to reach Gabriel Casales. It's taken some time as he left Valencia a while ago. He's now living in Cádiz, so not far from Ronda, ironically, and he sounded exactly the same. He was very surprised to hear none of his letters had reached his father and he was happy to let you call him. I've got his number here.'

'Excellent! Well done, Pedro. You've done your friend a good turn. I'll be delighted to speak to him. Go ahead...'

'His number is 956-267749.'

'Thanks.'

'Let me know what happens.'

'Of course. I'll be in touch.'

Sebastián hung up and looked at the number in front of him. He dialled it quickly on his mobile and waited impatiently until it picked up.

'Hello?'

The voice on the other side of the phone was husky, that of a smoker Sebastián guessed.

'Hello, Gabriel. I'm Sebastián Ortez, the new owner of Las Nevadas.'

'Yes, yes, Pedro Lantro's told me all about you and how

you found my letters in the attic. It's truly amazing. I'm very grateful to you for getting in touch with me. I've no idea how they ended up there, unless my father decided to store them.'

'It certainly seems to be quite a mystery. Nobody quite knows why those letters were in the attic here. More importantly, your father's lawyers were keen to get in touch with you. Apparently your father left you quite a substantial amount of money in his will, but the lawyers weren't able to locate you so the estate was divided up between your siblings.'

'Yes, so I've been told by Pedro... I was really very surprised to hear that. It's the last thing I thought my father would do. He knew where to find me but he never got in touch.'

'We're wondering if someone could have hidden your letters from him.'

'I'd very much doubt it. Why would they do that? I can certainly tell you it wasn't Luciana,' Gabriel said, affirmatively.

'Luciana?'

'She's the gypsy woman at Las Nevadas who I entrusted my letters to. She was always a hundred per cent loyal and she was under instructions to deliver the letters directly to my father.'

'I'm sorry, should I know Luciana? She lives near here, does she?'

Gabriel laughed and then went off into a smoker's coughing fit.

'She lives on the farm, in Las Nevadas itself. Always has done.'

'What? I don't think so. I'm sorry but I don't know of anyone of that name here.'

'She used to live in that broken-down little cottage next to the Pinsapo trees in Las Nevadas. To be honest I don't know if she's still alive or not.'

Gabriel sighed reminiscently.

'Did Emilio know about her?' asked Sebastián, suspiciously.

'Of course. He worked the farm. My family always thought she was as mad as a hatter but they didn't have the heart to evict her. She never bothered anyone. She was the only one back then who was willing to help Rebekka and me get away together.'

Gabriel paused for a moment, as though the memory was painful to him. Sebastián waited patiently for him to continue.

'She kindly let Rebekka stay with her at the cottage, because Rebekka's family moved on from the farm that winter. Once I was able to get enough money together for us to leave, Rebekka and I took off... Everyone else was against us.'

'So what are you going to do now?'

'I'm going to get in touch with the lawyers and arrange to meet them. I want to claim my rightful inheritance, although I've heard it might take a while. It'll benefit my two children and any grandchildren I might have.'

'If you do come to Ronda please be my guest here in Las Nevadas. I'd very much like to meet you and I'm sure Emilio Gordillo will be delighted to see you too.'

'Emilio Gordillo? Is he still alive?'

'Yes, he's doing pretty well for his age, actually.'

'Wow, that really does bring back memories from the past. I'll be delighted to stay there, thank you.'

Sebastián gave Gabriel his mobile number and signed off cordially.

He spent a long time sitting on his chair, staring into space. Was this woman Luciana still living on his estate?

Maybe it was time for him to visit the famed Pinsapo trees and see what else or who else was there too. It seemed strange to have a vagabond woman, which was all he could think of Luciana as, living in a broken-down cottage on his estate.

Someone should've damn well told him. Tomorrow he was going to head out to the Pinsapo trees and see for himself if Luciana was living there.

33

Early the next morning Sebastián set off on the quad bike to the far north of the Las Nevadas estate. After twenty minutes he could see the pointed tips of the five Pinsapo trees that were protected by law in Spain. Most Pinsapo trees preferred the rocky mountainside terrain. Why they had decided to grow on this particular spot was a mystery.

Sebastián suspected they'd been deliberately planted by someone. There was no Pinsapo forest nearby, so what were the chances that five of them would grow here?

They looked like ordinary pine trees from a mile away but they were actually beautifully unique. Each branch had bushier, sturdier pine needles than the standard pine and they didn't loosen when touched, either. Each needle was solidly attached. The trees looked like perfectly symmetrical, plump green cones from a distance.

Sebastián stopped the quad bike when he'd got as close as he could to the trees without diverting off the farm track. He then set off at a quick pace across the soft, crumbling earth towards the five pines.

Sure enough, on the right hand side of this Pinsapo copse he could see a dilapidated stone cottage that looked as though it had been abandoned to the elements. Half of it had crumbled, so there was no roof or indeed any walls, just abandoned limestone bricks. The other half didn't look much better; Sebastián reckoned it wouldn't be long before this side fell as well. It didn't seem possible for anyone to inhabit such a small dwelling.

He walked around the back, looking for a doorway or entrance. He saw a large piece of plywood leaning against a doorway. There was no bell so he knocked uncertainly on the plywood.

'*¿Quién es?*' croaked a voice from behind the plywood door.

'Hello. I'm Sebastián Ortez, the new owner of Las Nevadas farm.'

He heard a dragging noise and then saw four fingers grab hold of the plywood door before pulling it to one side.

From behind the door an old woman peered up at him. She was almost bent double and her eyes were a strange milky white. The few strands of long white hair left on her scalp fluttered in the slight breeze. Her face was a shrivelled mass of wrinkles and her mouth sunk inwards. Sebastián was prepared to bet she didn't have many teeth left. She was dressed in black from top to toe, looking like a frail old crow.

What on earth was this woman doing living here? She should be cared for in a home! Sebastián started to feel increasingly angry. This wasn't right.

'Luciana?'

'Yes. That's me.'

Her voice lisped, no doubt because of her missing teeth.

'Luciana, I'm sorry for asking this, but how on earth are you surviving out here?'

Luciana cackled to herself.

'This has always been my home, I'll move out of here only

when I'm dead. The foxes can eat me then.'

'You cannot possibly continue to live here. It isn't healthy. What on earth do you do for food?'

'Nuria brings me a weekly shop.'

'Nuria?'

'Yes, Nuria.'

The old woman's facial expression clearly showed she was the one thinking Sebastián was losing the plot.

'Do you even have running water?'

'A little. Enough for my needs. Come in and see for yourself.'

Sebastián squeezed in through the doorway and looked around.

In one corner there was a tap, just like any outdoor garden tap. There was a mattress on the floor, a rickety table and chair. Three worn plastic buckets were positioned against a wall. A couple of plates and a knife and fork were reposing on the table. The rest of the room was completely bare. This woman was living like a nun in a strict convent.

He felt horrified. How could Emilio and Nuria have let this woman live here? It was appalling.

Sebastián walked out of the house and turned to face Luciana as she stood determinedly at the doorway.

'Luciana, I can't, as the new owner of Las Nevadas, have you living in these conditions. I'm sorry.'

'What do you mean? I've always lived here... Nobody's ever bothered me. They've left me in peace.'

'Well maybe they should have bothered you. It's not right for anyone, in this day and age, to live in these conditions, and certainly not someone of your age.'

A stubborn expression came onto the old woman's face.

'You can't force me out of my home. I have legal rights, you know.'

Sebastián was slowly beginning to realise this woman was a force to be reckoned with.

'No social worker would accept you living in these conditions. There are laws to prevent people living like this, Luciana.'

The old woman looked at him.

'How do you know my name, anyway?'

'Gabriel Casales told me about you. You were kind to him once.'

'Ahh. Yes. How could he betray me to you? I was quite happy minding my own business until you turned up.'

'He didn't "betray" you. He said he'd left the letters for his father with you. It turns out his father never received them.'

'Diego Casales never received them?'

'No, not a single one. All the letters were found in a box in the attic. We have reason to believe he never received any of them.'

Luciana spat viciously.

'That bitch.'

Sebastián, taken aback at the crudity of her language, was speechless.

'She's a *puta*. A snake. May God bring disaster upon her house!'

The woman was raving. Sebastián wondered what on earth he was going to do with her.

'I gave the letters to Silvia Casales. She said she would give them to her father. She lied to me, the bitch.'

'You gave them to Silvia Casales?' That would explain a lot... She must have hidden them from her father. Wow! I can see

178

there's going to be a family meltdown between Diego's children, if that's the case.'

Luciana looked hostilely at him and then sniffed disapprovingly.

'I'd like you to go away now, please. Leave me in peace... I don't need any hassle at my time of life.'

'Look, Luciana, you can't live in this shack. I'm warning you, I'm going to have to get the authorities involved. It's not right.'

'What's not right is you not leaving me to live out the rest of my life in peace, young man. You know nothing. We gypsies have lived on the land for generations, moving from one place to another. We don't need security and possessions.'

'I'm thinking more of a doctor, Luciana, or a nurse. I'm thinking of warmth and cooked food. I mean, what the hell do you do in the winter when it snows?'

'I've warm clothes and I know how to light a fire. I'm a gypsy after all,' she said sarcastically.

'I'll talk to Emilio and Nuria but I really think I'm going to have to get someone professional involved. You cannot carry on here.'

'Sebastián. Please...' Luciana grabbed hold of his arm. 'Please, don't do this to me. It would be cruel. I'd never survive in an old people's home.'

Sebastián looked at her. Fat, round droplets began to fall down her withered cheeks as she pleaded with him. He looked over her head at the dilapidated house. His heart sank. This whole situation was crazy. They were right, this woman was as mad as a hatter.

He shook his head slowly.

'I'm sorry. I'll have to speak to people and figure something out. This simply isn't right. In the meantime I'll get a couple of men to come and make repairs to the house, OK? They should at least make sure it's watertight and safe. I mean, anyone could get in and murder you in your sleep.'

'No one will. Anyone here who has any local knowledge thinks I'm a witch. They're scared of me, if anything. There's nothing to steal. I'm just an old woman... So no attraction there...' Luciana cackled heartily to herself.

She wiped her cheeks, slowly turned around, and without saying goodbye disappeared into her house again, firmly pulling the plywood door back into place.

Sebastián was left staring at the house in disbelief. His responsibilities since he took on this farm never seemed to end.

34

'Hi Nuria, would you mind coming to the office at your convenience today? I need to speak to you and Emilio.'

If Nuria was surprised at Sebastián's formal tone she didn't show it.

'Yes, I'll be up at lunchtime. Why don't you join us for some lunch? My father's always pleased to see you.'

'OK. Thanks. I'll see you then.'

Sebastián wasn't sure it was a great thing to accept the kind lunch invitation when he was feeling so much rage because of Luciana's situation. He shrugged. It was too late to change his mind now.

He looked at his watch. Twelve o'clock. Having decided he didn't have enough time to help out with the olive tree planting, he decided to pop round to the mews. As he walked round he had Caro in tow. The puppy, having just woken up from a refreshing nap in his basket, was ready for some fun.

A family renting one of the mews houses had rung up earlier that day to complain about the shower not draining properly. This could either be an easy problem to fix or an emergency call out for the plumber, costing him a fortune in the process. Because of this he liked to go and see the problem for himself, before calling in the technical experts. He could manage the basics.

He rang the doorbell at number 5 and waited patiently. Eventually the door opened and Sebastián found himself looking at his brother.

'Felipe? What are you doing here?'

'I came round to fix their shower. It's all working fine now, you'll be glad to know.'

'Hi Sebastián! Good to see you. Your brother's fixed the problem for us but thank you so much for coming round,' said Heidi, coyly. Sebastián recognised Heidi as the blonde girl Felipe had been paying a lot of attention to in the farmhouse courtyard the day before. She was dressed in a skimpy kaftan that left nothing to the imagination. Her coltish tanned legs seemed to extend forever.

Sebastián looked suspiciously at his brother. Felipe smiled back at him in good humour, although a disturbingly mischievous twinkle at the back of Felipe's eyes was blatantly challenging Sebastián to confront him with his suspicions.

'OK. Great. I'm glad it was easily resolved. Felipe, are you heading back now?'

'Eh. Actually, no. Heidi's invited me to stay for a drink and an *aperitivo*. I'll catch you later.'

'OK. See you later.'

Sebastián turned and stalked off back to the farmhouse courtyard, Caro happily waving his little tail like a flag beside him.

Two hours later he was seated in the apartment with Nuria and Emilio, swallowing spoonfuls of ice-cold *gazpacho* laced with chopped peppers, onions and boiled egg. He ate hungrily and silently, enjoying the refreshing coolness of the soup after the heat of the morning.

It was midway through July and the heat was suffocating.

He found it hard to breathe in the stifling air.

He finished his last spoonful, sweeping the bowl clean with a piece of bread as all Spaniards have traditionally done for centuries. His grandmother had told him since he was little that bread was the staple of a Spanish meal.

He sat back, noticing Emilio and Nuria looking at him with barely concealed concern on their faces. José Luis, oblivious to his family's uneasiness, leaned back on his chair comfortably and smiled pacifically at Sebastián.

'How's your day going, Sebastián?' José Luis asked politely. Sebastián smiled back.

'Good thanks, José Luis. How about yours?'

'I've managed to sell fifty of my wooden bowls in the last month. I have a lot of work to do to catch up,' said José Luis, as usual jumping into a different topic without an opening.

'I know, it's fantastic. Your work's selling really well. You must've been making a good deal of money in the process. What are you planning to spend it on?'

'I'm saving up to buy some better equipment for the workshop.'

Sebastián nodded, and then got up to help Nuria carry the soup plates through to the kitchen, shortly returning with a mouth-watering dish of Basque chicken casserole.

Midway through his plate of casserole, Sebastián sat back with a contented sigh, and decided to take the bull by the horns and explain to Nuria and Emilio his concerns about Luciana's situation.

'I went to the Pinsapos this morning and met Luciana.'

Emilio and Nuria looked at each other but didn't say anything.

'I was horrified. Actually, more than that, angry, to see what conditions she was living in. Total squalor, no amenities. I don't think that place even had a toilet from what I could see. Any municipal council would have condemned that cottage. How could you two have allowed her to carry on living there?'

Emilio cleared his throat.

'I don't think she sees it as living in squalor.'

'I don't care what she sees it as. She's clearly not quite right in the head.'

'What makes you think she's not right in the head?' asked Nuria.

'The way she behaved, the fact she wants to stay there for a start.'

'She might be eccentric but she's totally with it. I would be careful with what you say about her. She's not senile, if that's what you're implying.'

Emilio nodded in agreement.

'She's sharp. She has a better understanding of people than you'd give her credit for. She lives there because she wants to. Always has done.'

'Yes, but at her age it's simply not right.'

'Why?' countered Nuria, to Sebastián's surprise.

'Because she might need medical treatment, because anyone could break in there and attack her and none of us would know anything about it, because she has no heating in the winter and she's an old woman, and as for her hygiene, don't even get me started. When did she last have a bath or a shower?'

'I take her once a week to the clinic in Ronda to get her washed and they look her over. We also pass by her house once a day to check on her. What you don't get, Seb, is that some people prefer to live life to the full, even at the risk of shortening it,' Nuria said impatiently, putting her spoon down to fold her arms defensively across her chest. 'If it was a choice between living in what she sees as her home and having a shorter lifespan, or moving to a residential unit to be kept alive for much longer, she would still choose to live at her cottage. Taking her out of there would kill her soul. Literally. She loves nature and her beloved Pinsapos. It would destroy any joy she has left to be taken away from her home.'

Sebastián was silent as he pondered this, resuming his mouthfuls of sweetly scented stew. He knew he couldn't leave Luciana to live in those conditions. If she couldn't be moved out of her home, he would have to make improvements to it so at least it could qualify as a dwelling, not a tumbledown shack.

He looked up only to catch Nuria staring out of the apartment window, looking absolutely devastated. He was so unused to seeing any raw emotion on her face that he was thoroughly unnerved by her expression.

He peered out of the window to see what she was looking at, only to see Felipe snogging Heidi passionately in the courtyard.

'Right! That's it. I've had it with Felipe!' he said angrily, throwing down his napkin and getting up from the table. He turned towards the door but suddenly found his arm being held in a surprisingly strong grasp.

'Seb, I don't need you to fight my battles,' Nuria whispered fiercely in his ear. 'I can sort my own problems out.'

Sebastián looked at her and then sat down obediently at the table again.

He could well believe Nuria could look after herself. In fact, it occurred to him that Felipe had no idea what was coming his way.

You didn't mess with Nuria, who'd spent most of her working life standing up for herself in a male-orientated environment. Most people around these parts wouldn't take a woman gardener seriously. Nuria had to continually prove herself more capable than any other male gardener in the area.

He looked out of the window again but Felipe was no longer in sight. He must have been very drunk to allow Heidi to kiss him like that, right here in the farmhouse courtyard. Some *aperitivo* that must have been! Drat his brother! All of a sudden his presence in Las Nevadas was proving too hot to handle.

35

Sebastián put his desk light on and looked closely at the calluses on his hand. Planting olive trees had taken its toll, even with him wearing gardening gloves. Still, he enjoyed the outdoor, manual work. It was better than being a pen pusher.

He looked down at the paperwork on his desk. He had all the accounts for the last six months listed, as well as the financial forecasts for the next year.

The business manager from Unicaja Bank was arriving after lunch today to offer his advice and Sebastián had requested Manuel, the farmer who'd been kind enough to offer him a helping hand, to come and join the meeting.

Manuel had a profitable business up and running, so Sebastián felt his opinion would be invaluable. In fact Sebastián felt he could trust Manuel more than Rodrigo, the financial manager. At the end of the day, Rodrigo was a bank employee, who dished out advice to clients that he never had to take himself.

Felipe was still hanging around at Las Nevadas despite the fact that Heidi, the young girl he was enjoying a liaison with, had now left the mews house that her family had been renting for the holidays.

Nuria seemed to have let Felipe off lightly which surprised Sebastián. He'd asked Felipe what had happened between him and Nuria. Felipe had just shrugged and said, 'It's over.' Relieved that he didn't have to deal with a hysterical Nuria (which wasn't her style, admittedly) and an irate, remorseless and ingrate brother, Sebastián figured he'd been let off lightly over what could've been a big domestic drama.

The farm had a habit of drawing an odd assortment of people close together, sometimes uncomfortably close. Working together on a daily basis there was nowhere to hide one's flaws or idiosyncrasies. Sebastián felt so sucked up into this little world that he was starting to wonder if he was in danger of losing himself. He knew sooner or later he would have to take a break from it all and escape out of Andalucía to get some perspective. The irony was that people were coming here to Las Nevadas to take a break from their lives.

Luciana had a newly renovated cottage now. Sebastián had phoned Piedra and had recruited two of his builders to make upgrades and repairs to her home. None of which she appreciated, of course. In fact, when they'd first arrived she started screaming and cursing like a banshee, trying ineffectually to hit the poor men with the handle of a brush. Sebastián had been forced to call on Nuria to calm Luciana down and take her out for the day while the two builders worked on the cottage.

Two weeks later Luciana had a watertight home with a rudimentary bathroom and a solid front door. Sebastián fervently hoped there were to be no more unexpected surprises hiding out of sight on the farm...

There was a sharp rap and the door opened. Nuria poked her head in.

'Seb, have you got any spare wire at your house?'

'There might be some in the garage,' he said, leaning over to pick up his keys and handing them over to her.

'Thanks.'

As she headed out of the door Caro whined and pawed at the door. Sebastián got up to fetch his lead.

'I think Caro's ready for his third walk of the day.'

Nuria giggled.

'He has you around his little paw.'

'Yes, he does, curse him. He's ruling the roost at the moment. Even the chefs upstairs can't resist stealing down and feeding him leftovers. He's starting to develop a bit of a paunch.'

Nuria bent down to stroke his soft tummy. Caro rolled over onto his back and obligingly lifted up his paws.

'No, come on, Caro, if you're going to make me get up from my desk to give you a walk, you're going to have to stand up properly.'

Nuria stood up and Caro, looking disappointed, rolled upright again. Sebastián attached his lead and walked out after Nuria.

Slamming the office door shut behind him, he turned right, walking past José Luis's workshop and out of the back courtyard into the path leading to the orchard.

He loved having a look at the orchard at this time of year. It was wonderful to see things growing so fast: watermelons, melons, tomatoes, peppers and aubergines were all coming to fruition. The fruit trees were heavy with produce and he had bowls filled with locally grown plums and figs in his kitchen.

He walked past the partially shaded glasshouses and took a straight path out to the outskirts of the farm, a path that eventually led into a neighbouring sunflower field.

An hour later he was strolling along the side of the sunflower field. Having cheekily broken off one of the sunflower heads, he was cracking its pips with his teeth and eating their soft inner kernels. Caro had his head down, sniffing interestedly along the path, sometimes yanking on the lead when a particularly enticing smell beckoned him.

A wall built of limestone was on the other side of the sunflowers and he stopped occasionally to have a look and see if he could spot any fossils. Eventually he was rewarded when he found what was undoubtedly a sea urchin fossil.

He carefully prised it loose from the wall and looked at it. The delicate sea urchin markings were all intact and its circular shape could clearly be seen. Sebastián chucked the sunflower head back into the field and continued on walking, carrying the fossil in his hand. He was taking this one home. He fancied building a fossil collection just as Manuel had done.

By the time he got back to the farmhouse it was after lunchtime and he barely had time to grab a sandwich at the farmhouse kitchen before heading to his office to await the arrival of Rodrigo and Manuel. He put the fossil on his desk in pride of place, hoping Manuel would give him some guidance on cleaning it up so it would show to its best advantage.

36

'The problem is, Sebastián, you're not really making enough of a profit. You need to be building up a rainy day fund. You're covering your loan repayments but not much more. If there's any drop in your bookings you'd find it hard to make ends meet,' Rodrigo had said, after studying Sebastián's accounts in minute detail.

There was some advantage in being a business owner who did his own accounts, thought Sebastián; at least he was in the position to answer the multitude of questions Rodrigo had thrown at him.

'I know, that's why I'm in the process of planting the olive trees. I'm hopeful that once I'm able to harvest them yearly that will be a boost to the income the farm generates.'

'Yes, but by your own admission that's five years away.'

'Well, what are you suggesting?'

Rodrigo pursed his lips. He was in his late fifties, dressed in an expensive suit, in stark contrast to Manuel and Sebastián who were wearing jeans and T-shirts. Rodrigo looked at Sebastián over the top of his glasses.

'You might have to diversify even further with your business.'

Sebastián's heart sank. The last thing he needed was more projects. He was barely keeping up with his current ones.

'So have you any suggestions?'

'You could make the restaurant at the farmhouse big enough to accommodate bookings from Ronda. Several people have set up successful restaurants in this area.'

'I think that's a bit risky, Sebastián,' said Manuel quietly. 'So many restaurants don't make it. It's a fickle market.'

'What other alternatives are you recommending, then?' Rodrigo asked Manuel sharply, clearly not appreciating his advice being dismissed so summarily.

Manuel smiled to himself.

'I've often thought that piece of land Diego Casales cleared of olive trees, so as to build a small airport, would be perfect for a riding school. You have the stables as well. Diego always had horses and he used to enjoy riding in the mountains around here.'

'A riding school? I know absolutely nothing about horses and I'm prepared to bet no one who works here does either.'

'Exactly, but don't you see, there's no riding school anywhere near here. I'm prepared to bet there isn't one in a hundred-mile radius. You could attract interest from all the villages around here, as well as Ronda.'

'Yes, but after purchasing horses, equipment, feed and a trainer I'll be back to where I started. Completely broke and stressing about making my loan repayments.'

Sebastián and Manuel turned simultaneously to look at Rodrigo, who'd been silent during their discussion.

'It might be worth getting some initial estimates,' said Rodrigo, cautiously. 'It's true there isn't a riding school anywhere near here and the area lends itself perfectly to horse riding. I would've taken my children to a riding school had there been one. But again it's a risk. However, there are going to be risks in any business that's branching out or trying to improve its profits.'

'You might also get some volunteers who like spending time with horses to help out with their upkeep. I know of riding schools where they get interested teenagers to come in and help out at peak times in return for free rides on the horses,' said Manuel, enthusiastically, clearly sold on the idea.

'I'll have to have a think about it and I'll need to speak to Piedra again, seeing as he'll be the one building the arena and improving the stable area.'

'You only need to start with a couple of horses. Small beginnings until word gets around,' said Manuel.

Sebastián nodded half-heartedly.

'Don't look so downhearted, you've done incredibly well for the first year. You've taken on an abandoned farm and restored it into a viable business. It really is remarkable,' said Rodrigo, getting his papers together and slotting them neatly back into his briefcase. 'I would say you're over the worst and if you keep a steady hand on the tiller you'll soon have a very lucrative business on your hands. Do get in touch if you have any concerns or questions.'

He handed his business card to Sebastián. After they'd shaken hands he nodded and disappeared out of the office door.

Manuel and Sebastián looked at each other for a moment.

'Well, I would say you've been let off lightly. I can't say my bank manager was as easy-going as that when I started,' said Manuel. 'By the way, I've been itching to ask you, is that a fossil on your desk?'

'Yes, it is. I found it next to a neighbouring sunflower field but I think it needs some cleaning. Only I thought I'd better get your advice first.'

Manuel picked it up and looked keenly at it.

'It's a very good specimen. You need to get yourself a sharp chisel and gently work it over these bits of rough stone, try and dislodge them gently. If a piece isn't willing to loosen, it probably won't without taking out some of the fossil. You have to leave what doesn't want to budge. I sit by the pool so I can clean the fossil as I go along and any loose bits of stone just fall to the ground as I work on it...'

Sebastián took Manuel up to the farmhouse later to have a look around. They then sat in the dining room at the Juliette window, as Sebastián liked to call it, and had a sherry with some olives.

The swifts in the courtyard had quietened; many of them were probably swooping acrobatically over the swimming pool trying to get a drink of water before night came. As dusk fell the bats would take over and hover around the pool, catching the insects attracted to the water.

Sebastián sighed contentedly. His first annual meeting with the bank had gone well and hopefully he'd get a good report. He'd sleep well tonight in the knowledge the farm was pulling together slowly but surely.

37

Manuel stayed for dinner. Once he'd left, Sebastián walked to his car, listening with approbation to the steady chirping of the crickets around him, which by now had become an oddly soothing sound in the solid darkness of the night.

He got into the car and switched on his headlights as he drove out of the farmhouse courtyard and down the drive to his home.

Moths could be seen in the headlights as well as odd glimmering red dots: the eyes of unspecified nocturnal animal life. Rabbits, foxes, wild hog and country mice, as well as rats; all roamed the farm when the sun went down.

Sebastián turned the car into the open gates of his garden and then got out to close the gates for the night. He was glad to be home at last.

Felipe had left for the farmhouse a good few hours before him; he could see the lights were on in the sitting-room.

Sebastián listened appreciatively to Caro's steady barking on the other side of the front door. Caro knew he was out there in the garden. Sebastián turned the key in the lock and let himself in quickly before Caro jumped up on him in excitement. He patted the puppy whose tail was wagging so hard his little body was moving from side to side.

He went to the kitchen, grabbed a beer from the fridge and

walked into the sitting-room, plonking himself down on the soft cushions of the sofa with a sigh of relief.

He looked across at Felipe, who was watching a tacky game show on television. There was something odd about him.

Sebastián stared at Felipe, trying to work out what was different.

'Felipe, is that my shirt you're wearing?'

Felipe looked at his brother for a moment.

'Yes, it is,' he answered shortly.

'I don't mind you borrowing it, but don't you have any shirts of your own?'

'No, as it happens I don't any more.'

Sebastián's tired brain mulled over his words.

'Felipe, I'm tired. What are you talking about? Have you run out of clean shirts?'

'No, go along to my room and you'll understand what I mean.'

Sebastián put down the beer, got up off his seat and marched to Felipe's room. He wasn't sure what was happening.

He switched the corridor light on and then reached into Felipe's room to switch on his bedroom light.

A scene of devastation greeted his stunned eyes. The bed and the floor were covered in mounds of shredded material; it looked like a tiger had been let loose in a cloth shop. Scraps of denim and bits of cloth in every colour and pattern lay scattered in uneven piles across the room. The cupboard was lying empty, as were the open drawers of the wooden cabinet.

Sebastián hurried back to the sitting-room.

'Felipe, what on earth has happened? What the hell's going on?'

'Nuria's what's happened. You gave her the keys to the house, remember?'

The penny dropped in Sebastián's head. He suddenly remembered Nuria asking him if he had any spare wire and borrowing the keys to his house.

He looked at Felipe, aghast.

'Nuria destroyed your clothes?'

'Yes,' said Felipe, bitterly. 'My designer jeans shredded, my Lacoste shirts destroyed, my Calvin Klein underwear, everything.'

Sebastián stared at his brother, not knowing what to say.

'I know, I know, it's my fault. But, Seb, the woman is *vicious*. I've never had any woman behave like this before. It scares the hell out of me, to be honest with you. I thought she was OK with it all.'

'Felipe, firstly, how on earth was she going to be OK with it all?' asked Sebastián hotly, remembering the look of devastation on Nuria's face when she caught Felipe snogging Heidi in the courtyard. 'Secondly, she's clearly still very upset about it. I'm not sure what we're going to do.'

'Well, hopefully she'll be feeling a good deal better since she destroyed my entire wardrobe.'

The two of them looked at each other for a moment.

Felipe smiled at his brother with a good deal of comprehension in his eyes.

'I know what you're thinking, Seb, and you're right. Maybe now's the time for me to move on to pastures new. I'll take the train to Madrid tomorrow, assuming there's an available seat.'

There wasn't much more to say. The two of them turned in shortly afterwards, Sebastián handing Felipe some pyjamas and clothing for the next day.

Sebastián felt genuinely sad at the thought of Felipe leaving as he lay in bed that night, but he also felt it was the right thing for them all. He couldn't have Felipe getting involved with the tourists arriving at Las Nevadas, and Nuria was too valuable an employee to upset. Up to this point she'd hidden well her feelings about Felipe's infidelity, but clearly she'd been simmering with volcanic fury inside.

The house, and the farm, would feel empty without Felipe's magnetic presence. Felipe had brought companionship and friendship, as well as a much-valued contribution to the work of Las Nevadas. It wouldn't be the same without him.

Sebastián felt Caro's whiskers tickle his cheek as the puppy snored gently beside him.

At least he still had Caro. Maybe Felipe had somehow known when he'd purchased the puppy that Sebastián would have need of him one day.

38

It was the Ronda festival, the *Feria de Pedro Romero*.

Sebastián was charging phenomenal rates for these few days of festivities. In fact, this week of gaiety was bringing in a month's worth of income to Las Nevadas. People from all over the world liked to appear for the Ronda festival. The popular bullfight was on the first Saturday of the month but before that there was a procession of horse-drawn carriages through the streets of Ronda, with everyone dressed in eighteenth-century costumes.

The festival was created relatively recently, in 1954 in fact, on the 200th anniversary of Pedro Romero's death. Pedro Romero, considered the biggest influence on modern bullfighting, had been a third-generation bullfighter based in Ronda.

Everyone dressed in what were called 'Goyesque' costumes for the procession, clothing that came from the era of the well-known court painter, Francisco de Goya.

Sebastián knew Goya's paintings well, having visited the Prado museum in Madrid. Goya was the eighteenth-century court artist who famously painted portraits of the Royal family looking completely imbecilic. It was a sign of the Royal family's blind conceit that they didn't at all object to the way they were portrayed in Goya's paintings.

Sebastián had always wished he could have known Goya personally. To get away with painting such derogatory portraits of the Royal family showed some guts.

He found it hard to believe that with most Spaniards disappearing on vacation for the entire month of August, Ronda had somehow managed to squeeze in yet another long public holiday in September.

None of his regular staff at Las Nevadas had wanted to work this week so Sebastián had been forced to advertise and recruit staff from the city of Málaga, an hour and a half away, in order to provide staffing cover.

This was another reason why tonight he was sitting on his own, in the dining room of the farmhouse, drinking a delectable bottle of Valdepeñas from La Mancha. All of his guests were out tonight in Ronda, so the staff members had been signed off and Sebastián had decided to stay up at the farmhouse until his guests were safely back.

Knowing how people liked to party during the festival, he was prepared for a long night.

Caro had pattered off to his basket in the office and the farmhouse was quiet.

Sebastián decided he might go into the sitting-room and watch some of the fun on the television later, if the waiting became too boring. For now, he was absorbed in García Lorca's *Gypsy Ballads*.

An hour later, he heard the downstairs door slam shut. He woke up with a start, realising he'd fallen asleep at his table in the dining room... His cheek was actually resting on the white tablecloth.

He sat up guiltily, tidying his hair and looking down

frantically, in the hope he hadn't been drooling in his sleep.

'Seb, what are you doing here?'

Sebastián turned and saw Nuria at the top of the stairs, in her dressing gown and slippers, staring at him in surprise.

'I'm waiting up for the farmhouse guests to return. There wasn't any point keeping the office staff up tonight when everyone's away in Ronda.'

'You gave me a fright. I knew everyone had gone out to Ronda tonight so I didn't know who was still left here in the farmhouse. No one's come back yet.'

'I know, I think they'll struggle to find taxis after tonight's celebrations.' Sebastián rubbed his eyes. 'It's going to be a long night.'

'So you thought you'd drink out the wait?'

Sebastián looked at the empty bottle in front of him.

'Actually it's a good wine. I think I'm going to get some more. Care to join me?'

Nuria smiled.

'Sure.'

Sebastián trotted off to the kitchen larder for another bottle and Nuria took a seat at the table.

'Are you guys still keeping an eye on the farmhouse? Clearly old habits die hard,' said Sebastián, pouring out a glass of wine and handing it to her.

'You forget, this is our home. We're still getting used to seeing complete strangers milling about the place every day.'

'Safer this way, I would have thought. I mean, I still can't believe the three of you lived here for seven years by yourselves. Did no one ever try to break in or steal something?'

'They did, twice,' nodded Nuria in agreement. 'But I have a

licensed rifle. A hunter's rifle, which is technically supposed to be used when the wild hog population gets out of control on the farmland. Actually, to be more accurate I have a licensed rifle but my permit is overdue for renewal. It's come in handy on the odd occasion.'

Sebastián choked on his wine and started coughing. God, he thought, Felipe had a luckier escape than he realised.

Nuria waited patiently for him to finish coughing, swallowing down her glass of wine so fast that he found himself refilling it before he'd even got properly started on his.

'You're right, the three of us aren't much of a deterrent for anyone wanting to break in, but do I feel safer with a bunch of tourists around?'

She took a mouthful of wine as she considered this.

'Probably not, actually. Where there are tourists there's money, and that'll always be an attraction for a thief. You're right to wait up tonight. Can't leave the farmhouse empty when there's probably hundreds of euros' worth of stuff over in those bedrooms.'

Nuria jerked her head in that direction.

'I wouldn't know. I've never gone to have a look.'

'Seriously, have you never even taken one peek?'

'Nope.'

'I'm sure the cleaners have seen plenty of their stuff.'

'That's true. They probably have.'

Sebastián looked at Nuria and he could see the same thoughts running through her head as his.

'Why don't we take a look? It's got to be more exciting than reading your García Lorca,' said Nuria, cajolingly.

Sebastián shook his head.

'I can't afford to let my clients catch me in their rooms. It would be a disaster. I'd look like a thieving Spaniard, for sure.'

Nuria didn't argue the case but she stuck her tongue out at him, mocking him for his cowardice.

She finished her glass of wine and held it out for some more. Sebastián poured her another glass.

He wasn't sure this was a good idea, the two of them getting drunk together. Although he could virtually guarantee his guests would be in the same state.

Nobody came back sober from the *feria*. The smell of alcohol lingered on in the main square for days after the festival.

In no time at all there were three empty bottles on the dining table. They looked at the bottles blurrily, each wondering if they could manage any more.

Sebastián wasn't even sure he could remember anything they'd talked about but the wine had certainly given them both a loquaciousness they wouldn't have had normally. He felt like he'd spent the evening in the company of a cherished friend.

Nuria stood up and reached a hand across to pull Sebastián up.

'Come on, Seb. Let's take these bottles to the recycling in the kitchen and have a quick five-minute peek at the bedrooms. I've not seen them since they were renovated.'

'Oh, all right then. But quickly,' Sebastián said, looking at his watch. 'They can't be too much longer.'

They both ran from the kitchen, giggling like children, and went down the long corridor to the far end of the farmhouse where the fancier bedrooms were.

39

Sebastián took his master key out of his pocket and opened the door of the bedroom nearest the chapel. He walked in slowly, automatically grabbing hold of Nuria's hand for reassurance. They both stood in the middle of the vast room and looked around.

'Wow!' said Nuria, starting to spin around in the centre of the room, gazing in admiration at the decor.

Sebastián went over to the Italianate balcony window leading out to the front garden and kept a nervous eye on the driveway in case any of his guests arrived early.

'You've been in this room before, haven't you?' asked Sebastián, surprised at her over-reaction.

'Yes I have, but it was falling apart. The floor was completely dipped in the middle of the room and the floor tiles were cracked... There were huge cracks across there,' Nuria said, pointing to the right hand side of the ceiling. 'The furniture was old. This is beautiful... absolutely beautiful. I love the wallpaper, the curtains, and the bed's stunning. It's like what a king would expect to sleep in.'

She walked across to the four-poster bed and began to stroke the carved wood as if she couldn't bring herself to believe it was real.

Something about the way she reverently touched the bed

brought a lump to Sebastián's throat. Money had never meant much to him but he realised looking at Nuria just how privileged a life he'd had.

She'd never had a home of her own to decorate, nor had she ever been able to escape from her duties as daughter, sister and gardener to stay in a hotel.

He threw caution to the wind and moved away from the balcony to join her. He encircled her waist with his arms and started to nuzzle her neck. She arched back into him and reached her hand back to touch the side of his face.

She smelt of musk and very faintly of soap, and her skin was surprisingly soft. Because she was so tough and hardened by her job he'd always had the impression she would be rough in all aspects, but her kisses as he savoured them were surprisingly gentle.

Before he could help himself he'd tugged her dressing gown belt loose and reached for her breast. She responded by determinedly pulling his shirt off.

They both paused for a minute as if unsure if they should proceed, before he quickly undid his belt and dropped his trousers and boxers to the floor.

She smiled mischievously at him, appreciating for once his boldness. Still staring at him, challenging him, she threw off her clothes and they both collapsed together into an embrace that was cushioned by the mattress of the bed.

Both of them soon forgot where they were and only later, when they were both happy and satisfied, did they lie panting side by side and look at the ceiling of the gigantic room.

'I can't believe we just did that,' Sebastián said, eventually. He turned to face her. 'It's not going to change anything, is it?'

Nuria looked at him with her black eyes glowing. She put an elbow onto the mattress so she could look at him more closely.

'In what way?'

'I mean, are we still going to be able to work together after this and be friends?'

'Friends? Is that what you want to be?'

Sebastián lay back on the mattress to ponder this.

'I don't know,' he said, treading cautiously. 'I mean, if we start a relationship and it doesn't work out things could get very complicated.'

Nuria started to trace circles on his chest with her finger but he was determined not to be distracted.

'I mean, if it goes badly wrong like it did with Felipe, how on earth are we going to carry on working together, with you living here too?'

'Oh, are you unfaithful as well?' Nuria asked, with an edge to her voice.

'No, no! I mean I've never done that to anyone... To be honest with you, I haven't had that many relationships. Women never seem to find me attractive in the way they do my brother.'

Nuria bent down and kissed him on the lips, letting it linger.

'I find you attractive.'

Sebastián looked at her sceptically but she was staring at him boldly, defying him to contradict her. Finally, he was the one to turn his eyes away. The sheer naked desire in her eyes was scalding him and leaving him breathless.

He bent down and took her nipple into his mouth again, at which point the lights of a car coming up the driveway shone on the wall above them.

'Hell!'

The pair of them bumped into each other as they clumsily tumbled onto the floor in their haste to get out of the bed. They raced to put their clothing on and hectically tidied the bedclothes.

'Hell! I really hope they don't see anything amiss.'

'It's fine, Sebastián. Stop freaking out. Come on, let's get going!'

They slammed the door of the room shut and raced down the corridor, through the main section of the house and into the dining room where four of the guests, looking worse for wear, were still chattering away to each other.

'Hello Sebastián!' they shouted gleefully when they saw him. Nuria, ashamed to be seen in her dressing gown, disappeared at speed down the staircase and out of the farmhouse.

'Hello. How was the *feria*?' asked Sebastián, casually.

'Fantastic. Amazing,' said Mónica, a young lady who hailed from Alicante. 'I didn't stop dancing, my heels were absolutely killing me.'

Sure enough, she was carrying her bright pink heels loosely in her hand. Sebastián wondered how long she'd been walking without them. Her feet must be filthy, he thought to himself.

'Do you not go to the *feria* yourself, Sebastián?' asked Pepe, Mónica's husband, with interest.

'No, I've been to it enough times already,' lied Sebastián, not wanting to give the impression he usually hated this kind of thing.

'Well, the people there were saying it's the best *feria* they've ever had. They had thirty carriages this year and they also had amazing lights decorating the road up to the bullring. We're pleased we'd booked everything in advance because all the restaurants and bars were absolutely packed,' said Celia, a friend of Mónica's.

Sebastián nodded politely, and waved towards the fireplace.

'You're welcome to have a drink and some tapas here if you like before you turn in.'

'That would be lovely, thank you, but I think we're going to crash. It's been a long night,' said Pepe.

The others nodded and followed him out of the dining room. Sebastián sat down on the sofa and took a few deep breaths. He still had to wait for the rest of the farmhouse guests. It could be a while.

He felt a cold nose prod his hand and looked down at Caro. He stroked the dog's soft ears as he sat obediently on the floor next to him. Caro knew he wasn't normally allowed up here in the dining area so he wasn't going to push it by attempting to climb up on the sofa as he did at home with Sebastián.

Sebastián didn't know what tomorrow held as far as his relationship with Nuria was concerned but he felt strangely at peace with it all. Maybe that was an added benefit of having spent so much time with her, working on the farm.

They knew each other pretty well; this was just a new dimension to their relationship. He was fairly sure if it didn't work out they'd still be able to keep their working relationship going. At least he strongly hoped so. She was as much a part of the olive farm as he was.

40

'Diego Casales and his daughter Silvia used to take their horses for a ride together in the early hours of the morning. You could tell it was a special time for them both. She rode on an ancient side-saddle, as the women did in the old days. So much harder for them to ride that way, but that's the way they did it in times gone by. As for all the others in the family, they used to lie in in the mornings...'

Emilio passed a photo of Silvia riding on her horse to Sebastián. Sebastián looked at it carefully, interested to see Silvia's face and expression. Irrationally, he wanted to see if her facial expression suggested someone Machiavellian enough to hide letters; letters addressed to her father from her brother Gabriel. Unfortunately, all he could see in the photo was a happy young lady with rosy cheeks, the bloom of exercise and health giving a pink tinge to a distinguished face.

He was seated with Emilio in the sitting-room at the apartment. Neither he nor Nuria had told Emilio about their new relationship, which was getting stronger and more intertwined with every passing day.

He felt like a new man, walking with a spring in his step, remembering stolen kisses and torrid nights when she would sneak to his house in the early hours of the morning, quickly driving back to the farmhouse before anyone else was up and about.

The secrecy added another element of excitement to their intimacy and neither of them wanted it to end.

Emilio was busy shuffling through his collection of photos this morning like it was a pack of cards. Eventually he found the one he was looking for and passed it to Sebastián.

'Diego's wife Amaya wasn't keen on the horses, look at this photo. It's hilarious! She's holding the horse's reins, posing for the camera, but could she be any further away from the horse? You can see she was terrified of it. But Silvia was fearless; she would spend most of her day in the stables. Diego governed the horses with ferocity, Silvia with bravery. The horses sensed it. They never tried to push their luck with her, and horses will if they sense fear or weakness in you...'

Sebastián smiled. He knew absolutely nothing about horses but he was certain of one thing: he wasn't keen on them at all. The horses would certainly be detecting fear or weakness in *him*. He would be completely dependent on the stable manager if he ever got that to that point in the project, but just now that possibility seemed far away.

'How many horses did they have in those days?'

'They had four, but really the only ones that got taken out by Silvia and Diego were the two Arab mares. The other two were farm horses.'

Emilio looked down reminiscently at the photos, his connection with the Las Nevadas of the past.

'They had cars, too, in those days. Diego splashed out on a Rolls Royce at one point but it was an expense he was later to regret as his family grew. He never had the money for repairs to the car.' Emilio held up a photo of an ancient Rolls Royce with Diego leaning against it, posing for the camera. 'Indeed, there was one time when they were invited to a prestigious wedding in Ronda and the passenger seat was broken, so Diego came up with the ingenious idea of tying one of the kitchen stools to the place where the passenger seat should have been... Amaya used to laugh until she cried when she recalled the look on the car valet's face at the wedding when he opened the car door, only to find her in her glamorous outfit sitting on the kitchen stool.'

Emilio laughed to himself and Sebastián could visualise Amaya Arismendi recounting the story to the family over the years.

'I think it would be a wonderful idea to bring back the horses to Las Nevadas,' said Emilio, looking approvingly at Sebastián. 'Animals were always a part of the farm. They had horses, pigs, and even a paddock of bulls here on the farm. Horses would make this place a proper working farm again.'

Sebastián sighed.

'I know. I'm looking into it. Piedra's here today getting some quotes for me to look at. It just feels like yet another commitment, another responsibility... Goodness knows, this place is demanding enough of my time; I can only imagine when the stables are full what it'll be like. On top of all the daily problems of running this place I can see myself taking calls every minute of the day requesting visits from the vet or more horse feed, or help to clear out the stables because staff are off sick or haven't turned up.'

'You're sounding very pessimistic, which isn't like you,' said Emilio, in surprise. 'Horses don't give you that much trouble. You'll always be able to enlist the help of other staff members. As long as they get the right food and exercise, as long as the stables are clean, they're pretty docile for the most part I would say. They might take exception to Caro here but they'll get used to him eventually.'

There was a knock and before Sebastián could get up to answer it, the door opened and Piedra peered in.

'Sebastián, have you got a minute? I've drawn up some quotes, only approximations of course, but I wanted to run them through with you and it's easier if we're in front of the stables so I can explain to you what's needing to be done.'

Sebastián nodded and followed Piedra out.

Piedra was a short man, bow-legged and edging towards sixty but there was a kind of dignity around him that aroused everyone's respect. No one looking at him would assume he was the director of a building firm because he was so down to earth and perfectly willing to go out personally to help his clients with minor repairs or problems.

Piedra was a family man who was honest and decent, which sadly was a rarity, as well as a valuable commodity, these days. The number of dodgy builders who'd sold poorly built properties to gullible foreigners on illegally developed land had made headline news too many times. Sometimes it felt like every man was out for himself in the trade, but in Piedra Sebastián had found someone who still had the old-fashioned virtues of pride in one's work and integrity too.

Time and time again in the development of Las Nevadas Sebastián had been advised by Piedra not to follow through on an alteration because the cost would far outweigh the benefit. Piedra wasn't out to get all the money he could; he always tried conscientiously to give his clueless clients the best advice possible.

So today Sebastián followed Piedra to the stables perfectly

willing to listen to his suggestions.

Sebastián wanted to build a small flat above the stable block for the stable manager. He felt this could be an attraction for anyone taking the job on and it would also be reassuring to have someone who knew about horses on site, in case of any emergencies. However, he still had to see how much this would cost.

'The stables, surprisingly, aren't in a too bad a condition, Sebastián. A lick of paint would make a big difference. There are no exposed beams used in their construction so there's been no *carcoma* damage and the roof is still solid enough. Though not, of course, if you want to build a flat above the stables. We'd have to reinforce the ceiling with steel girders. That's all included in the quote.'

Sebastián looked at the quote with trepidation, trying not to let his heart race at the sight of the five-figure sum written at the bottom of it.

'Then of course, there's the cost of the arena. I've quoted you as requested for a basic arena with no seating included, just the cost of the floor and the walls with a basic corrugated iron roof. I've also made up a quote for the arena with additional seating and café. Then I've added on separately the cost of the toilets at the arena, something I think you will find necessary if this is going to become a proper riding school.'

Sebastián nodded.

'How long would all this take, Piedra?'

Piedra smiled.

'It depends what you want done. We could renovate the stables completely, without the flat above, in a matter of weeks. If we're building the flat as well that's going to be at least a two-month project. As for the arena... I would say it would take about nine months, more or less? There's a lot of work involved.'

Sebastián sighed as he looked at the figures. The quote for the arena was way beyond his budget but he wasn't going to cut corners by looking for a different builder or cheaper quotes. He had implicit trust in the quality of Piedra's work.

'You know what, Piedra? I think I can have a working stable in place before I begin to think about an arena. As far as I'm concerned an arena is for competitive riding and I'm just looking at this stage to start a small venture and see how it grows. I think we should go ahead with the stable renovations and the flat, as well as the toilets, leaving the arena for the future. Many hotels have stables and horses that are used by the locals as well as hotel guests and they don't have an arena. I think we start small and then see where it takes us.'

'What about parking on the site? You don't want the locals taking over the farmhouse parking, that's going to nark your guests off no end because there's not a lot of space for cars at the farmhouse.'

'You're right. We'll have to have signs directing people to drive around and to the back of the farmhouse for riding. They mustn't come up the farmhouse driveway.'

'You might want to tarmac a specific space for parking, near the future arena and not too far from the stables.'

'Yes, that would certainly be very useful. Have you anywhere in mind?'

Piedra, with Sebastián following behind him, walked away from the stables and out of the back courtyard of the farmhouse, through the huge green wooden doors and out onto the road that encircled the farmhouse. He walked along the road until he reached a path that dipped down to where the refuse bins were stored.

'I would put the car park here, next to where the refuse is kept. This bit of land is just big enough for a small car park and I've noticed there's already a foundation of sorts. I don't know if they had ever planned to build anything there?'

'I've no idea,' said Sebastián, shaking his head. 'It's close to where Diego Casales cleared the land for an airport to be built so it could've been something related to that. If you could write me a quote for tarmacking, that would be very helpful. I don't want people parking irresponsibly anywhere on the farmland.'

'It won't cost too much. The base is already there.'

'OK, thanks Piedra. I'd also want a fence or wall to enclose the car park so it's not an eyesore. Like what we've done for the refuse collection site... I would also like a rectangular, securely fenced paddock next to the car park, about 8 acres in total. If you can get your men started as soon as possible that would be really helpful, thanks.'

'I'll get some fixed quotes to you as soon as I get in touch with my colleague who costs all the supplies. We won't be able to start until the New Year, I'm afraid, because everyone at the company is tied up on several other projects.'

'OK. December and January are lean for bookings so it might suit quite well to have the building work done in January. Let's go with that.'

Piedra nodded, scribbled down a few more quick notes in his notebook and then shook hands with Sebastián before they both turned their backs on the new car park site and walked back to the farmhouse.

41

Sebastián felt the soft juddering motion of the train and looked out at landscape flashing past his window. He put his head back on the headrest and stretched his feet out.

Like a child without a favourite teddy, he was missing the piles of paper he was accustomed to tackling on a daily basis. He was missing his rickety old desk. He was also missing the sight of familiar faces, faces that belonged to his small but cherished Las Nevadas community.

He felt like he was going through a Las Nevadas detox programme by removing himself from his project for two weeks.

He'd left Nuria in charge of the farm while he left to visit his family in Madrid for Christmas.

He could tell it had come as a shock to everyone when he announced Nuria would be deputising for him, and the surreptitious glances that passed between his employees clearly showed their surprise.

Sebastián stretched his arms and yawned.

Their secret was out now; they were now an official couple, whatever anyone else thought about it. Except that he hadn't told his family, and most of all he hadn't told his brother, Felipe. Felipe's reaction would be interesting, to say the least.

He felt so exhausted...

He hadn't realised how much life in Las Nevadas had consumed him. Now all he had to do was rest, and his thoughts were slowly ebbing away into blankness.

Yet still the worries niggled and tormented him, bringing back a rapid heartbeat as he thought about them.

How would Nuria cope managing the accounts? Sure, she'd managed her own accounts for years but keeping track of her income as a gardener in no way compared to keeping track of the farm's accounts.

Would she cope with all the unexpected problems that cropped up on a daily basis?

How would she deal with any customer complaints? Hopefully she'd be able to rein in her temper. Nuria didn't suffer fools gladly.

He was less worried about her looking after Caro. Sebastián missed his little dog as much as he would've if he'd left behind a family member. But Caro was quite capable of taking care of himself; he had everyone under his thumb.

He hoped no one would give Nuria a hard time. She was a gardener turned acting boss of the farm. If they did give her any trouble, he knew Nuria wouldn't tell him. She would want to be seen as capable of the role he'd entrusted to her.

Sebastián took his mobile phone out of his coat pocket and looked at it. No new messages. He tucked it away again and silently scolded himself for his anxiety. It was time he stopped thinking of Las Nevadas and prepared himself for two weeks with his family. He'd definitely be in need of a holiday after that as well.

42

Four hours later, Sebastián descended the steps of the train and walked along the platform carrying his travel case over one shoulder. In the distance, at the end of the platform, he could see his mother and father standing and peering anxiously into the crowd. He hastened his footsteps and in no time at all he was bending down to greet his mother and hugging his father before they turned around as one and headed out to the taxi rank.

'How are things at home?' asked Sebastián, as they sat in the taxi that was skilfully winding its way through traffic to his parents' flat in Calle Edgar Neville.

'Good, good. All good,' said his mother, happily. 'We have many, many parties organised over the holidays. We're meeting up at your grandmother's as usual on the 24th. On the 25th we'll be hosting everyone at ours. New Year's Eve will be at your Aunt Maite's, and on New Year I believe we're all congregating again at my mother's house. On the Epiphany we're going to your uncle's house.'

Sebastián nodded. The usual. He thought warmly, yearningly and also nostalgically of Nuria celebrating quietly with her father and brother at Las Nevadas.

Sebastián looked out of the car window at the bright lights of the city. He'd never appreciated before what people meant by light pollution, but he did now. Gone was the beautiful tapestry of the night sky from Las Nevadas with its stars, moon and planets. He felt blinded by the streetlights, the bright shop fronts, apartment blocks lit up like a Times Square billboard and the multitude of cars, all with their headlights on.

I really have become a country bumpkin, he thought to himself.

The taxi dropped them off at Calle Edgar Neville and Sebastián walked into the foyer, taking a trip down memory lane. His flat in Madrid had been rented out since he'd taken over the Las Nevadas project so he was staying at his parents' flat. The foyer hadn't changed from when he was a small boy, the same blue carpet and faded blue walls. Javier, the security guard, wasn't at his desk at this time of night but Sebastián looked forward to greeting him at some point tomorrow.

They all got into the lift. It had gained some interesting graffiti since Sebastián was last in it.

'These spoilt privileged kids who come back drunk at night and decide to write all over the lift! They keep removing the graffiti but it always comes back. Now the association's talking of installing a camera to catch them and charge them,' his father moaned.

Sebastián smiled to himself. That would set the cat among the pigeons! No one was more in denial about their children than some of the families that resided there. He didn't think even CCTV evidence would convince the parents that their children were anything other than angelic.

They arrived at the eighth floor and he waited patiently while his parents fumbled at the front door with the key. Eventually the door opened and Sebastián stepped back in time into his childhood home.

Nothing ever changed in this flat. The parquet wooden floor and the well-loved and well-worn furniture, the handsome impressionistic paintings on the walls and his father's beloved study with its neat bookshelves and cosy desk chair.

Sebastián sighed with relief, plonking his bag on the hallway sofa and making his way, out of habit, straight to the kitchen for some food and a drink. His mother scurried behind him in her high-heeled shoes.

Before long, Sebastián was seated at the wobbly old kitchen table with his mother, drinking coffee and munching on a *torta de aceite*. His mother continued her ceaseless flow of inconsequential talk. Her chatter was quite soothing, and it helped Sebastián catch up on all the family news he'd missed out on.

His father had disappeared to his favourite reading chair in the study; the study was his father's 'cave' where he hid from view and found his space in much the same way Sebastián did in his office at Las Nevadas.

'How's Felipe doing?' asked Sebastián, after listening to his mother for a few minutes.

'Felipe? Fine, I think. He's quite busy these days so we don't see as much of him as we used to. He's managed through friends to get a contract working for the television channel, Tele 4. He's working for their advertising department.'

Sebastián laughed loudly, his humour tickled by the thought of his brother working in advertising.

'That should suit him to the ground. He could sell a pair of glasses to a blind man if he wanted to,' Sebastián shook his head in admiration. 'He always falls on his feet, Felipe. I shouldn't have worried so much for him after he left Las Nevadas.'

His mother looked at him, concerned.

'Yes, I don't know what happened there, he won't tell me. Did you two fall out? Is that why he left Las Nevadas?'

'Felipe never stays anywhere for too long, Mum, you know that. But just to reassure you, we didn't fall out. He fell out with his girlfriend.'

'That lady who's a gardener?'

'Yes, exactly, Nuria.'

'Don't tell me, Sebastián. He screwed around and caused an upset. The usual,' said his mother angrily. 'He has some kind of mental problem I think.'

'Well, I certainly think he'd make an interesting case study for a psychologist, but then wouldn't we all?'

His mother didn't say anything. She looked worn and beaten. She reached across for a piece of *torta* and started to nibble it unconsciously.

Sebastián reached across and held her free hand. What must it be like to have a child who is constantly causing emotional dramas in his relationships? His mother still hadn't learnt to let go. It must be a guilt thing with parents, Sebastián mused, this constant desire or need to feel responsible for the peccadillos of your children, no matter how old they are.

'Don't worry so much, Mum. Nuria's not upset with him any more. In fact, we're an item now.'

His mother looked at him in surprise.

'You and Nuria are a couple?'

'Yes we are, and we're very happy. She's looking after Las Nevadas for me while I'm here with you. You've no idea how busy my days at the farm are. She's doing me a huge favour.'

'Isn't that a bit strange?'

'What? Both your sons falling for the same woman?' asked Sebastián, amused. 'I don't think so. It's never serious in Felipe's case. For him it's always a bit of fun, a bit of fooling around. For me, it's different.'

His mother nodded in agreement.

'I know. You were always more loyal. Nuria's found herself the better man.'

'No, Mum, I'm absolutely not the "better man". The better man for Nuria, maybe, but Felipe has a healthy attitude to life. He doesn't take life too seriously or let it affect him too deeply. There's a lot of merit in that. Goodness, sometimes the responsibility of taking on that farm crushes me. It's too much. But to live life like Felipe, on the light side, never worrying too much, it's no bad thing. He'll outlive us all, you wait and see.'

'Probably. Nothing would surprise me any more as far as Felipe goes.'

'Maybe it's time he stopped being the black sheep of the family.'

They looked at each other. His mother nodded silently and stood up to take their mugs to the sink.

43

The Spanish music belting out of the speakers at his grandmother's house was dominating the atmosphere in the
room. The family had gathered for Christmas Eve, as always
at his grandmother's flat, meaning that currently present were
his grandmother's three married children and all her grandchildren, in turn, with their families too. Everyone had spread
themselves out across the flat, monopolising the kitchen, the
dining area, the sitting-room and even some of the bedrooms.

Andrea, Sebastián's sister, had stopped her two children from
playing rap music at full volume but unfortunately two of
his grandmother's other great-grandchildren weren't so well
behaved, and had now started playing *their* favourite collection
of Spanish music.

The noise was deafening.

Sebastián had had his ears checked in Ronda after that
memorable night at the bullring, but had vehemently refused
a hearing aid when they showed him the results. He knew
he definitely had declining hearing, especially in his right
ear, apparently, but in the quiet of Las Nevadas this wasn't
a hindrance.

Tonight was different. His hearing loss was definitely proving
a handicap but Sebastián would rather suffer in silence than be
sitting on the sofa with his ninety-year-old grandmother, both

of them wearing hearing aids.

Nuria teased him constantly for his pride and denial, calling him her bull-headed boyfriend, and that didn't help make him one iota less stubborn about this sensitive subject.

Sebastián felt a hand grip his elbow and a raised voice in his ear said:

'Hey, Sebastián, want to come and join us in the pantry? We've discovered a secret stash of 1973 sherry.'

Sebastián turned and found himself looking at his brother. Felipe was looking very dapper, as usual, wearing an expensive suit and a smart tie for the occasion. Sebastián, used to living daily in jeans and a T-shirt, had opted for an open-necked shirt under duress from his mother.

He nodded and followed Felipe into the kitchen, where a small group of men from the family were sheepishly gathered. There was loud cheer as the first bottles were opened and passed out of the pantry.

Soon everybody waiting was rapidly filling up their glasses with glee and some of them even began toasting Sebastián's grandmother in extravagant terms, although she was probably totally unaware of the depreciation of her cherished alcohol hoard. His grandmother's mental faculties, undeniably, were not what they once were so there was a good chance she would never notice.

'Mmm. This is a good bottle, Seb. I wonder how long our grandmother has had these stored away. She doesn't even drink sherry; she's an inveterate whisky drinker. I suspect we owe this supply to our dear deceased grandfather... How's the farm doing in your absence?'

'Good, as far as I know. I left Nuria in charge.'

Felipe transferred his attention from his wine glass to Sebastián.

'Did you, now? Well, that's interesting... I'm sure she's doing a great job.'

'She is,' said Sebastián, defensively. 'And I might as well tell you now that Nuria and I are an item.'

Felipe grinned at him.

'I knew you liked her, Seb. Congratulations. How long's this been going on for? I hope it isn't a rebound affair?'

Sebastián hated how Felipe knew exactly how to reach his hand into his innermost fears and give them a sharp, mischievous tug. That's the problem with family. They always know what buttons to press.

'No, it's not. We're very happy together.'

Felipe looked searchingly at his brother and had the grace to look ashamed. He patted Sebastián on the back.

'I'm sure you are. You're a good fit.'

They drank in silence for a few moments, listening to the chat of the other men in the room.

Felipe turned back to Sebastián eventually and whispered: 'Has she forgiven me yet?'

Sebastián looked at Felipe with some amusement, recalling suddenly Felipe's bedroom in Ronda covered in his shredded clothing.

'Yes, I think so. I don't think she thinks of you too much. At least I hope not.'

'I'm glad of that at least. As I said before, the two of you are a good fit.'

Sebastián was surprised to see some lingering sadness in Felipe's eyes.

'Felipe, do you think you'll ever find a girl you can love and be faithful to?'

'I don't know. I hope so... Life on one's own sucks. You should know.'

Sebastián laughed. Same old Felipe! He suspected for Felipe the grass would always be greener with someone else and that he was constitutionally incapable of being satisfied with the status quo. But no one could put Felipe in a box. He could surprise them all yet.

'By the way, has Mum told you about Dad's heart attack yet?' asked Felipe. 'We missed you when it happened.'

Sebastián stood still in shock.

'What heart attack?'

'Do you mean to tell me Mum hasn't told you yet?'

'No! Why didn't you? When did this happen?'

'It happened at the start of November, early on the Saturday morning. I never *ever* want to go to A&E at the weekend again. It was mobbed with people. Mum and Dad didn't want you to know at the time. I thought it was wrong of them. As I said, we missed you badly. I asked Mum to tell you but she said you shouldn't come and they didn't want you to know about it.'

Sebastián suddenly felt overwhelmed with a sense of abandonment. He was bitterly hurt that nobody had thought to mention this to him. He sincerely hoped it wasn't because of his fractious relationship with his father. Maybe they thought he'd make his father worse?

'Any idea why they didn't want me to know?'

Felipe shook his head.

'No, I think you're better talking to them about it. They should've told you. Dad's doing OK, though, it was a minor heart attack and he's now on statins. Haven't you noticed how he's so subdued these days? It gave him a real fright. Nothing like a heart attack to put life into perspective...'

Sebastián swallowed his anger during the rest of the evening, which seemed to him eternally long. All the time that he was eating the paella and seafood buffet, talking to his relatives and joining in with the family jokes and tales, he kept glancing across at his father, who was seated with his two brothers-in-law and looking as though he didn't have a care in the world.

Should he confront his father when they arrived home tonight or should he wait until the next day? He decided he would do more harm than good bringing it up after a late night out. He would wait until the morning, Christmas Day.

That night, as he lay in bed, Sebastián listened to the Madrid traffic thundering and bellowing eight floors below him and thoroughly yearned for the gentle chirping of the crickets and the occasional hoot of an owl at Las Nevadas. He missed the empty stillness of the mountains during the day, the insects busily crawling in and out of the flowerbeds, and the train of ants climbing determinedly up and down the fig tree in the garden and across the terrace.

He missed the sense of purpose the farm gave him and the friendly faces he came into contact with on a daily basis. Most of all, he missed Nuria.

He no longer had any regrets about taking on the farm. It was home to him now.

44

Sebastián woke up late the following morning, his head-ache warning him he might've had more sherry than was required. He wondered how the others who'd partaken liberally of his grandmother's sherry were faring. Probably worse, he thought, given their exuberance at the time.

He looked at his watch. It was half past ten. He should've been up earlier, helping his mother in the kitchen. Christmas Day was not as big a deal in Spain as it was in some other countries like the UK and America. No presents were handed out today. That was for Epiphany. But people still expected a good meal.

Sebastián's mother, the super organiser, had been planning for this day for months so all Sebastián had to do today was follow instructions.

He jumped out of bed and opened the window, letting in the chilly December air. This room still had the sixties wallpaper from his childhood.

Some of Andrea's schoolbooks still sat on the bookcase, much to his amusement, and Andrea's old necklace stand had been hammered into the wall. It had a few forlorn brightly coloured strands hanging off it from a bygone time.

He quickly grabbed some clean clothing and went to the shower room to get ready for the day.

Half an hour later he met his mum in the kitchen. She'd clearly been up for a while. A banquet fit for a king was laid out on the kitchen surfaces.

'Hi, Mum,' he said, dutifully kissing her on the cheek. 'What can I do to help?'

'I need you to open up the dining room table with the two additional leaves. And to lay out the tablecloth I've put next to it.'

'Consider it done,' said Sebastián, heading out the door.

'Hold on, Sebastián! Don't you want to have your breakfast?'

'I'll have it later. I'll be back in a minute to get more instructions.'

When Sebastián returned his mother seated him firmly at the kitchen table with a cup of coffee and a croissant.

'We've plenty of time. I don't think anyone will turn up early.'

Remembering the boisterousness of his family yesterday evening, Sebastián had to agree.

'Mum, can I ask you something?' he said, through a mouthful of croissant.

'What?'

'Why didn't you tell me about Dad's heart attack?'

His mother looked at him uncomfortably, which only served to rouse his anger again.

'Your father didn't want you to feel you had to come and see him.'

'That wasn't his decision to make.'

'I know, but you see he's actually very impressed with what you're doing, underneath all the criticism and comments he makes to you. He doesn't find it easy to admit, but he admires your dedication to the farmhouse project and the courage you've shown with taking a financial risk.'

Sebastián's mother wiped her eyes as the tears began to fall.

'He could never have done something like that. He's always been too conservative and cautious. He's secretly a bit envious of you, although he'd never own up to it. And he didn't want to add more pressure because he could see you had a lot going on at the farmhouse...'

'Again, that's not a right decision from either of you. You're both morally in the wrong. How would you feel if I'd been diagnosed with cancer and hadn't told you?'

His mother hung her head sadly.

'I know, I know, I'm sorry, Son. But if your father asked me to do it again I would. How can you deny anything to a man who's just had a heart attack? You can't. Why don't *you* try and speak to him?'

'Because every single time I have a proper chat with him it ends up in an argument. Always. Without fail... We have a big problem with communication.'

'He's changed now. He's not as... as...'

'Overpowering? Controlling? Forceful?'

Sebastián's mother laughed.

'Stop it. Go and speak to him now, before everyone else arrives. He's in the study. Christmas is a time to make peace.'

Sebastián obediently got up and went to find his father, who was sitting behind a newspaper from the day before in his favourite chair in the study.

Sebastián stood looking at his father for a minute. As if sensing his presence his father lowered the newspaper, and then looked at him over his half-moon glasses.

'Sebastián? Everything OK?'

'Actually, no, Dad, it's not. I was really hurt to find out from Felipe you'd had a heart attack and didn't want anyone to tell me about it.'

'Ah.'

'Yes. Exactly.'

His father carefully folded up the newspaper, as if trying to buy some time in what was evidently going to be a tricky discussion.

'It's complicated...'

'Is it? Why's it complicated?' asked Sebastián, praying silently for patience with his obtuse father.

'I know how busy you've been with the farm and I had your mother, Felipe and Andrea, as well as our entire extended family. There are so many of us here as you know. And, to be honest, I've worried a great deal about you and all that you've taken on so far from Madrid. You've no family out there; none of us can help you with anything. So I felt it would be easier on you if you didn't know...'

'Dad, I know that in a crazy kind of way that might sound rational but you're more important to me than my bloody farm. I would hope you would rate me in the same way. I had a right to know. I feel you keep pushing me out of this family...'

Sebastián's father reached across to him.

'No, no, that's not true, Sebastián. All I've wanted for you, for all of you, is for you to be happy. I'm not pushing you away. I think about you all the time. I just feel you've got a lot on your plate at the moment... Felipe, despite the way he behaves and the upset he causes, he's a happy person. I don't worry about him. Andrea's buried happily in her family here. It's you I worry about the most. I sometimes don't think you're always at peace with yourself. It's like you have to prove something to us.'

Sebastián looked at his father in surprise.

'Me? I'm not trying to prove anything.'

'Why did you feel you had to buy that derelict farm, then?'

Sebastián thought about it for a moment.

'I think deep down I've always yearned to live in the country. I love being surrounded by nature. And I didn't know how much until I started to look at properties in the country for a holiday home. Las Nevadas just enthralled me and wouldn't let go. I wasn't trying to prove anything. I don't know. Maybe I just needed to escape and start my life again in the country.'

His father looked at him dubiously.

'Son, there's easier ways of moving to the countryside. That don't involve mortgaging yourself to the hilt and setting up a demanding business enterprise.'

'I know, I totally know that. Do you think that hasn't tormented me on many occasions? You're wrong. There have been so many times when things have gone awry that I wished I'd gone for the easier option. That's why I was so grateful to have Felipe there for a while. He puts life in perspective. But it's all worked out. Las Nevadas feels like home to me now.'

Sebastián's dad nodded.

'I see that in you... Nothing to do with Nuria, is it?' he asked, slyly.

Sebastián smiled.

'She's a big part of it. But every person that works there is a part of it. We're a family in a way. A big community.'

'Good, Son. I'm glad to hear it.'

'However, we seem to have digressed from your heart attack. Please don't keep me in the dark again. It causes me unbearable pain. I want to be with you all when these things happen. Don't shut me out. Las Nevadas is home to me but you're my father and I love you.'

His father looked at him with eyes that were suspiciously shiny.

'I love you too, Son. I'm sorry for upsetting you. Next time if I'm still conscious, or even if I'm not, I'd like them to let you know.'

'Thanks, Dad, but hopefully there won't be a next time.'

'There will be, sooner or later. It's the life cycle. You'll be there too one day.'

45

Sebastián stepped off the train at the Ronda railway station and saw Nuria standing next to the neat white arches that looped along the platform.

This station was so provincial compared to Madrid. Madrid's Atocha railway station was vast and cavernous, giving a similar impression of size and space to Monet's paintings of the Gare Saint-Lazare. Atocha had numerous cafés and even a nightclub. In the centre of it there was also a huge green space, Atocha Station Tropical Garden, full of trees and plants native to countries as widespread as the Philippines, Brazil and Cuba. Turtles swam in the water around the trees. This oasis of greenery, he'd been informed, so startlingly at odds with the surrounding industrialisation of the train station, was planted to celebrate life.

Here in Ronda the train station was predictably minuscule in comparison, with only one small platform to its credit. Sebastián realised he was about to make the big adjustment again from a metropolitan city to a rural one.

Nuria, dressed as usual in her dungarees, ran up the platform to greet him. Sebastián kissed her fondly and they left holding hands, Sebastián carrying his bag on his shoulder. They walked companionably in silence, not needing to talk. They'd been talking on the phone at the end of each day he'd been away.

He looked out of the front window of the car as it took him out of Ronda and along the road to Las Nevadas. As soon as they were on the eucalyptus-lined driveway he felt a lump build in his throat. He'd missed the farm and its stately beauty so much while he'd been away.

Lines of neat olive trees on the soft red earth stretched into the distance, protected by strong plastic tree guards against all the herbivores that roamed the farm during the day and night.

Sebastián knew Piedra's men had started work on the stables so he wasn't at all surprised to see the chaos in the back court-yard of the farm when he got out of the car. Supplies were scattered across the cobbled courtyard, a cement mixer was revolving and men were climbing like ants over the stables, busy with their work.

Caro, who'd been barking excitedly as soon as the car had driven into the back of the farm, ran up to Sebastián and jumped up on him, his tail wagging with happiness. Sebastián bent down to stroke him until the dog's ecstasies abated.

Sebastián was relieved to see Caro wasn't in a huff with him for being away so long. He'd heard some pets could be in a strop with their owners when they returned from a trip away. Clearly Nuria had done a good job of looking after him.

'How's José Luis dealing with all this mess?' Sebastián asked Nuria, pointing to the shambles of the builders' materials dispersed across the back yard.

She shrugged her shoulders.

'He doesn't like it any more than he did when you were reno-vating the farmhouse. He's started going to the workshop really early, before the men arrive, and he works with headphones on, to block out the noise of building. Still, the stables are the last

235

thing to be built in the farmhouse itself, aren't they?'

'Yes, once the stables and the flat above it are finished, everything inside the farmhouse walls will be done. Which will be a great relief to all of us I'm sure, and will give me a great sense of achievement at having got this far without bankruptcy.'

Nuria giggled.

'Silly, you've no need to worry about that. There've been so many good online reviews and the bookings haven't stopped coming in... We've a party of hunters here at the moment, and they're ideal guests because they all disappear early in the morning and aren't back until late, just in time for dinner.'

'Sounds perfect. I wish we had more of those kinds of bookings.'

'I suspect this won't be the last of the hunters. The government needs to keep the ibex numbers in check so they're encouraging licensed hunters to come to the area.'

'When do they normally hunt?'

'The hunting season runs from October to May for the ibex. These groups are hunting for the Sierra Nevada ibex and the smaller Ronda ibex.'

Sebastián shook his head and grimaced in distaste.

'I've never understood the lure of hunting game but I guess for some it's the thrill of the chase.'

'Probably. It's not easy hunting ibex in the mountains. They're wary of all predators and have an excellent sense of smell and hearing. It's a real challenge for the hunters... Anyway, I'm off to see Dad for a coffee so feel free to join us if you want to. Now you're back I don't need to be buried in the office every minute of the day.'

Nuria stuck her tongue out at Sebastián cheekily and

disappeared off to the apartment.

Sebastián turned and walked to José Luis's workshop. He pulled open the sliding door and looked inside. Sure enough there was José Luis with his headphones on, curved over the workbench as usual and enthralled in his woodwork. Sebastián waved at him. José Luis smiled and waved back before resuming his chiselling.

Sebastián walked over to the stacked shelves and had a look. He picked out a wooden wine rack. José Luis was obviously introducing variety into his woodwork.

'José Luis?'

José Luis didn't answer. Obviously the volume in his headphones was turned right up.

'José Luis?' yelled Sebastián.

José Luis pulled his headphones down and looked at Sebastián enquiringly.

'These are new, aren't they? They're very good.'

José Luis nodded.

'Yes, I'm also working on some large wooden serving spoons with different animals carved into the handles. Local animals, of course.'

'Sounds fantastic. Well done. Eagles are a well-known icon in this area, they'd be a cool carving to do.'

'Yes. I was thinking of doing those as well...'

Sebastián looked at the shelves again.

All the items that didn't sell were sent on to other shops in the district and anything that was left José Luis gave out as presents. Sebastián had accumulated a collection of olive wood bowls in his house thanks to José Luis's generosity. None of his work was wasted.

Which must be very satisfying when you're spending your life slaving over wood, thought Sebastián.

He looked across to José Luis, who'd put up his headphones again and was back to working over his latest project.

For some reason Sebastián found it very reassuring to see José Luis working away in the workshop, as he'd done every day religiously over the past year. There was a comforting stability in seeing that life at Las Nevadas remained unchanged. Greeting familiar faces and seeing familiar surroundings gave Sebastián a real sense of homecoming.

Sebastián left the workshop with a sigh, tempted by Nuria's offer of coffee but steeling himself instead to confront his office and the paperwork on his desk. Caro followed faithfully at his heels, reluctant to let him out of sight.

46

Three hours later, as Sebastián pored over the bookings that had been confirmed in his absence and made a small start with bringing the accounts up to date, going through the pile of invoices stacked neatly in his in tray, he heard a sharp knock on the door.

'Come in!'

To his surprise, Iván, the gardener who worked with Nuria on the estate, poked his head around the door.

'Hi Seb. Do you mind if I have a quick word?'

'No, of course not, Iván. Take a seat.'

Iván sat down gingerly, and for an instant Sebastián hoped he wasn't going to complain about the way Nuria had managed things when he was away. Inevitably, nobody liked a change in management or routine, least of all himself.

'How can I help you?'

'I've heard you're trying to set up a riding school here in Ronda, is that right?'

'Yes, it is,' said Sebastián cautiously. 'Actually, it's a very small start-up at the moment so I'm not sure I would call it a riding school yet.'

'But Nuria said you'd be looking for a riding school manager to manage the stables and live in the flat above them?'

'Yes, that's true. We're looking for someone who knows as

much as you can know about horses because, to be quite frank with you, I don't have a clue. I haven't ridden a horse in my life.'

Iván nodded.

'Are you asking me these questions because you have some-one in mind?'

'Yes I do, actually. Have you heard of the Ronda Reservatauro?'

'Yes, of course. You mean the working ranch on the Campillos–Ronda road? They do tours for tourists, don't they?'

'Yes, they basically breed fighting bulls and have a practice arena for the bullfighters. They also breed Andalucían horses. Tourists get to have a look around their facilities and see the ranch in action, so to speak.'

Sebastián nodded politely but he was still unsure where Iván was going with all of this.

'My sister Mari-Carmen used to work with the Andalucían horses on the ranch. In fact, she worked with them for years, ever since she left school. But it all came to an abrupt end. Six years ago, returning home late one night, she was raped...'

Sebastián stared at Iván in shock. No words came to him. Iván, meanwhile, seemed immovable, expressionless. Maybe he'd worked through it all a long time ago.

'Anyway, she decided to keep the child, a boy, and she's been a single mum living in a council flat in Ronda ever since. I've always thought it such a waste of her talent and ability. She's always been horse mad and loved the open spaces. Now she lives cooped up in a small flat next to a busy main road. Her boy, Alejandro, is at school now. And so when I heard about this job you were creating it seemed too good an opportunity to miss. I know you might want to interview others but I just wanted to speak for my sister and see if you could maybe give her a chance?'

Sebastián swallowed.

'Iván, firstly, I'm so sorry to hear about your sister's tragic story. I mean, it's horrific. Did they ever catch the guy who did it?'

'No, they didn't. I suspect my sister knew who it was. It was so frustrating at the time but she was traumatised enough by the whole thing.'

'I was wondering if she'd be strong enough emotionally after that awful experience to deal with the demands of managing a business, which is in effect what she would be doing here. That would be a concern to me.'

Iván nodded.

'I know, it's totally normal for you to think that, but my sister's very strong. I wouldn't risk my own reputation recommending a relative who'd fall apart. And she's horse mad; working with horses would be heaven for her because she adores them. If she still has any issues, the horses will heal her of them. I'm sure of that. Besides, haven't so many of us been given a second chance working for you here?'

Sebastián looked at Iván. He felt cornered. He wouldn't go as far as to say this was emotional blackmail but Iván was making it very difficult to say no.

'Iván, I can't give you an answer today on this one. Why don't you give me your sister's contact number? I'll get in touch with her and arrange to meet with her. I'm afraid, at the moment, that's the best I can do.'

Iván nodded in agreement.

'Thanks Seb... at least for giving her a chance. I won't hold a grudge if you decide not to hire her.'

He gave Sebastián his sister's number and left shortly afterwards. Sebastián sat staring at the opposite wall for a few minutes, oblivious to the open spreadsheet before him.

Sebastián *was* attracted to the idea of having a woman in charge of the stables. Nuria was the only woman who worked outside in the farm and it would undoubtedly be nice for her to have some female companionship around the farm. But he was still concerned about Mari-Carmen's potential vulnerability.

However, weren't all of them working here vulnerable in different ways? All of them were significantly fragile in some areas of their lives, yet they worked as a community and unlike most organisations, where you found a percentage were always off sick, here in Las Nevadas attendance happened to be surprisingly good. The employees' commitment to working here was an asset of the business.

He decided he would text Mari-Carmen in the morning and arrange a convenient day to meet with her.

47

January 2019

In the end, Sebastián didn't meet Mari-Carmen Rosales until the end of January. The whirlwind of life at Las Nevadas swept him up and he didn't remember to get in touch with Mari-Carmen until Piedra proudly announced work was finished on the stables, and showed him around the newly finished building project.

On 26th January Sebastián drove into Ronda and parked in the parking lot on the outskirts, having discovered long ago this was an easier bet than trying to find a parking space anywhere near the centre of town.

He was making his way first of all to Pedro Lantro's flat at the Avenida de la Serranía, keen to hear any news about Gabriel Casales and to have a proper catch-up with Pedro.

Mari-Carmen was meeting him later on, at lunchtime, at a café in Calle Molino.

The shops in Ronda today were bustling with people, as after a week of constant rain the sun had finally decided to come out. Climate change seemed to be hitting the city hard. Summers were hotter than the older residents remembered and the rains in autumn and spring were causing problems with flooding.

The River Guadalevín had become a waterfall of substantial proportions compared to the trickle it usually was in the summer months. Sebastián reckoned it was a question of time before the old bridge above the river would need to be reinforced; he just hoped the council wouldn't be lackadaisical about it.

The thousand-year-old Arab wall in the old town had been washed away by the engorgement of the river the year before. Beautiful trees along the river had all been swept away as it broke its banks.

Today several houses along his route were getting their walls repainted snowy white; clearly things had been on hold until the sunshine broke through the rain. Sebastián wondered how Pedro's arthritis had fared in the inclement damp weather they'd been having over the last couple of weeks.

Oranges on the trees in Avenida de la Serranía had withstood the frost in early December and were hanging like lanterns among the foliage. Sebastián wished lemon trees would grow as profusely. Lemon trees were his favourite fruit trees, but unfortunately they were more sensitive to the cold so it was a thankless task trying to coax a lemon tree to grow in Ronda's climate.

But maybe with climate change that would revolutionise too, thought Sebastián. These days they had vineyards in the south of England, something that would have been unheard of a hundred years ago. Change could be reaching Ronda too, soon, and then he could maybe start to grow lemon trees...

Sebastián rang Pedro's buzzer and waited patiently. This time the door buzzed open without him having to speak to anyone. They were obviously expecting him.

'Hi Sebastián,' said a confident, middle-aged and rather squat lady with sharp brown eyes, when he reached the first floor. 'I'm Flores Lantro, Pedro's daughter.'

She kissed him enthusiastically on both cheeks, then waved him in and closed the front door.

'He'll be pleased to see you. Would you like a drink?'

'Yes, a soft drink would be great if you have one. Thank you.'

'*¿Fanta de limón* or Coca-Cola?'

Sebastián shrugged.

'*¿Fanta?*'

'*Bien*. Please go through to the lounge.'

Sebastián went through and was greeted by Pedro, who was seated in the same armchair as the last time Sebastián was in his house.

'Pedro, how are you doing?'

'Good, good, thank you. It's good to see you. Take a seat.'

Sebastián sat down opposite Pedro and looked at him. Pedro was dressed neatly in a shirt and tie but the dark shadows under his eyes suggested a man who struggled to get enough rest, mostly, Sebastián suspected, because of his arthritic pain.

'I'm sorry it's taken so long for me to drop in and see you, Pedro. There always seems to be something needing to get done up at the farmhouse. How are you keeping? Is the arthritis still causing you bother?'

'Yes, sadly, having arthritis is a case of learning to live with pain, and you never get used to it. I'm the first to admit I'm not very stoical. My poor family have accustomed themselves to my continual grumpiness and complaints.'

Flores came into the room with Sebastián's drink and handed it over to him.

'Don't believe him, Sebastián, he doesn't complain that much. He's stronger than he realises.'

She kissed her father affectionately on the forehead.

'Do you want anything to drink, Dad?'

'No thank you, Flores. I'm fine.'

Flores smiled and left the room.

'You said on the phone you'd gone home to Madrid for Christmas. How did that go?'

'It had its ups and downs, but more ups I think,' said Sebastián, thoughtfully.

'So you're not tempted to return to your business and life in Madrid? I wouldn't blame you if you did. Ronda's a sleepy, slow sort of place. It feels at times like it's a backwater, cut off from the rest of the outside world.'

'I know what you mean, Pedro. I could see many of my relatives and old friends feeling that way about Ronda but it genuinely feels like home to me now. I think even if my business here went bust I'd still want to live here. The awe-inspiring mountains and the clear night skies have cast their spell on me.'

Pedro chuckled with delight.

'I'm glad to hear you say so. Too many of our young people leave to find work elsewhere. It's nice to meet an outsider who actually chooses to be here all year around. Is the business going well?'

'It's ticking over. There are plenty of advance bookings and good reviews but I can't get complacent at this stage. I'm still paying off loans to the bank. I think we'll be OK, though. The estate's greatest asset is the staff, actually. I've not had to deal with any misconduct or irregular absences. It's quite incredible really.'

Pedro touched the wooden arm of his chair superstitiously.

'Long may it continue. You've been fortunate if that's the

case. There are plenty of people pushing the boundaries these days. I'm lucky I'm so well looked after by my family, because an old man like me would be easy pickings for people that like to take advantage of others. You have to keep your wits about you.'

'Yes, I know. I've been very lucky but I've also had good advice and recommendations from Emilio and Nuria. And Piedra has been an inspired choice. He's been straight as a die. But I was going to ask you if you'd been in touch with Gabriel Casales? I was wondering how his situation with the lawyers was getting on?'

'Oh, well! That's all been very dramatic, as you'd expect. As a nation we're experts at drama. His siblings had all been given a portion of money and of course none of them want to give any of it back. I mean, would you? I believe that they were warned that if Gabriel made an appearance things would have to be reallocated, but some of them have already invested all their share of the inheritance. It's a mess, to be honest with you, a melting pot of recrimination and anger.'

'Did they ever find out who'd hidden Gabriel's letters from his father?'

'Oh, yes, Silvia's admitted to keeping the letters hidden. She's not in the least remorseful. She says her father was deeply hurt and damaged by Gabriel running away from home, and disappearing out of their family like that, and she didn't want Diego to be hurt any more than he already was.'

'God. I can't see Gabriel accepting that lame excuse. He could've communicated with his father before he died. She took that away from him.'

Pedro sighed. He straightened the cuffs of his shirt.

'I'm not making excuses for her behaviour, but if one of my children disappeared like that, I'd want to boil them up in a cauldron. Until you've had children you cannot possibly imagine the pain of being cut off from your child.'

'I guess it's all going through the courts at the moment, then?'

'It's been a while since I spoke to him, but yes. I think it's going to have to be settled in court. It's very sad, really. I hope after all the shouting and bawling they'll be able to establish some kind of relationship.'

'I'd be surprised. I mean, all the stuff that was in Las Nevadas, that'll have to be divvied up again too, won't it? It's not going to be something any of them forget, that's for sure.'

'It's better for the court to sort it out. The rights of the case can then be settled without too much emotion. It's amazing how people change where there's money to be had. They become like a set of vultures, all circling for the best pickings.'

'Yes, a lesson to die leaving nothing behind to be fought over.'

Pedro burst out laughing.

'People will always argue about the stupidest things. The smallest, most insignificant gift in a will can cause a rift that can last generations. People are naturally crazy about ownership.'

Sebastián nodded at the truth of this.

If someone else were to take over Las Nevadas he'd find it extremely difficult to sit back and watch it happen. Maybe like the Buddhist monks we needed to live a simpler life, he mused, with less attachment to our possessions. Not a very realistic proposition though, he thought, dismissing the idea. Materialism was too embedded in our capitalist society; people would have to go into rehab to overcome their addiction to possessing things.

48

El Perico Café on Calle Molino was tucked away inconspic-uously on a corner of the long street. Sebastián, who'd left Pedro's flat later than he intended, found himself jogging down the street, much to the amusement of a passer-by. Nobody ran in Ronda. Most people there tended to amble about their daily business.

He opened the door of the café and blinked at the colourful brightness of the interior decor. Tropical flowers were painted on all the walls amidst the bright green leaves of what was obviously meant to be a jungle. Here and there on the walls a painted monkey's face peered out from among the greenery.

At the end of the large room there was a huge cage filled with blue and white, as well as green and yellow, parakeets. The sound of their chattering was drowned out by the rumble of chatter from the tables where people were doing what Spaniards were best at: talking about anything and everything.

Sebastián scanned the room and saw a table in the corner where there was a petite brunette nursing a large coffee and scanning a newspaper.

Could that be her, he wondered. He wasn't sure why, but in his complete ignorance about horses he'd assumed someone who looked after them would be tall and muscular.

'Mari-Carmen?'

'Yes, hello!'

The lady stood up immediately and greeted him with the double kiss on the cheek.

Sebastián felt an immediate liking for the diminutive lady in front of him. He thought it was funny how within the space of a minute you could make a judgement about someone. He'd instantly acknowledged the warm expression on her face and the guileless manner with which she'd greeted him.

'I'm sorry I've arrived so late. I was caught up talking to an acquaintance of mine in Ronda and lost track of time.'

Mari-Carmen looked surprised at his apology.

'*Hombre*, it doesn't matter. I'm often late myself.'

Sebastián smiled to himself; tardiness was a very southern mindset. Here in Andalucía, time was a flexible concept, unlike in Madrid. If he'd been meeting someone in Madrid they would have left by now, instead of waiting patiently reading a newspaper as Mari-Carmen had done.

'I've spoken to your brother and he says you have years of experience working for the Ronda Reservatauro?'

'Yes, that's right. I worked there since school. I started as an apprentice and worked my way up to horse trainer.'

'You must miss it, these days.'

A spasm of pain crossed Mari-Carmen's face.

Sebastián felt like kicking himself for being so direct; however, he also knew intrinsically he wouldn't be able to work with someone if he had to tread on eggshells all the time.

Mari-Carmen recovered quickly and looked at Sebastián calmly.

'Yes, of course. No doubt my brother told you what happened. I live with the memories of that night every single day, but I don't regret the consequences for one moment. Alejandro is a beautiful boy, inside and out. He's the shining light of my life and anything I do from now on will always be for him.'

Sebastián nodded quietly.

A buxom waitress came up to their table, dressed in a bright pink and red dress, with white linen flowers tied into her hair. Obviously the tropical decor extended to the café's uniform, too.

'Could I have an espresso, please? And a *bocadillo de tortilla*? Mari-Carmen, what would you like?'

'A *bocadillo de chorizo*, please.'

The waitress wrote down the requests impassively in her notebook and walked off into the kitchen at the back of the café.

'How many horses are you planning to have on the farm?'

Sebastián looked at Mari-Carmen worriedly and leaned back in his chair, carefully weighing up his words.

'To be honest, Mari-Carmen, this venture is making me a little nervous. I know nothing about horses, nor do I have any desire to learn anything about them. I manage the farm, the staff and the bills. I'm a city boy turned country bumpkin, but my ignorance runs deep. I've to rely on people who understand the countryside and how it works. If you work for me I'll be depending on you totally to manage that side of the business. I know it'll take time to get established but the idea is to have a riding school for all ages.'

'Will it just be me working there?'

'No, no! Of course not. At the start, we'll need at least one other staff member to look after the horses too, but I would expect the manager of the stables to recruit them and to carefully choose the horses we'll be buying.'

'Wow! You really are depending on your staff members.'

Sebastián smiled ruefully and then gratefully took a big bite out of the sandwich that had just arrived at the table. He was hungry.

'I still have contact with the people who own the Reservatauro and I'm pretty sure they'll be willing to find you some good horses. How many were you thinking of getting?'

Sebastián, busy munching his sandwich, held up three fingers.

'I want to start with just three and take it from there,' he said, with his mouth full of food.

'That makes sense. I would recommend getting foals. It's best to train them from a young age. That way they tend to be more biddable. Three foals who've known each other in the paddock will usually get along very well and cause little trouble.'

Sebastián put down his half-eaten sandwich just as Mari-Carmen made a start on hers, holding it daintily in her hands.

'That makes sense, Mari-Carmen. I guess, just as with every animal, horses each have their own individual traits. If we're going to be a valid riding school the temperament of our horses will be very important. The insurance payments are astonishingly high for this venture, too, so it would be good to have horses who won't constantly try and unseat their inexperienced riders.'

'Yes, accidents are common with horse riding, which is probably why there are so few riding schools around. But I don't want to alarm you. With the right horses, as long as they're well looked after, there'll be no problems.'

'How did you learn to horse ride?'

'My family had nothing to do with horses. My father works

as a plumber and my mother has cleaned offices in Ronda for a living...'

Mari-Carmen took another bite of her sandwich and chewed it thoughtfully.

'I became obsessed as a young child with horses, when my friend at school took me up to the Reservatauro. Her parents both worked there as horse trainers and from then on I spent every available weekend volunteering to clean out paddocks and stables, learning to feed and brush the horses and then, of course, ride them. After I left school at sixteen they took me on as an apprentice. They were some of the happiest years of my life so far...'

Mari-Carmen smiled mischievously.

'I actually find horses easier to deal with than people.'

'Yes, I can see how that could be the case. People are never easy. My staff members are all wonderful but some of the guests we have at Las Nevadas can be an absolute nightmare. Dealing with the public isn't easy at all... in fact, it's very demanding.'

'On that subject, I think it should be made very clear that the minimum age for anyone learning to ride at Las Nevadas should be seven.'

Sebastián took a sip of water and looked at Mari-Carmen, who was still munching her sandwich sedately, oblivious to the fact he'd wolfed his down a while ago.

Mari-Carmen had evidently taken for granted that he'd be hiring her. He had to reluctantly admit he admired such confidence; she seemed to have no self-doubts at all.

'Iván hasn't told you what the salary is, has he?'

'No, he hasn't. Why?'

'You're clearly wanting the job. Don't you want to know the

salary? Most people do.'

'Is this a warning it'll be paltry? Because for me to work outside in the countryside with horses again is a dream come true. I'm not in this for the money.'

'How's your boy going to get to school? Won't he miss Ronda?' Mari-Carmen grinned.

'I'm going to get a second-hand scooter. That's what I had before everything fell apart for me. I'll take him to school in the mornings on that.'

She seemed to Sebastián to have it all worked out.

He wondered to himself how many evenings she and Iván had sat together discussing this opportunity, weaving new hope for a second chance around a job that hadn't yet even been advertised.

'OK, Mari-Carmen, the starting salary is 1,300 euros a month and that includes the flat and all the bills for it. Obviously depending on how successful the school is, and how it increases in size and profit, the salary will be amended accordingly.'

Mari-Carmen nodded, looking very pleased. Sebastián heaved a sigh of relief.

'There are probably going to be unsocial hours worked within that, I'm afraid, but if you love horses that shouldn't be too onerous for you. I suggest you start looking for someone to help you out at the stables as soon as possible. I need to find out which of the current staff are willing to get involved with the horses too, especially for the times when we have absences and the horses need to be taken care of. Does Iván know anything about horses, for example?'

'Iván? Yes, he's fine with horses. He's a good rider, actually. He'll be happy to fill in I'm sure.'

'Right, then, you'll want to have a look at the flat too. I suggest Iván drives you up one morning and you take a look and see if it's suitable for you. I think it will be, it's only just been built.'

'I'm sure it'll be fantastic. How soon can we move? I need to give notice to the council to move out of my current place.'

'As soon as you like.'

'Right, then I'll aim to move in at the end of February with Alejandro. This is absolutely brilliant. Thank you so much.'

'Not at all. I'll leave you to sort things out with Iván as far as looking at the flat goes, but we'll look forward to you moving in at the end of February.'

Sebastián caught the eye of the colourful waitress, who was busy picking at her teeth while she looked through her notepad, and motioned for the bill.

Twenty-five minutes later he was in his car heading back to Las Nevadas, feeling satisfied that yet another important administrative task had been dealt with.

The landscape passed by, as unwaveringly constant as the surrounding mountains.

Somehow bringing horses into Las Nevadas felt like finally the farm was coming back to life. Horses were restoring the estate to something of its former glory, a faint echo of the farm as it must have been in 1856 when it was built.

49

March 2019

It was the end of March and Las Nevadas had its newest acquisitions, a colt and two fillies, both chosen from the Ronda Reservatauro by Mari-Carmen. Sebastián was confident that in years to come he would find no fault with Mari-Carmen other than in her choice of their colt, named Malo (naughty) and with good reason.

Malo turned out to be more trouble than everything and anyone else on the farm.

He began his eventful career inauspiciously. Sebastián was working in the office as usual when he heard a man yelling out: '¡Mierda! ¡MIERDA!'

The shouting came from the back yard.

Startled, Sebastián left his desk and hurried to the back courtyard only to see Iván hobbling and cursing loudly to himself like a madman in King Lear's shadow. Everyone else was gathered at the other end of the courtyard where the stables were. A horse trailer was open in the middle of the courtyard.

'Iván, what's happened?'

'That bastard of a horse is what happened. We brought him out of the trailer and he turns around and deliberately kicks me in the shin.'

Iván lifted his trouser leg where there was a round bruise

already beginning to form.

Sebastián's lips twitched but he manfully contained his mirth. He patted Iván on the back consolingly.

'I'm sorry, Iván. He seems to be a bit of a handful.'

Iván looked askance at him.

'I warned Mari-Carmen he'd be trouble but she fell for him and wouldn't listen.'

'All I can say is he'd better get tamed or he's not going to last long here. We don't need a disruptive horse to add to our daily problems.'

'You're telling me. You'd better speak to Mari-Carmen. I'm keeping out of that horse's way.'

Sebastián strolled across to the stables and looked at the three horses lined up in their commodious stables, watched by a crowd of admiring onlookers. Two of them were a pale grey colour with white spotting on their heads and hindquarters, but the third was ebony black with a white star on its forehead.

'Which is the one that kicked Iván on the shin?' he asked.

Mari-Carmen turned quickly to look at him and pointed silently to the black horse.

'Mari-Carmen, it's not inspiring me with confidence to have a feisty horse, one that's just kicked my gardener's shin, planned for a riding school. Are you sure you've made the right choice?'

Mari-Carmen walked up to the black colt and fondled his head.

'Of course, Sebastián. He'll settle down. He just objected to being put in a trailer. He'll get there. These horses are only young, barely two years old. They'll grow up and calm down.'

'Has he been castrated?' Nuria asked Mari-Carmen.

'Yes, he has.'

'Aren't they supposed to calm down after that?'

'Yes, of course, they're much easier and more biddable after that.'

Nuria and Sebastián looked at each other doubtfully, neither of them wanting to contradict Mari-Carmen, who was supposed to be the resident expert on horses. Sebastián smothered his misgivings and decided to trust his equestrian manager.

'Sebastián, what names would you like to give them?' asked Nuria.

'How about Dulce (sweet) for that one and Bonita (pretty) for this one with the white nose?' he said, pointing to the horses.

Mari-Carmen smiled her assent.

'Those names are perfect. They suit them very well.'

'What about the colt?'

Sebastián looked at the black colt musingly.

He sensed there was a spark of challenge in the horse's eye. He was clearly more intelligent than the fillies, looking unswervingly at him, almost measuring him up, he thought to himself.

'This one should be called Malo (naughty),' he said, affirmatively.

Mari-Carmen frowned.

'I'm not sure that'll create a good impression with visiting riders.'

'I don't care. He's proved his mettle out there and I'm not sure we've seen the last of his antics. You know I don't know anything about horses, Mari-Carmen, but if I were you I'd only let experienced riders mount him for now.'

'Maybe,' said Mari-Carmen, with pursed lips, not relishing being told what to do by a complete amateur.

Inevitably, in the following weeks Malo proved to be more hassle than the other two horses put together. Malo very quickly established whom he liked and disliked, and wouldn't be budged from this standpoint. He didn't like Iván at all. Mari-Carmen reckoned this was because Iván had been the one to put Malo into the trailer that had taken him away from his team of horses at Ronda Reservatauro.

Malo, spoilt rotten by Mari-Carmen, who had a soft spot for him, very quickly became eager to please her and very possessive, getting jealous if she spent too much time giving the other horses blandishments. But even Mari-Carmen was pushed to the limits of her patience by Malo's mischievousness.

A week later Sebastián wandered out to watch the horses in their paddock. He often enjoyed watching them running freely, frisky and boisterous, as they shook off their pent-up energy.

Today, though, was somewhat different because Malo was playing with a new toy: the water bucket. He was happily rolling the plastic bucket up and down the paddock like a football. Sebastián could see the puddle where he'd spilled the water.

He went to find Mari-Carmen who was cleaning out the stables.

'Hey, Mari-Carmen, I've found Malo playing football with the water bucket. Is he supposed to be doing that?'

'Oh, please don't tell me he's knocked over the water again. Bloody horse. We're going to have to get a stone water trough if he keeps doing that. I don't have the time to be continually replenishing the water in the bucket.'

She marched out to the paddock and climbed in, grabbing hold of the bucket and walking off with it before Malo tried to kick it again.

Malo looked irresolutely after her, standing still in the middle of the paddock, looking like a naughty child who'd just had their favourite toy removed. Dulce and Bonita, meanwhile, came across to Sebastián to get their noses rubbed, sniffing eagerly to see if he'd brought them any carrots, which he hadn't.

Two weeks later, to stop everyone getting complacent, Malo decided to escape from his stable.

50

Mari-Carmen had seen the warning signs, but didn't believe the horse would ever actually manage to open the stable door. Malo had spent the quiet hours in his stable investigating the bolt on the outside of its door with his mouth.

Clearly he'd been watching how it opened and closed because one afternoon he managed to pull the bolt back with his mouth and escaped into the farm.

Mari-Carmen didn't see it happen and only found out when she came to top up the oats in their feed.

Sebastián was on the phone when Mari-Carmen burst into the office in a panic.

'Sebastián, Malo's escaped!'

Sebastián looked at her, dumbfounded.

'Sorry, can I call you back later? Something's come up,' he said quickly into the phone, hoping his supplier on the other end wouldn't take offence.

'What's that damn horse got up to now?'

'He's figured out how to open the bolt on his stable door. I saw him playing around with it, never thinking he'd actually manage to move it across.'

'So he's out on the farm somewhere?'

Mari-Carmen hung her head.

'Yes.'

Sebastián stood up.

'How on earth are we going to round him up?'

'I don't know, I can't see him,' Mari-Carmen said, miserably. 'I'm hoping he won't go too far because he knows his feed and the other horses are here. He'll be scared if he goes too far away.'

'There's no barrier or boundary between the farms around here,' said Sebastián, trying to think clearly. 'He could end up on someone else's farm if he goes far enough. I'm wondering whether to call in some help.'

'Not yet,' said Mari-Carmen. 'I think I'll take Dulce out with me and get one of the others to ride Bonita, and see if Malo decides to join us. No horse likes to be on its own. He'll want company.'

'OK. Let me know if you need me to call the police.'

'That's the worst possible thing to do for a frightened horse. Give me time, I'll let you know how it goes.'

Mari-Carmen exited the office, leaving Sebastián sitting at his desk in a daze.

He didn't hear from Mari-Carmen until an hour later, by which time he'd gnawed his fingernails to ragged bits. He picked up the mobile call on the first ring.

'Sebastián?'

'Yes, it's me. What's happening?'

'We've got him. He was by the orchard and as soon as he saw Dulce and Bonita he came to join them.'

'Great! Fantastic. Is he back in the stable yet?'

'Yes, Mateo's trying to fix the door so he can't get out again.'

'Thank goodness for that. Dratted horse... Is he getting bored or something? Why on earth would he want to make a break for freedom?'

'I don't think he can be bored. He's the most popular horse in the stables by far. He's out a good chunk of every day.'

'So he's just being naughty?'

'Well, on the ranch we'd be looking at whether he was getting bullied by the other horses, or if there might be a problem with the stall itself. There's nothing wrong here. Dulce and Bonita are two softies. The stall is fine, no bees' or wasps' nests, no damp, no nothing.'

'They're brand new, so of course there's nothing wrong with them,' Sebastián said impatiently.

'I don't know. I'll get him some more toys. He should really be satisfied and he's not difficult or problematic with the riders.'

'Just as well. He'd be up for sale by now if he did play up with our riders. There's only so much we can take. Just make sure he doesn't get out again. The next time it might not be so easy.'

'Yep. I don't want to go through today again.'

Sebastián managed to forget about the horses for the next few weeks but then in April Malo decided to upset everyone again, both his trainers and his devoted riders, by becoming ill with a bad case of colic that never seemed to improve. He lost weight and became listless, the curious sparkle in his eyes fading to dullness.

Sebastián, dealing with a growing pile of vet bills, went along one morning to visit Malo in his stable. According to the vet there was nothing wrong with the feed, so it was evident Malo just had an incredibly sensitive stomach. The vet had used his arsenal of medication and was reluctant to continue the treatment for too much longer as the side effects would end up negating any positive outcome.

He walked into the stable where Malo was standing listlessly and was surprised to see Caro lying on the floor next to Malo's stable. The horses had always viewed Caro with intense suspicion, barely tolerating him. Sebastián hoped his dog wasn't causing Malo more agitation than necessary, but with the other two horses in the paddock he might be company for the sick horse.

Malo looked as though he was beyond caring if Caro was in the stable with him or not.

Sebastián was shocked at the sorry state Malo was in. He had protruding ribs and his sleek black hair had lost its healthy sheen. He stroked Malo's nose and neck, feeling sad for this horse that had lost his lively spirit. Mari-Carmen reckoned if things didn't change soon he'd have to be put down.

Sebastián wondered if he should get a second opinion. He remembered Manuel had a wise employee on his farm called Nicolás who was a genius with animals. He wondered if Nicolás would have any new advice to try.

He rang Manuel's farm and spoke to Nicolás later that day. 'Hi Nicolás, I've been told you're the equivalent of Dr Doolittle around here and we desperately need some help with one of our horses. He can't seem to overcome his colic.'

'Yes, that's a very common problem around here, partly because in this climate we don't have an endless supply of soft green grass for them to eat and all the other foods are harsher on their digestive system. Also, historically these animals are used to continually grazing. I'll come up later this afternoon and have a look at him.'

Nicolás turned up at the stables and to Sebastián's surprise came up with some rather unusual remedies for Malo. Mari-Carmen was sceptical at first but, with so few options left, submitted to Nicolás's treatment plan.

Nicolás was an advocate for natural remedies and offered to spend the rest of the week giving Malo a combination of equine acupuncture and acupressure, equine massage therapy and Di-Gize Essential Oil. He also recommended feeding Malo the natural supplement colocynthis.

Sebastián agreed to all of this and hoped for the best.

Unexpectedly, Mari-Carmen popped into the office a few days later to inform him she thought the treatment was working.

'He's eating more and he's not lying down as much as he used to. I think whatever Nicolás is doing is working. It really is amazing.'

Sebastián agreed, thinking of all the vet bills he'd had to pay to no avail and marvelling how this strange horse whisperer turned up at Las Nevadas with his natural remedies and suddenly things started to get better. He hoped they'd all learnt a valuable lesson and would turn to Nicolás in future. What a gem Manuel had working for him!

Sebastián paid Nicolás handsomely for his help and advice. Mari-Carmen continued to adhere to his treatment plan and slowly but surely Malo returned to his former self.

One day Mari-Carmen came to fetch Sebastián to the stables.

'Sebastián, I think you need to see this.'

Sebastián observed her closely, worried that yet another equine problem was about to be thrown his way, but Mari-Carmen looked remarkably cheerful.

Sebastián walked to the stables and stood at the door with her, watching in surprise the scene before him.

Malo was holding onto the handle of a red inflated plastic ball with his mouth, and seemed to be playfully teasing Caro by bending his head down so Caro could jump up and take a bite at the toy. Then, a minute later, the horse would pull it back up again, out of reach. Caro would sit patiently by the stable door and would then leap up as soon as the horse bent his head over the stable door and offered him the toy again.

It was quite extraordinary to watch, Sebastián thought, thoroughly surprised.

After a few minutes, Mari-Carmen turned to Sebastián, who was by this time grinning fatuously at the absurdity of it all.

'I think they've built a friendship.'

'Yes, it certainly looks that way.'

They both beamed at each other complicitly.

Over the next few days a steady stream of visitors appeared at the stable, in the hope that they too would get a chance to see the novelty of the horse playing with Sebastián's dog.

Regardless of his newfound friendship, Malo's recovery seemed to impact positively on everyone at Las Nevadas, and Malo found himself a new set of admirers as a result. Sebastián was very aware that for better or worse they were stuck with Malo now. Malo had managed to worm himself into everyone's affections and had become an integral part of their small community.

51

The loud blast of the fishmonger's horn resonated up the driveway as he drove to the farmhouse. Three times a week the fishmonger turned up early in the morning with fresh fish from the coast.

Sebastián groaned as he lay in bed, halfway between sleeping and waking. He turned onto his side only to find himself spooning neatly into Nuria who was sleeping next to him. The warmth and closeness of her body was slowly allowing him to drift off again when his alarm clock went off.

Cursing it, Sebastián sat up suddenly and hit the switch to silence the alarm.

Nuria stretched out and turned towards him smiling sleepily. Sebastián leaned over her and kissed her gently on the lips. Before the kisses became any more intense he suddenly remembered what day it was and sat up hurriedly.

'Nuria, the wedding!'

'Yes, calm down Sebastián, it's all organised and prepared,' said Nuria patiently, reaching up determinedly and softly pulling his head down again.

She'd become used to Sebastián's moments of stress, acknowledging them with good-humoured complaisance. Seeing what the responsibilities of running the farm did to Sebastián, she'd told him she was glad she just had to worry about her gardening. Sebastián was perceptive enough to see that his episodes of intense anxiety did affect her, so he tried to curb them as much as he could.

Therefore, despite the fact today was the day they would host their first wedding at Las Nevadas, he bent down and resumed his lingering kisses, allowing himself to get lost in exploring Nuria's body, enthralled as usual by her willingness to offer herself to him.

Later on as they ate breakfast companionably together on the terrace, his mind kicked into gear. He went over any final arrangements needed that morning before the wedding guests turned up.

Piedra's daughter, who was in her thirties, was getting married at Las Nevadas. Piedra's wife was so delighted to have her only daughter marry at long last that she was determined the wedding had to be the finest and most expensive in Ronda that year (much to Piedra's disgust, as he was footing the bill). As a consequence the wedding preparations had become ever more detailed and complicated.

Add to this the fact that, in Piedra's blunt words, his daughter and the groom were behaving like love-struck teenagers and were making a sickly affair of the ceremony and speeches, the wedding seemed to be a recipe ripe for disaster.

It certainly looked to be an entertaining experience for the bystanders. The wedding guests, who were coming from all corners of Spain, had taken over the mews and the farmhouse the day before. When Sebastián had left to go home late last night the atmosphere was at fever pitch.

For months the bride's family had been selecting florists,

hairdressers, make-up artists, musicians, photographers, wedding outfits, wedding lists, a horse and carriage, the wedding cake and, of course, the wedding menu.

Four chefs were working on the wedding lunch under the direction of Agustín, the head chef. Agustín had visibly lost weight over the last few weeks and yet Sebastián wasn't really surprised at this because Piedra's wife, Carmela, was driving him demented. She'd evidently decided Sebastián was a sympathetic ear and any small drama or alteration in the arrangements meant she contacted Sebastián to share her anguish with him.

Sebastián felt Carmela had put him off weddings for life. Every detail had to be absolute perfection; it was as though Carmela felt the wedding was a direct projection of her. After seeing first hand the fuss created over his sister's wedding in Madrid, Sebastián was already aware weddings were mainly to placate family members, not so much the bride and groom.

However, he really felt Carmela was taking things to a different level. With the amount of money she was spending, any young couple wouldn't just be able to put down a deposit for a home, they'd be able to buy it outright. Were the months of debating over the exact shade of a wedding tie or wedding dress worth it for an event that would be over within 12 hours?

Sebastián had to confess, though, this wedding was making him introspectively examine his relationship with Nuria. How deep were his feelings for her? Did she feel the same way? What kind of wedding would Nuria opt for? He had no idea...

52

'Seb, are you OK? You're awfully quiet this morning,' Nuria asked as she watched him over the top of her mug of coffee.

Sebastián looked across at her, drawing comfort from her familiar presence. The depths of her black eyes were twinkling with amusement.

He smiled.

'Yes, sorry. This wedding of Piedra's is bursting my brain at the moment. I'll sleep well tonight once it's over. Carmela has been so demanding. I can see if things don't go to plan I'll be getting all her ire and complaints. It makes me feel like a punch bag.'

'I know, *querido*, it's not easy. I suspect Carmela will be as relieved as you when it's all over. She's invested in this so much emotionally and economically. The silly woman's put all this pressure on herself. Try and relax. It's too late to undo anything that goes wrong. As you know, with life you just have to roll with the punches.'

Sebastián nodded half-heartedly, unconvinced.

'It all needs to go well because the best advertisement for a wedding venue is word of mouth,' he explained. 'It's a chance for Las Nevadas to prove it can compete on an equal footing with other well-known venues in the area. Anyway, I'd best get up there and see how everyone's coping.'

'What would you like me to do, Sebastián? How can I help you?'

Sebastián looked at her with affection.

Today was a Saturday, Nuria's day off, supposedly, and he was touched and grateful she was willing to help him out.

'It's OK, Nuria. I don't think there's anything you can do, to be honest. The wedding planner will call on me if there are any major problems but so far, thank goodness, there're no messages on my mobile. Fingers crossed it continues that way. I'll just hang around the office as usual in case anyone feels the need to speak to me. If you can walk Caro today and take care of him that would be a great help.'

He got up and stretched, bent down to take their coffee mugs through to the kitchen and kissed Nuria on the lips in the process. What better start to the day could there be, he thought to himself complacently.

He arrived at the farmhouse at half past eight and clearly the wedding organisers had been there even earlier because all the tables in the dining room were made up for the celebrations and the outside courtyard was liberally festooned in an eclectic mix of garlands: ivy, star jasmine, gladioli, roses and eucalyptus fronds. Above the perimeter of the chapel entrance an extravagant arch of white roses encircled the wooden door, red carpet led directly into the chapel, and the music system, attached to a generator, had been set out at the far end of the courtyard ready for the DJ later in the day.

As the chapel was small for the number of guests expected, they had set up television screens on either side of the chapel door so the guests who weren't able to join the congregation could sit and watch the ceremony from outside.

All the way up the driveway and at the entrance to the estate there were festoons of white silk material draped from eucalyptus tree to eucalyptus tree, leading to the cobbled entrance of the farmhouse gardens. At intervals large red rose-shaped lanterns were hanging from the white drapery decorating the driveway.

At the entrance to the cobbled road leading to the farmhouse and its gardens, there was a huge heart-shaped arch made of red and white roses. A bit tacky, thought Sebastián aggrievedly.

The front facade of the farmhouse was suffocated by a mass of gigantic floral garlands of red and white roses. Small rose-shaped lights hung in a criss-cross pattern from the trees in the front garden. Sebastián had had to arrange for adequate lighting all along the side roads to the car park at the rear of the farmhouse.

The back entrance was decorated in a similar manner to the front of the farmhouse and tables had also been set out in the back courtyard to offer guests a drink of champagne as they arrived.

Sebastián was pleased he had had the forethought to reach an agreement with the bridal party to use some of their photos on his website. Not many people would go to the extremes of Piedra's family for a wedding but the photos were certainly going to be dramatic and impressive enough to attract any browser's notice.

Sebastián stood irresolutely by his office, trying to work out where he would be most useful. He decided he would make his way to the kitchen, even if only to give poor Agustín some moral support.

Carmela had insisted on some extremely unusual dishes for the wedding food. Unusual for a Spanish chef, that is: goose foie gras, duck à l'orange, sushi starters. Agustín was an extremely talented chef but he was also a Spaniard through and through, used to cooking up varied but traditional Spanish dishes for the guests who stayed at the farmhouse. His eyes had boggled at the list Carmela had presented him with for the wedding. No wonder he'd lost weight.

Sebastián walked into the kitchen to find it full of white-coated people purposefully chopping, cutting, frying, rinsing and mixing. He blinked, startled at all this industrious activity.

It was only just past eight thirty in the morning.

Waiters were laying out a breakfast buffet in the dining room to allow the chefs time to focus on the main event of the day.

Sebastián looked around and saw Agustín talking with another chef.

'Agustín, how are things going?'

Agustín turned and clapped Sebastián across the shoulder.

'Hi Seb, good to see you. It's all under control but obviously we're trying to be prepared. There's a lot to do today.'

'I've full confidence in your ability, Agustín. I've not had a single complaint about your cooking in all the time you've worked for us. You'll be fine.'

'Yes, well, we're talking about Carmela this time, Seb. She's set herself up as a food critic extraordinaire.'

'Yes, I know, but don't you worry about her today. She'll be busy concentrating on her daughter and the guests, she won't have time to focus on the food for once. Hopefully some of the guests will make sure she gets tipsy. Then she won't even remember what she ate...'

Agustín laughed out loud.

'Here's hoping.'

Sebastián nodded in heartfelt agreement and after greeting the other members of staff exited the kitchen, feeling he would only be a hindrance.

The dining room had been transformed from that of a rustic Spanish *finca* into a white-and-red-themed state room; red velvet chairs surrounded snow-white round tables and each table had a bouquet of red roses at its centre. A huge red circular rug had been placed at the entrance of the dining room and the sofas had been covered in red and white loose fabric. The fireplace had bouquets of red and white roses hanging down above the mantelpiece.

Sebastián felt he would be having red and white nightmares about this day for years to come; his farm had been taken over by a garish, monstrous decorative scheme and he didn't like it.

He decided to hide away and work in his office until some-one needed him.

53

Sebastián looked on with satisfaction as the wedding guests spread themselves out across the courtyard. The sun was shining and the atmosphere was one of festivity and joy. The wedding ceremony had been a long one and now everyone was enjoying the freedom of moving around the courtyard, having tapas and a drink in preparation for a three-course meal a short time later.

The little flower girls and pageboys had managed to dirty their pristine white outfits. Fruit juice, tomato stains from the tapas and dirt vied with each other to liven up the children's staid appearance. Two of the pageboys had decided to have a fight with swords made from branches found in the front garden and one of them had managed to cut his face in the process. He now had a big white plaster across his tanned cheek. Sebastián was immensely relieved the wedding photos had been taken before this happened.

The bride was looking resplendent in her satin wedding dress, embellished with hand-sewn silk embroidery and fresh water pearls (as a wedding guest had informed Sebastián in a snide aside). She was loaded down with a great volume of jewellery; every part of her exposed skin was covered in it. She looked like an advert for a royal dowered bride. The bridegroom, looking splendidly neat and prim, was grinning happily and downing drinks in quick succession.

Everything had gone to plan except for one part of the ceremony. For some reason best known to the bride and bridegroom, they'd insisted on an owl bringing their wedding rings to them. Apparently they had been to a wedding in Germany where the owl had swooped in carrying a cushion with the two rings in it and had decided they wanted the same for their wedding.

The only problem was, in the middle of the wedding ceremony the owl had become disorientated in the chapel, probably because of the noise of the congregation, and had accidently flown straight into the wall behind the altar and fallen to the floor in a heap of tousled feathers. Its owner, dressed in jeans and a T-shirt, had rushed up the aisle to rescue the bird, but not before the rest of the congregation had fallen apart with laughter.

As the hiring of the owl had nothing to do with him, Sebastián was relaxed about this one small mishap.

'*¡Hola Sebastián!*' Carmela bustled up, beaming with pleasure and kissing him on both cheeks. She was wearing a tasteful blue dress that hung down to the floor in flowing lines.

'Carmela, I hope you're happy with everything so far.'

'Oh, yes. Absolutely. It's been the best day of my life,' said Carmela. Her expression darkened suddenly. 'I'll be speaking to the owl trainer though. If they weren't able to do their bit properly they should've told us so. It's made a laughing stock of us all.'

'Not at all, Carmela,' said Sebastián, suddenly feeling intensely sorry for the owl and its trainer. 'Things like that always happen at weddings. Nobody will remember it. And look, everyone seems to be having a great time.'

He pointed to the crowd in front of them.

'Yes, I know. It's so lovely to have everyone here. I must go and speak to the members of the family but I hope you'll be with us until the end, Sebastián. I'm relying on you...'

'Of course, Carmela. I'll be here at your disposal. Don't you worry about anything.'

'Thank you, you've been my rock. Piedra! Huh! He couldn't care less about the wedding and it's for his only daughter, too. I don't know what I would've done without you, Sebastián, I really don't.'

She gave Sebastián a tearful hug and walked away to greet more of her guests. Piedra, who was watching them both, caught Sebastián's gaze and raised his eyes up to the heavens.

Sebastián smiled sympathetically at him and went to get another glass of champagne. When he got to the waiter he picked up two glasses, deciding to take one to poor Emilio who had to put up with a full-blown wedding party literally on his doorstep.

He'd offered the use of his house to Emilio and José Luis for the night, but neither of them wanted to move out of the apartment.

Sebastián walked to up to Piedra, who was busy talking to a couple of wedding guests, and waited patiently until he got his attention.

'Piedra, I'm just popping over to see Emilio. If you or Carmela need me, that's where I'll be.'

'Of course, Sebastián! Thank you for helping us with the wedding. We're both of us very grateful. My wife would've driven me insane if it hadn't been for you. At least I could field her questions to you when it got too much.'

'I'm actually really grateful you both decided to have a wedding here in Las Nevadas. You're our first, but we hope to have many more in future. It's a stressful business, though. I don't think I'd grasped just how complicated weddings can be.'

Piedra grabbed Sebastián's arm and looked him firmly in the eye.

'Sebastián, Son, I don't want you to think this wedding is in any way normal or representative of what weddings are like,' he said, waving his arm at the busy courtyard. 'It doesn't have to be this complicated at all. Carmela and María between them made it phenomenally elaborate...'

Piedra scowled and took a long swig from his glass. Sebastián, diplomatically, didn't say anything.

'Believe me, when I married Carmela we had the ceremony in the Cathedral in Ronda and then straight away we went to a restaurant for lunch. That was it. Easy. All this fuss and botheration is to pander to their pride. I mean, seriously, an owl? Wanting a horse-drawn carriage? An extortionately expensive wedding dress, which had to be handmade by the nuns in Alicante? It's all ridiculous, all of it.'

'Well, you have to try and keep the ladies happy, Piedra,' said an eavesdropping guest, humorously.

'I know that. Why do you think I ended up paying for all of this?' said Piedra, impatiently. 'They'd have had my balls on a plate otherwise.'

Everyone around Piedra nodded in agreement. You didn't mess with a girl's dream wedding.

Sebastián made his excuses and disappeared to Emilio's

apartment. Emilio had left the front door slightly open for him, knowing he was going to drop in at some point.

54

Sebastián walked into the sitting-room and found Emilio glued to the window, watching all the commotion outside.

'It's interesting to watch, isn't it?'

Emilio turned and smiled.

'Hello, Sebastián! Yes, of course, for an old man like me it's fun to watch. Can't remember the last wedding I attended. Have you been enjoying yourself?'

'Yes, now the first part of the wedding's over I do feel more relaxed. I'm sure Agustín is in a panic right now, however, preparing the wedding lunch. I must go up and see him in a bit, although I'm sure he'll have everything well in hand.'

'Oh yes, I would say so. He'll do everything well because he's a perfectionist, that one. I wouldn't worry about Agustín.'

'Where's José Luis, by the way? Is he hiding away somewhere?'

'He's in the workshop as always, of course. He'll probably come home later when he hears the guests going upstairs for their lunch.'

Sebastián sat down gratefully on the sofa and passed a glass of champagne over to Emilio.

'It's nice to have the chapel used once more. It's been lying empty for so long. Did they ever use it in Diego Casales's time?'

Emilio mused for a bit.

'They did, but not very often, it has to be said. Diego Casales always went on Sundays to Mass at the Cathedral in Ronda. He baptised his children in the chapel and one of his grandchildren had a wedding there if I remember rightly. But really most of the time it was shut up and unused...'

'It makes you wonder if it was commonly used back in the nineteenth century when the *finca* was built. I mean, was it like the stately homes in England where the entire family went to worship at the chapel? Did they have a priest living on site?'

'Chapels in the *fincas* back in those days were widely used by the family as well as any of the farm workers who were devout. It was a different era, of course. In those days it was a status symbol, and also for some it was like having a papal blessing on their land at a time when the climate was fickle and crops were vital to the prosperity of the landowner.'

Sebastián thought about this. It was amazing how religion had changed from the old days. How could people claim Spain was a Catholic country these days when so few people bothered to go to church?

He wasn't sure why the church had declined so much here in Spain because in Latin America the Catholic Church was booming. It was undeniable that suffering seemed to move people closer to faith. For so many in poverty and distress faith was the only hope they had, and how could one live one's life without hope?

He would never mock people for clinging on to the one thing that made their lives bearable and gave them a sense of purpose when they needed it. He personally didn't have the discipline to follow Catholic traditions but he did have respect for well-meaning people who did.

Unfortunately the church in Spain had suffered from the

abuse of power. Memories still rankled in many people's minds.

Sebastián's mother, who'd been expelled from a Catholic school as a child, still harboured bitter memories of the nuns who had taught her. As a child she had been left-handed and was forced, by corporal punishment inflicted on her by the nuns, to write with her right hand.

Boy, his mother really hated those nuns and to this day moaned about them, but she still went to church occasionally and had some belief in God. She was moved enough to contribute funds to the elderly nuns who worked around the clock in a special needs residence near their home in Madrid.

So she wasn't totally embittered.

Sebastián remembered the day when Nuria had taken him and Caro for a walk up a steep hill called Colina de la Penitencia (Hill of Penitence) forty minutes away. Once they'd reached the top she'd shown him the sheer drop on the other side and a plaque commemorating the women who'd died there. Apparently during the days of the Spanish Inquisition women who were considered witches had been ruthlessly tossed over that hill to their death.

Nuria reckoned in a different age Luciana would have been pushed off that hill, as well as herself. Anyone who was different or eccentric back then was considered a threat to the status quo. Europe had a dark history of destroying women in the name of heresy and witchcraft.

Sebastián looked outside to the sunny courtyard filled with well-dressed wedding guests gathered in joyful groups, enjoying a chat and a laugh. He smiled as he saw the children naughtily chasing each other among the throngs of people gathered to celebrate the marriage of Piedra's daughter. He felt grateful to be living in a freer age, a different epoch to those dark days, one that wasn't without its problems but that at least gave people the freedom to express themselves.

55

Gabriel Casales and his son, Enrique, had arrived at Las
Nevadas at last. After dropping their bags at Sebastián's
house they walked up with him to the farmhouse.

Sebastián had seen Gabriel's features as a young man from
the pile of photos Emilio had in his apartment. This version of
Gabriel was just an older one. His shock of white hair showed
no sign of receding, his eyes were just as kind and intelligent
as they'd been in the photos, and he still walked at the steady
pace of a much younger man.

However, he rarely had a cigarette out of his hand, and his
husky voice, and at times his hacking cough, revealed he was
a hardened smoker.

A short time later Gabriel was standing dumbstruck in the
dining hall, looking at Sebastián's transformation of the farmhouse, and he was certainly trying hard to remember the place
from when he was there.

It was undeniably an emotional experience to be returning
to his childhood home after so many years away, and Sebastián
suddenly worried that he would disapprove of all the changes
that had happened since he was last there as a young man.
His son Enrique, who'd never known the old farmhouse, was
admiring and politely complimentary about it all.

Gabriel walked in a circle around the renovated sitting-room and then went to peer out of the French windows, as if to try and reassure himself this was the same Las Nevadas he remembered from years ago.

He was conspicuously quiet throughout the tour of the farmhouse until he went to the back courtyard and saw the stables, at which point his eyes seemed to brighten.

'You've done a fantastic job with the stables, Sebastián. My goodness, these horses are living in the height of luxury,' he said, stroking the horses' noses. 'My sister, Silvia, was the best rider in our family.'

He fell silent again and continued to gently stroke the horses, his thoughts clearly flying back to the past.

'Did you have a horse in those days, Dad?' asked Enrique.

Gabriel shook his head.

'No, I never had my own horse. Occasionally I'd borrow my father's, but that's as far as it went. I was too busy hanging out with the farm workers' children in those days and none of *them* rode horses.'

'Are you planning to meet with Adolfo at Casa Valiente tomorrow? I can take you into Ronda if you like,' offered Sebastián, who'd picked both of them up from the train station.

'Yes, that would be great, thank you. I've to drop off my identification documents and I think Adolfo's going to go through what the court proceedings have achieved so far. I think my sisters and brothers have finally agreed a settlement. It just seems a case of jumping through administrative hoops at the moment.'

'Hopefully the legal side of things won't take too long. Come and have a coffee with Emilio. He's looking forward to meeting you after all this time. He's so delighted you managed to make it.'

They walked through to the front courtyard and knocked at Emilio's front door.

After a minute Emilio opened the door and his face broke into a broad smile as soon as he saw Gabriel, clearly recognising him right away. The two men gave each other a heart-warming hug, Emilio extending his hug to Enrique too when he was introduced as Gabriel's son.

'It's been too long, Gabriel. Too long... You look just the same, so it's evident life's treated you well. Come in and get a drink.'

Everyone trooped into the small sitting-room and Sebastián disappeared to make some coffee. When he came back Emilio and Gabriel were busy comparing notes on their respective families and Enrique was listening to the pair of them patiently.

'Sebastián, don't you agree it's a shame Rebekka, Gabriel's wife, didn't make it here too? It would've laid a few ghosts from the past to rest.'

'She's busy with the children in Cádiz, Emilio. How are Nuria and José Luis getting on?' Gabriel asked politely, not wanting to venture too deeply into the painful past. He'd lit a cigarette and the smoke was rapidly filling the room. Sebastián went to open the window slightly.

'Nuria's working out on the farm right now. She's doing fine, isn't she, Sebastián? They're a couple now, Sebastián and Nuria. Pulled the wool over my eyes for a long time, too, the rascals, but I'm very happy about it. Did you not see José Luis in his workshop?'

'I didn't take them in there because I didn't want to disturb José Luis. He's not keen on getting too many visitors to his workshop,' explained Sebastián.

'Same old José Luis,' Gabriel said fondly. 'I'm so happy he's managed to find his vocation.'

'Yes, he makes some beautiful creations with wood. He's an absolute genius with it. At least I think so,' boasted Emilio, unabashedly showing off. 'He made that wooden engraving over there on the mantelpiece.'

Both Gabriel and Enrique dutifully looked across at the engraving. Gabriel stood up after a minute and walked over to the mantelpiece, picking up the engraving to look at it in more detail.

'It's wonderfully intricate,' he agreed. 'Such detail! No wonder you're so proud of him.'

Sebastián restrained a smile. Emilio was in his element with this appreciative audience.

'Have you met your brothers or your sisters since we last spoke?' Sebastián asked Gabriel, interestedly.

'Nope, I haven't. Not likely to, either. Silvia and her family aren't talking to me. Although if you think about it I should be the one aggrieved with her for keeping my letters to my father hidden from him for all those years. I'm not going to bother with her any more. You know her, Emilio, stubborn as a mule. She's made her bed and she can lie in it for all I care. My brothers and Miriam... I suppose I'll keep trying to establish some kind of communication sporadically, but all this legal stuff needs to get settled first.'

'Gabriel, they'll come round in the end. I'm sure they will,' Emilio said, distressed at this state of affairs. For most Spaniards family was the most important thing in their lives. Family bust-ups, of course, were common, but long-running family feuds less so.

'When, exactly?' said Gabriel impatiently. 'When I'm on my deathbed? At our age we don't have endless time at our disposal, Emilio. I'm thankful to have a beautiful family in Cádiz, with good friends around us, and this legacy will help us all live better. I don't need to get involved with my extended family. If they don't want to know me, or my family, that's their problem, not mine. That's the end of it.'

Sebastián looked across at Enrique and could see he was looking embarrassed at his father's impassioned outburst.

'Enrique, I'm going to go upstairs to the kitchen and grab some tapas. You're welcome to come and join me if you don't want to hear these two going down memory lane for the next two hours.'

Enrique nodded gratefully and got up. Neither Emilio nor Gabriel seemed to notice them leaving. They were too busy trying to compartmentalise thirty years into one short afternoon.

56

'Thanks, Sebastián,' Enrique said as he and Sebastián climbed the wooden staircase up to the dining room.

Sebastián turned and patted Enrique on the back.

'No problem! I guess you're finding this trip down memory lane a bit overwhelming.'

'Yes, I mean in Cádiz we just have a small flat and that's where we've always lived. It's hard to imagine my grandfather owned all of this,' said Enrique, gesturing with his hands.

'Yes, it's sad you never had a chance to get to know your grandfather but he'd be happy if he knew you were here now. Better late than never. The way he wrote his final testament, it's clear Diego Casales held Gabriel very much in his heart, in spite of everything that happened between them. That's the important thing. You're as much a part of the Casales family as any of the others, so their past belongs to you as well.'

Enrique nodded politely but Sebastián could see he would rather not be involved in all this family history and its associated complications. Like any other person who was occupied living life to the full it was obvious he'd prefer to live in the present not the past.

Sebastián smiled to himself. Enrique's general attitude to life was suddenly making him feel very middle aged...

The next day Gabriel and Sebastián left Enrique to laze

happily around the house and garden as they made their way to Ronda.

'You've done a great job with Las Nevadas, Sebastián. I can see how much work you've put in to restore the place, you should be proud of yourself,' said Gabriel as the car ate up the distance to Ronda.

Sebastián felt his eyes tear up.

It meant a lot to him that Diego Casales's son should give his blessing to all the changes he'd made to the farm since he bought it.

He felt the farm's past history touch him every day and he felt more like a custodian than an owner of this uniquely situated property. He wanted to leave Las Nevadas as nurtured and cared for as he possibly could. He was deeply in love now with the landscape around him and he felt that taking good care of the farm would ensure its preservation and viability for the future.

'Thanks, Gabriel, that means a lot to me, although I appreciate it can't have been easy to return to Las Nevadas yesterday and see it all changed from what it once was.'

'Yes, it's an emotional rollercoaster to return after all these years but seeing things as an older man, rather than an impetuous and reckless young one, is always going to be different. My father never managed the upkeep of the place very well. The farm, from what I can gather, was falling apart well before the American pension fund bought it up.'

Gabriel coughed, a dry, hacking cough that always made Sebastián wince when he heard it.

'I can remember all of the things that were a serious inconvenience but never fixed, let alone my father's DIY attempts at renovation,' Gabriel continued. 'He'd too much on his hands with his high-pressure job in Madrid, and with his five children. Las Nevadas was way down his list of priorities...'

Sebastián couldn't disagree with him. The farmhouse had been on its knees when he'd bought it up. Given another ten years, it might never have been possible to restore it.

Sebastián parked at the car park on the outskirts of Ronda and he and Gabriel made their way to Casa Valiente, Adolfo's office.

Gabriel had asked Sebastián to join him for the meeting, feeling he needed moral support to get through the intricacies of the legal system and his family's obstinate sense of entitlement.

As he sat down on the padded leather chair in Adolfo's office, Sebastián pondered the power of solicitors. There was no doubt that any settlement would have a large impact on Gabriel's family, allowing them to do things they'd never dreamt of before. Yet all of this was in hands of the solicitors, who would no doubt be recouping a hefty fee for their work.

If humans were more reasonable they'd be able to bypass using lawyers for these things but it was clear lawyers made their money quite often on the back of inherent, and never-ending, human weakness and irrationality.

'Right, Gabriel, I'll get my secretary to take a copy of these documents before returning them to you,' said Adolfo, efficiently putting Gabriel's passport and identification papers to one side. 'The settlement that's been agreed is larger than you might think. Las Nevadas was sold to the American pension fund for an incredible twenty-five million euros. I'm afraid to say, though, some of your siblings made a lot of very unwise investments with their share of the money, so that capital was reduced substantially... Still, the lawyers have done an excellent job of tracing where all the funds went. There's still a decent amount left of the Las Nevadas money. Remember, also, your father's flat in Madrid was sold when he died. So, all things taken into consideration, your share of the money would amount to near enough two-and-a-half million euros.'

Gabriel looked blankly at Adolfo.

'You mean I'll be getting two-and-a-half million euros?'

'Yes, that's right. That's what you're entitled to. It should have been more, of course, but a lot of money was lost through bad investments and general waste. Not all your siblings were wise with the money they received.'

'Goodness. That's a huge amount of money. I never imagined I would be receiving so much. I can't believe Las Nevadas sold for so much either, it's incredible.'

'It sold at the height of the market, before the housing market crashed in Spain... The ones who lost out were those who invested in the American pension fund. The fund bought Las Nevadas for an astronomical price, but after ten years it realised it wasn't going to recoup its money from the farm and sold it to Sebastián here, for a tiny fraction of the price it had paid.'

Sebastián thought of the poor pensioners who'd invested in the fund and who'd had their, no doubt hard-earned, money go up in smoke. He hoped the fund's other investments were more profitable.

Gabriel looked at Adolfo in shock as this information sunk in.

Sebastián, seeing he was still struggling to process it all, felt obligated to step in and help him out, buying him time while he absorbed the news.

'Adolfo, when will Gabriel get his money?' asked Sebastián.

'The money should be in Gabriel's account in less than a month's time. There's also the furniture and other belongings of your parents' estate, Gabriel,' said Adolfo, turning to face him again. 'That's been a bit trickier to follow through on. In the end your siblings had to put all they had into equal ballots. Your share will be with you as soon as you want it... at present it's all in storage here in Ronda. I have a list of the items.'

Adolfo picked up a typed sheet of paper and handed it over to Gabriel. As Gabriel carefully read through the list, Adolfo fidgeted with his ballpoint pen.

'I suggest you get a removal company organised as soon as possible. Aside from the cost, it's always best when there's some bad feeling among family members to deal with things quickly and not leave them to fester.'

Gabriel nodded.

'I'll have to thank them all. This money will transform my family's life.'

Adolfo looked at Gabriel pensively.

'Of course, that's up to you. If you take my advice I wouldn't expect too much from them. They were extremely difficult to work with, putting up obstructions and delays at every possible point in the process. Forgive me if I cause you any offence, but I can't say I found them particularly amicable or helpful. Quite the reverse, in fact.'

Sebastián could tell Adolfo's words were a great understatement. Adolfo was given to expressing himself as neutrally as possible, so the underlying disapproval in his tone suggested he'd been grossly offended by the behaviour of the other Casales siblings.

Gabriel shrugged.

'I can at least try. And Sebastián, I'm very grateful to you for working so hard to track me down after finding my letters. Without you, none of this would've happened.'

Sebastián felt embarrassed.

'Come on, Gabriel. It's what any decent person would do. You always had a right to all of this. At least Diego Casales will truly rest in peace now, his final wishes honoured.'

Gabriel nodded in heartfelt agreement.

Ten minutes later they shook hands with Adolfo and made their way out into the warm sunshine.

Gabriel took a deep breath as they strolled back to the car park.

'I'd better not let my children know about all of this or they'll never give me a minute's peace. They'll be begging me for things they want to buy,' he joked.

He laughed gleefully, his breath rasping harshly.

'I think I'll buy my boys a flat each,' he said decisively, talking more to himself than to Sebastián. 'They're desperate for independence and fed up with living at home. Properties in Cádiz are so expensive and they didn't want to waste money renting a room. Now they can have their own places...'

All the way back to the car Sebastián could see Gabriel was in a silent world of his own, busy weaving future plans and dreams, and no doubt thinking happily of his wife's reaction to the good news.

57

Two weeks later Sebastián received an unexpected call from Gabriel, who was now back home in Cádiz.

Gabriel was wheezing, as well as coughing, down the phone line due to a severe cold. Although Sebastián struggled manfully to understand him, he could make very little sense of what Gabriel was trying to tell him. In the end he had to hang up.

Depressed, Sebastián looked down at the telephone. Between his bad hearing and Gabriel's rasping, breathless voice, there was no hope of having a conversation with Gabriel today. He wondered what Gabriel had wanted to say to him. Hopefully it wasn't important.

He thought sadly of Gabriel's poor, much-tried lungs that now needed to fight the dual challenge of a bad cold as well as his addiction to nicotine.

Sebastián had an uncle in Madrid who'd been in rehab twice (unsuccessfully) for nicotine addiction so he knew how difficult it was to overcome. His uncle had been told by doctors he only had 20 per cent lung capacity left due to his smoking, and that if he carried on he wouldn't live much longer, but still he continued, much to the despair of his family.

Sebastián sighed heavily and went back to dealing with the day's post.

Caro was sleeping peacefully at his feet, with his head across Sebastián's ankles.

Sebastián's office didn't look any tidier than when he'd first started at the farm. Shelves and chairs were crammed with paperwork and all the paraphernalia he'd gathered over several months of working at Las Nevadas. On the plus side, as Sebastián kept reminding himself, he kept his house scrupulously clean, perhaps compensating for the chaos of his office life.

Behind the office was the room with the old olive press. Occasionally, if guests at the hotel or the mews showed enough interest or enthusiasm for the farm, Sebastián would bring them in to see the old press. He felt it added to the uniqueness of the farm, even though it was redundant, and futilely occupied most of the space in the unused room.

The phone rang again a few minutes later, the piercing tone startling him this time: he'd been totally absorbed in reading through his mail.

With trepidation Sebastián picked the phone up, hoping that he and Gabriel weren't about to embark on another round of hopeless communication.

'Yes?'

'Hi Sebastián. It's Enrique, Gabriel's son.'

'Oh, hello Enrique! How's your father doing? He didn't sound too good when I spoke to him a few minutes ago.'

'He's not in great shape but it's just a cold. He's insisted on me calling you because he was struggling to speak on the telephone...'

That's an understatement, thought Sebastián, remembering their tortuous efforts to understand each other.

'Yes, I couldn't quite understand what he was trying to say so I ended up having to hang up,' agreed Sebastián.

'He said that. He just wanted me to say to you that he's had all the Las Nevadas furniture that was in storage in Ronda transported to Cádiz. Everything's now on its way to us. But he requested they leave behind two things that he wanted to gift to you. One is a leather side-saddle that was used in Las Nevadas when my father was there, and the other is the life-sized portrait of Amaya Arismendi, my grandmother.'

Sebastián was so surprised he was momentarily unable to speak.

'Hello? Sebastián?'

'Yes, Enrique... sorry, I'm here. I was just a bit surprised, that's all. I don't understand this at all. Doesn't Gabriel want the portrait of his mother? I would've expected him to want it.'

'The problem is, Sebastián, we don't have a flat big enough for it. I mean, it's a huge portrait. It used to hang in the sitting-room in the farmhouse and that room's enormous. We only have a small flat here in Cádiz and there's literally nowhere to put it. My dad liked the idea of having it hanging up in Las Nevadas again, as it did in the old days.'

Sebastián quickly thought back to what was currently in the sitting-room, trying to visualise where he could put the painting without spoiling the expensive interior decor.

'Actually, I think I can see where it could be put in the sitting-room here... It would certainly be a very special addition. Can you thank your father very much for me?'

'Of course, he'll be very happy to know you have both those things in Las Nevadas. He says, though, that two of you will have to go along to pick them up today if possible, or the storage for the two items will continue to be charged to us. It's a very heavy picture so you'll need two men to lift it.'

'Absolutely. I'll ask the two gardeners Iván and Jorge to go and fetch it today. Do we need to show any ID?'

'No, I don't think there'll be any problem with that. He's explained it all to them.'

'OK, then. Well, tell your father to take care of himself and I'll give him a call in a few days when hopefully I'll be able to understand what he's saying.'

Enrique laughed.

'Will do. Bye Sebastián.'

Sebastián put the phone down and stared for a moment at the wall in front of him.

He remembered seeing the portrait of Amaya Arismendi in the photos Emilio had shown him. It was a beautiful and very majestic painting, clearly painted by a talented artist. It would be a fantastic picture to have in the sitting-room of the farmhouse.

Sebastián rang Iván's mobile, which rang out, and then he tried Jorge's mobile but that was switched off.

He decided to get up straightaway and try to locate Iván and Jorge. Where on earth would they be working today? Sebastián ruminated for a moment. They could be anywhere on the farm.

He suddenly remembered Nuria was working in the orchard that day, so he decided to find her first and ask where Iván and Jorge were working. She was bound to know given she was their boss.

As he stood up Caro groaned sleepily, realising his rest was coming to an end. Really, thought Sebastián, this dog gets lazier by the day.

Sebastián exited the office, slamming the door shut behind him. He left the courtyard and turned down the path by the side of the gardens.

58

Sebastián loved smelling the scent of jasmine as he walked by the exterior wall of the farmhouse. Jasmine had flourished in this south-facing garden and, helped by artificial nutrients, it had grown rapidly, covering the front of the house. The cascades of the star-shaped white flowers gave out a potent, intoxicating scent that wafted in the air.

He made his way to the orchard and found Nuria piling lettuces, peppers, cucumbers and tomatoes into a cardboard crate in her wheelbarrow. Agustín would use these supplies later on in his kitchen. Sebastián was prepared to bet there would be *gazpacho* on the menu this week.

'Nuria, where are Iván and Jorge working today? I need them to do something for me.'

Nuria smiled affectionately at Sebastián.

'It had better be important. They're both occupied cleaning out the swimming pool and fixing the profusion of weeds on the tennis court.'

'Gabriel's giving Las Nevadas a side-saddle that used to belong to the farm, as well as the full-sized portrait of Amaya Arismendi. You know, the big painting of her that's in the photo of the sitting-room, the one your dad has at home. I need Iván and Jorge to fetch these items for me from the storage facility in Ronda today.'

'Wow. That's kind of Gabriel. Are you going to put it in the sitting-room where it used to hang?'

'Yes, I think so. Anyway, I'm going to go now and get the pair of them to bring it here.'

Sebastián disappeared to find the two men, and shortly afterwards the red van left Las Nevadas to go and pick up the items.

Sebastián forgot all about it until he suddenly got a call forty minutes later from Iván.

'Seb, the portrait's too big to fit in the red van. We'd have to leave the back doors open but that could damage the picture, so I've phoned a friend who has a truck and he's making his way to us. We're going to hang on here until he arrives.'

'OK. Thanks for that,' said Sebastián, starting to worry this enormous portrait might actually be too big for the area on the sitting-room wall where he was planning to hang it.

The existing decor of the sitting-room already had a tasteful range of mirrors and pictures and he was reluctant to disturb or move anything that was already there. Maybe Nuria could help advise him later when they put the painting up.

Later on that afternoon, Jorge, Iván, Nuria and Agustín stood in front of the painting.

It had taken four of them just to get the picture up the stairs of the farmhouse and into the sitting-room.

The sitting-room had two sets of French doors leading out to two external terraces, one on the back wall and another on the left hand side.

Sebastián had decided on putting the portrait next to the French doors on the left hand side of the room, because the right hand side had two enormous wooden doors leading into the lounge next door, and the back wall of the sitting-room already had a large, tasteful landscape painting of some olive trees.

However, the others all said this was a bad idea and agreed the portrait should be on the back wall, opposite the room's entrance. So they'd moved the landscape painting to the left hand side of the room before putting the portrait of Amaya Arismendi up in its place.

It was undeniable the portrait had a magnetic presence; it drew the eye straight to it. It was the first thing you saw when you walked into the room.

The artist was called Stefano Gutiérrez.

Sebastián had looked him up quickly on his mobile and it turned out he was a Spanish impressionist artist, now dead, who'd made a name for himself painting portraits.

Sebastián loved the colour palette used in the painting. Amaya Arismendi was dressed in a long white silk ballgown but the muted warm tones of her skin, the highlights reflected in her dark brown hair, the bright cherry red of her lips and the kaleidoscopic blues of the background were very striking and brought the painting to life.

It was also incredible to see the different colours the artist had cleverly used when portraying the white dress. You could see violets, blues and even greens hidden among the different shades of white.

The artist had used thick and thin brushstrokes on the portrait, creating a vibrancy and immediacy that Sebastián hadn't seen in many other portraits.

'Seb, it's beautiful,' breathed Nuria, looking at it round-eyed. 'How could Gabriel bear to part with it?'

'I just think they couldn't see it fitting in their flat in Cádiz.

But I also think Gabriel wanted to leave her portrait here in Las Nevadas so the Casales name wouldn't be forgotten in future. Three generations of them lived here after all.'

'From what Emilio says, Amaya Arismendi was quite short,' said Iván, looking at the painting. 'You can see how the artist has tried to compensate for that by making her dress hang down low so you don't see where her feet should be.'

The others nodded in agreement.

'Well, I guess we'd all better get back to work now,' said Sebastián affirmatively, trying to sound humorously managerial in tone.

The others laughed at him but obediently trooped out of the sitting-room to finish their tasks for the day.

Sebastián took one last lingering look at Amaya Arismendi and then left the sitting-room, knowing she'd still be standing there on the opposite wall the next day, and hopefully for many more years to come.

59

Sebastián looked down at Nuria who was beside him. She was lying on her front and her face was squished into the pillow so her lips billowed out and her tousled black hair covered half her face. Not the most attractive pose, he thought to himself, smiling slightly.

'Nuria!' he said loudly.

There was no response.

Nuria always slipped away into a deep sleep, as completely cut off from the world as someone who'd passed away. Sebastián reckoned her ability to conk out so completely must be a result of the many hours of physical work she did with her gardening. It was her body's way of healing and restoring the wear and tear of a working day.

'Nuria!' he repeated impatiently, nudging her firmly with his elbow.

'What is it, Sebastián?' Nuria said crossly, turning over onto her back with her eyes tightly shut.

'You know today will be exactly a year since we got together?'

'Mmm.'

'I was wondering... if we should make our relationship more official. I mean, would you be willing to marry me?'

There was no response.

His heart beating rapidly, having spent most of the night working up to this moment, Sebastián looked at Nuria.

There was no expression or movement whatsoever on her face.

Aggrieved, he nudged her firmly again.

Nuria groaned complainingly and turned onto her side, with her back to Sebastián, as a pointed rebuke to him for disturbing her slumber.

Sebastián started laughing silently to himself.

What a ridiculous situation to be in. He'd just made the world's worst proposal and his girlfriend was oblivious to him, far away in the land of slumber.

He had to come up with a better plan. No doubt that would keep him occupied the rest of the day although he was determined to propose on their one-year anniversary as a couple.

Sighing resignedly, he pushed the sheet away and put his feet on the cool tiled floor.

The Ronda festival was in full swing and there'd be plenty to do up at the farmhouse as well.

All three of his horses had been hired for the procession through the city later on that afternoon. Sebastián had warned the organisers that Malo could be feisty and temperamental but they hadn't listened to him. Malo was such an impressive majestic horse, with his distinctive white markings, that the organisers were particularly keen to use him in the procession.

Sebastián had to acknowledge Malo had matured but Sebastián never fully trusted him. The horse was too damn intelligent for his own good. He hoped the organisers would take good care of all his horses. If not, this would be their last ride in the festival procession.

Before he could start worrying about it, as he was prone to do, he looked out at the view from the bedroom window. The mountains of Sierra Blanquilla stretched away into the remote distance and already the early autumnal rains were slowly changing the colours of the surrounding landscape, dipping nature's brush into swathes of orange, red and emerald green.

Sebastián decided he liked this time of year.

The guests at the farmhouse and mews were the same visitors to the festival as the year before, and he knew them well by now. It was nice for a change to have people you knew hanging around the place. It was also gratifying to know they'd booked to stay again this year, as clearly they'd enjoyed their last stay at Las Nevadas.

Sebastián disappeared into the large en suite bathroom and ran the shower. Dropping his pyjama shorts he looked into the mirror before it steamed up.

He needed a shave.

He needed a haircut as well, but there was no hope he'd manage to get his hair cut this week. Everyone in Ronda was too busy partying.

He yawned and walked into the shower, letting the warmth of the water soothe him into blissful wakefulness.

He poured the shower gel into his hand and instantly got knocked out by its powerful citrus scent. He felt his nostrils and sinuses gearing up for the assault.

Nuria liked expensive soaps and gels. Sebastián, who was used to throwing into his shopping basket the cheapest and most basic of shower gels, was getting educated in the art of upmarket cosmetic products.

He stayed in the shower for longer than usual, until it was

so misty he couldn't see across to the other side of the room. When he finally stepped out he quickly reached for the towel before he felt himself cool down. He was unwilling to lose the warmth he'd been enveloped with.

The door to the bedroom opened and Nuria appeared in the doorway, wearing her delicate nightdress, one of the straps sliding enticingly down her arm. Sebastián felt the early stirrings of arousal as he watched her.

'Seb, what are you doing up so early? It's a Saturday. Aren't you lying in today?'

'No. I couldn't sleep last night.'

Nuria came up to him and put her arms around his neck, standing up on her tiptoes until her head touched his.

'My poor love. Are you needing me to make you feel better?'

'Absolutely,' said Sebastián, reaching down to kiss her on the lips. They started to kiss passionately as the steam began to trail out of the bathroom and into the bedroom. Sebastián's towel slipped to the floor unnoticed.

Sebastián suddenly shivered.

September was always a cooler month and Nuria wasn't keen on having the heating turned on in the bedroom until the season really became unbearably cold.

Nuria took his hand and pulled him gently back into the shower, grinning mischievously. She reached out and turned on the tap, running the hot water again so it drenched them both in its flow.

Sebastián chuckled as he struggled to take off a nightdress that was now wet and sticking obstinately to Nuria's lithe figure, revealing her taut nipples through its flimsy fabric. Once he managed to remove it, Nuria reached up and wrapped her legs around him as they kissed passionately in the shower, both of them oblivious to the steam that was clouding up the bathroom once more.

After a moment Sebastián let himself slide down the wet tiled wall of the shower until he was sitting on the hard floor with Nuria on top of him.

They made love in the practised manner of a couple that each knew everything there was to know about their partner but with the added tenderness of recognising they were both vulnerable and needed one other.

60

'Iván, could you give me a hand today? I'd really appreciate it if you could. I want to set up my new telescope in the garden for tonight and it's complicated to assemble.'

'When were you thinking of putting it together?'

Sebastián looked at Iván. He knew Iván was hoping to sign off by midday so he'd be able to take part in the festivities in Ronda.

'Are you free now? It shouldn't take long.'

'Yes, of course,' said Iván, relieved he wasn't going to be asked to stay late and miss the fun.

'When did you get the telescope, Sebastián?' asked Iván interestedly, as the pair of them walked down the long driveway to Sebastián's house.

The leaves of the eucalyptus trees rustled and whispered in the slight breeze. It was rare to get strong winds here but Sebastián could already feel the weather was building up to the gusty weather forecast later on in the week.

'I got it a month ago, actually. I had my parents send it to me from Madrid. The night skies are so clear and beautiful around here and I was keen to take a closer look. This telescope is actually very powerful and should give a clear view of the moon, some of the planets and the stars. I just hadn't got round to setting it up.'

If Iván wondered why Sebastián was so keen to set it up today of all days, he tactfully forbore to ask, much to Sebastián's relief.

An hour later the pair of them had it more or less put together. Its three sturdy legs held up the huge cylindrical telescope. They'd tested it out, zoning into the mountain range in front of them, exclaiming in surprise at the level of detail you could see.

Sebastián had placed it next to the grapevine in his garden as the floor there was completely level and was unlikely to cause any imbalance for the telescope.

'That's perfect. Thanks, Iván, I really appreciate it.'

'You're welcome. It's very fascinating. I'd like to have a look myself one night.'

'Of course, Iván. Any time you like.'

Iván said his goodbyes, then walked back up to the farmhouse to get his car, keen to get into Ronda in time to get changed and ready for the festival. He was going out with a group of friends and Sebastián had no doubt it was going to be a heavy night for them all.

Sebastián cleared up the telescope's cardboard box and the plastic wrapping, disappearing into the house to find the expensive bottle of Dom Pérignon champagne he'd kept hidden in his study for the last few weeks. He came out of the house and hid the bottle and two champagne flutes in a bush in the garden, close to the telescope.

The last thing he had to fetch was the ring.

The ring had given him a lot of angst, because Nuria was so unconventional and unpredictable. He was fairly certain she wouldn't want a rock on her finger and he also knew she wouldn't want something too expensive. He'd also had to think of her gardening work, for a ring that got in the way of her gardening would only end up being an annoyance. So in the end he'd requested the jeweller in Ronda to make a bespoke ring.

Sebastián opened the box and looked at it.

It was a plain, thick, gold band but on it was delicately enamelled a circular green pattern of leaves intertwined. It was certainly unusual and Sebastián hoped she'd like it.

He'd managed to get her ring size by letting Emilio in on the secret.

Emilio had decided one afternoon to take Nuria aside and show her a box of her mother's rings, letting her try them on and finding one that fitted her perfectly. Emilio had then given Sebastián the ring to take to the jewellers, telling Nuria he was having it cleaned for her.

Emilio was a good ally.

In the old-fashioned way, Sebastián had asked his permission to marry his daughter, at which point Emilio had burst out laughing. He laughed until he cried, much to Sebastián's bemusement.

'Come on, Sebastián,' he'd said, gasping with laughter. 'We don't live in the medieval age. You're free to do anything you want. You don't need my permission.'

'No, but I'd like your blessing.'

'You have it. Of course you do. How could you ever think otherwise?'

61

Sebastián sighed contentedly as he drank his glass of Rioja on the terrace with Nuria.

They'd had dinner and, as was their custom, both of them were sitting out in the terrace this evening listening to the cricket's chorus and watching the barely discernible dark shapes of the bats occasionally flitting close to the swimming pool.

Nuria had looked at Sebastián strangely when he went for his fifth glass of wine but hadn't said anything. Sebastián was feeling the need of some Dutch courage this evening, even if he ended up regretting it in the morning, so he was happily drinking his way to relaxed serenity.

Moths danced above and around the terrace lights, sometimes flapping in desperation against the glass doors.

An hour later, when the night was as dark as it was going to get, Sebastián took Nuria down to the telescope in the garden. In the early evening, when the moon was out, he'd adjusted the telescope so it was positioned with the moon in its sight, even though he knew he'd have to readjust it later on for Nuria.

Sebastián had been stunned by the moon's beauty when he'd viewed it through his telescope. Luminous white, you could see its craters in sharp detail, the edges marked as accurately and beautifully as if a pencil had drawn them. The shadows cast on the pock-marked surface of the moon rippled across its circumference.

Once Sebastián had positioned the telescope correctly Nuria bent down to look through it. She was almost immobile for a good five minutes.

'Wow! This is amazing, Sebastián. I can't believe how much detail you can see... I hadn't realised the telescope would be this strong.'

'It is incredible, isn't it?' said Sebastián, pleased with her reaction. 'If you give me a moment, I should be able to focus in on Venus, too.'

He stepped in to look through the telescope and began to turn the dials, looking through the lens but occasionally looking up at the night sky to orientate himself as he tried to get the focus right on the planet. He soon had the light of Venus in the circumference of the lens, so much brighter than any of the other stars around it.

He moved aside to let Nuria have a look.

'That's Venus?' she asked, incredulously.

'Yes.'

'It looks like an exceptionally bright star; the light from it almost flickers as you look at it. I didn't think a planet would look like that. It hasn't got sharp edges, just hazy ones, almost like seeing the sun from a distance.'

'Yes, it looks like a very bright white star. Yet the stars around it are just like pinpricks. I hope with time I can manage to learn what all the constellations are.'

Nuria stood upright and looked up at the night sky.

'It's so awe inspiring and it makes you feel so very small in comparison. We're just little insignificant crumbs in comparison with what's out there.'

Sebastián nodded. He went over to Nuria and enveloped her in a big bear hug.

'Nuria, I've been wanting to ask you this all day. Will you marry me?'

Nuria gasped and turned to look at him in confusion.

'I know you probably haven't remembered, my love, but today is a year from when we became a couple.'

Sebastián fished out the ring box from his jeans pocket and opened it.

Nuria stared at it, tears starting to form in her eyes.

'It's beautiful, Sebastián,' she whispered.

Sebastián laughed.

'You haven't said yes yet,' he scolded, hiding the ring behind his back.

'Yes, you dope. Of course, yes,' she said, giggling.

Sebastián reached into the box and picked the ring up, gently sliding it onto her ring finger. It fitted perfectly, the gold metal shining brightly against the dark skin of her hand.

Nuria reached up to kiss him and they stood for a long while under the canopy of the starry night sky, the orb of the benevolent moon shining brightly down on them from its vast empty perch in space.

62

26th October 2019

In the early hours of the morning Sebastián got out of bed and went to unlock the terrace gate. Caro brushed past him once it opened and quickly disappeared into the garden, pleased to be out so prematurely. Sebastián stepped outside and moved a chair so he could sit in his cherished position on the terrace. The terrace had multiple arches on two sides, allowing a view out into the garden and the landscape beyond it, but without doubt his favourite aspect was of Sierra Blanquilla.

In the stillness of the sunrise, he gazed out at the magnificent view of the grey mountain in front of him. This morning the mountain was covered in the early haze of dawn so its colours were muted, a softer palette than usual. He never ceased to wonder at the constantly changing colours of the landscape, but one thing always remained the same and that was the mountain in front of him.

And yet, because today was Sebastián's wedding day, irrationally he couldn't imagine things would ever stay the same after it. He was embarking on a new phase of his life and like countless others in his position he couldn't help speculating if it would be a change for the better.

He rubbed his face wearily.

It was ironic how on the day he most needed Nuria beside

him she was incarcerated up at the farmhouse, a prisoner to their wedding preparations.

He decided to try and call her mobile, although he knew if she happened to be asleep she wouldn't hear it.

He looked at the time. Five thirty. There was no chance she'd be awake but he decided to try anyway.

She picked up on the first ring.

'Hi Seb. Are you OK?' she whispered.

'Nuria, why are you whispering? I can barely hear you.'

'I don't want to wake up the others. Give me a minute.'

Sebastián waited, listening to Nuria opening the front door of the apartment and escaping outside into the courtyard.

'How are you doing?'

Sebastián pondered the question.

'OK, I guess. Just feel like I don't know where we're heading.'

Nuria was silent for a moment.

'You getting cold feet?' she asked, disbelievingly.

'Not about us, Nuria, you know that. It's just all the wedding stuff. It feels like everything's going to change and I don't really want things to change. I'm happy with the way things are with us.'

'Seb, I'm not understanding you. How are things changing? We're not even going on a honeymoon. We'll be right here in Las Nevadas.'

'I know that. It's hard to explain. I missed you last night. It doesn't feel right when you're not here.'

'Today is all about us spending the rest of our lives together. Look at you, you're falling apart when we're not together for one night.'

Sebastián chuckled ruefully, feeling his spirits rise.

'True.'

'Why don't you come up to the farmhouse?'

'What, now?'

'Yes. I'll meet you outside in the gardens. I don't want you to be a bundle of nerves on your wedding day.'

'It's not just me having pre-wedding nerves, Nuria. There's no way you would've picked up my call if you'd been asleep. What were you doing up this early?'

There was no reply.

Sebastián laughed out loud.

'OK. See you soon, my love.'

Ten minutes later he parked the car at the bottom of the cobbled driveway and walked sedately up to the gardens. Caro padded along happily at his side, occasionally pausing to sniff at something interesting and getting distracted in the process.

In front of him he could see Nuria in her dressing gown and slippers, arms folded as she tried to keep warm in the early morning chill. Nights in this area were very cool in autumn, and it took a good hour or two of daylight to warm things up.

They hugged and kissed each other tenderly for a long moment.

'Are you going to be all right now?' Nuria asked, looking at Sebastián anxiously.

'I'm going to be fine. It was last-minute anxiety, that's all. I love what we have so much. I just don't want it to change in any way.'

'It won't. Why would it?'

'I don't know. You might become a fishwife after we're married, harping on at me until you drive me demented.'

'Well, you already drive me demented at times so you'll only be getting some of your own back.'

They looked at each other and giggled.

'Right. I'd better get back to my bed. I need my beauty sleep.'

'Me too,' said Sebastián, bending down to kiss her one last time.

Sebastián arrived back at his house and collapsed into bed fully clothed.

His mother woke him up after what felt like only a few minutes but turned out to be a good three hours.

'Come on, Sebastián. No sleeping in on your wedding day.'

Sebastián reached out for the coffee his mother was carrying. As he pushed back his blankets she stared at him in surprise.

'What on earth are you doing dressed? Didn't you bother getting your pyjamas on last night?'

'It's a long story, Mum. I don't think I'm up to explaining it all this morning.'

'OK. Fine. You've got an hour and then we need to go and pick up Nuria's flowers from the florist in Ronda and the wedding suits for you and Felipe,' said his mother, full of bristling efficiency.

'Sure. No problem.'

To Sebastián's profound relief his mother left the room so he could slowly waken up. He didn't understand how falling back asleep again could make him feel so groggy, worse than he'd felt in the early hours of the morning, but it did.

Downing his coffee in one, he made his way to the bathroom. He filled the sink with cold water. This water came from an underground well so it was freezing, and as he stuck his head into it he could feel its iciness make his hair stand on end. He felt his brain gradually gearing up into action. Lifting his head from the sink he dried it on the towel and then went to sit back down on the bed with a pen and paper.

He didn't want to forget anything today and he felt himself quite capable of doing so. He frequently forgot things when he felt stressed.

Poor Felipe bore the brunt of his pre-wedding jitters that morning with admirable patience, running necessary errands and answering Sebastián's questions when needed.

Soon after having returned from Ronda, Sebastián found he'd crossed almost everything off the list. Felipe had dropped off Nuria's flowers at the apartment as soon as they'd got back from Ronda, they'd picked up their suits and now both of them were freshly showered and dressed, waiting in the sitting-room for their parents and Felipe's new girlfriend Paola.

'Felipe, have you got the rings?'

'Yes, I have. They're safely tucked away in my suit jacket. No need to worry, bro.'

Sebastián smiled.

It was easy for his brother to say. Felipe was so laid-back Sebastián was sure he'd have forgotten everything if he hadn't been handed a list.

He looked at his watch.

It was twelve o'clock. Not long to go.

He was looking forward to getting on with the wedding now. Knowing all his family and friends would be there helped, and having Nuria by his side was all that really mattered to him at this point in time.

Nuria, with typical restraint, had organised the wedding to be as simple an affair as possible. There were to be no special arrangements; this was a Spanish wedding at its most basic with a service and then a meal out in the courtyard of the farmhouse.

The guests staying at the mews and the farmhouse had been warned a wedding would be in progress when they'd made their bookings. Needless to say this hadn't deterred anyone, and no cancellations had been made. Sebastián was sure some of them would be coming along to observe the proceedings, no doubt gawking at the sight of them all.

Everyone liked a wedding, especially tourists, as they would probably feel they were watching a slice of Spanish culture.

'Right, I think we'd better make our way up to the farmhouse. The priest will be arriving any minute now.'

'Yes, good idea Sebastián,' said his mother, who was dressed up smartly in a fuchsia-pink silk outfit.

Sebastián glanced at his father, who was in good form. He'd lost weight since his heart attack due to the strict diet his wife had put him on.

He'd confessed to Sebastián that when he couldn't take it any more he'd hidden peanuts and chocolate biscuits in his study. So far Sebastián's mother hadn't found any suspicious fatty food items in the house but Sebastián reckoned it was only a question of time before she did. However, for today at least his father could forget about his diet and enjoy himself.

Paola, Felipe's girlfriend, stood quietly next to Felipe and waited to be told what to do. Sebastián liked her. She was a rather plain young girl, shy and timid, but she also had a great deal of sweetness about her. She was not at all the type of girl Felipe was prone to dating. Sebastián wondered for the first time if on this occasion his brother's relationship was serious... For Felipe's sake he hoped so.

At half past twelve all of them trooped out to the car and

made their way up to the farmhouse. While most of their guests would be parked at the rear car park, they parked their car at the cobbled entrance of the farmhouse.

They walked into the large courtyard where numerous round tables had been laid out in preparation for the wedding lunch. Sebastián was sure he was going to miss Agustín's inspired cooking at lunchtime but today Agustín would not be cooking for them; he was going to be a wedding guest, as were all the people who worked on the farm.

The front courtyard was awash with colour since Nuria had turned her attention to it. Whenever Sebastián walked into this courtyard he never failed to marvel at her talent. Nuria seemed to have an endless capacity for creative gardening.

She had trained a bougainvillea to grow on the far wall where all the storage rooms were located. The plant seemed to rejoice in its south-facing position and the cascades of purple flowers shimmered in the bright light of the day.

Large white ceramic pots with bright red geraniums were scattered across the courtyard, adding a splash of colour against the white walls of the farmhouse and enhancing the mantis green of the wooden window shutters.

The chapel door was open, and despite the loud calls of the swifts in the palm tree Sebastián could hear the babble of voices coming from inside the chapel. He took a deep breath and walked bravely in, closely followed by the others.

A silence descended as people turned round to look at them.

The priest, who had an acerbic expression on his face, nodded grimly to Sebastián as he came to stand at the front of the chapel. The cleric's long gown and mass of fluffy white hair made him look as though he'd been transported from another time. However severe his expression was, though, Sebastián and Nuria knew him to be a kind man who did a lot for charity in his parish in Ronda.

Nuria and Sebastián had met with the priest several times in the run-up to the wedding and both of them felt he was a highly intelligent man, firmly rooted in the world around him. Nuria, rather disrespectfully Sebastián thought, had taken to calling the priest Santo rather than Padre García when she spoke about him in private. Still, there were worse nicknames she could've found for him, he reflected amusedly.

As he stood at the altar he wondered if Nuria was in the apartment, peering out of the windows to make sure everyone arrived before she made an appearance.

Sebastián pretended to look relaxed, exchanging mindless inanities with Felipe while they waited. He wondered how long Nuria would take to get ready. At home she would throw on her clothes in less than ten minutes before racing out to work. How much time would she expend in getting ready today?

It was evident when he finally saw her standing at the entrance to the chapel that she had actually taken a great deal of time.

She was dressed in a long, dark green gown that had large ivy leaves printed on it from top to bottom. Her dress was sleeveless and, as far as Sebastián could tell, simply cut, but with a big bow of embroidered ivy leaves at the back, the ends of which gave the dress bustle and volume.

Nuria had gone dress shopping with Sebastián's mother who'd decided she needed some feminine support and guidance in the wedding arrangements.

However, looking at Nuria now Sebastián was a hundred per

cent certain his mother must've been shocked at her unconventional choice of wedding dress and no doubt, behind the scenes, there'd been a battle of wills between them. Nuria had clearly won.

In her hands Nuria had a bouquet of her favourite flower, the white dendrobium orchid. Her black tresses were pinned up in a tight bun and she also had white orchids skilfully placed in her hair.

She was wearing no jewellery apart from her engagement ring and Sebastián thought she looked beautiful.

At that moment in time he felt everything around him fade into the background. Suddenly it seemed as though it was just Nuria and himself standing there in the chapel.

He smiled fondly at her. Oblivious to everyone else sitting in chapel he thought, not for the first time, how lucky he was.

Nuria walked slowly up the aisle on Emilio's arm.

Emilio was looking pleased, beaming with a combination of pride and pleasure. The only one obviously absent was José Luis. They'd all acknowledged José Luis would find attending the wedding a form of torture so they'd put no pressure on him to attend. Sebastián could sympathise with his aversion to the wedding; right up until this point he hadn't really been looking forward to it either.

The priest cleared his throat, startling Sebastián from his reverie and bringing him back down to earth. As the words of the mass resounded and echoed in the chapel Sebastián kept his gaze intently fixed on his wife, relying on her strength to see him through.

Strangely, afterwards Sebastián couldn't remember much of the service.

He remembered how the candles on the altar and in the chandelier flickered and bent with the drafts that occasionally blew in through the cracks in the door. In the moments of silence the sound of the swifts' excitable chatter could be heard outside. Nuria's black eyes had reflected the light of the candles and shone, gleaming brightly like the black marble pillars behind the altar. The rise and fall in the cadence of the priest's intonations sounded like the peaceful wash of the ocean sea.

As soon as the short service was over they both turned to the congregation for a moment, as loud cheers resounded and echoed around the chapel. Sebastián and Nuria looked at each other and laughed stupidly with relief. Finally it was all over.

Gazing back out at the congregation with a self-satisfied sense of achievement, Sebastián felt himself relax, happy to be surrounded with all the people who mattered to him most. His grandmother was there, as was his sister with her family, but because both he and Nuria wanted a small, intimate wedding they hadn't invited his enormous extended family.

Instead he had here his other family, all his colleagues at Las Nevadas. Included in this family was Piedra, who was there with his wife, daughter and son-in-law. Without Piedra's invaluable contribution Sebastián would never have managed to realise his ambitious dreams for Las Nevadas.

Oblivious to the human drama unfolding today the swifts outside in the courtyard carried on with their business. Hidden in the large palm leaves they were shrieking loudly as always. No doubt later on they'd hoover up any spilt crumbs from the wedding banquet.

As the guests poured out into the courtyard Sebastián could see the paying farmhouse guests watching them all through the window grille up in the farmhouse dining room. He waved playfully at them before seating himself at his table. By his side Nuria was in a silent daze, as if struggling to believe this day was really happening.

Sebastián poured her a glass of wine, hoping she'd be able to relax and enjoy their wedding day now the hardest part was over. Nuria wasn't used to being the centre of attention.

'Are you all right, Nuria?'

'Yes. It's just hard to believe after all the preparations we've finally done it. We're married.'

'I know. It's incredible. I get to call you wife now.'

Nuria pondered this for a moment, much to Sebastián's amusement.

'I think I'd rather you stuck to Nuria. Wife's too formal.'

'I was only pulling your leg. You'll always be Nuria to me.'

He could see Nuria was itching to kick him under the table but she was valiantly restraining herself. She was bravely trying to play the role ascribed to her today and that did not include kicking her husband. Sebastián wondered briefly if there were any other ways he could make use of Nuria's newfound docility. During the short time it lasted, of course.

Turning to look at her, he thought once again how beautiful she was.

Sebastián thought of the portrait of Amaya Arismendi hanging up in the sitting-room. In the same way as Diego Casales had wanted to have his wife's portrait painted, Sebastián decided he wanted a nice photographic portrait of Nuria in their home.

Nuria nudged him with her elbow.

'Stop staring at me, Sebastián.'

'I can't help it. You look beautiful.'

Nuria's face and neck turned crimson under her dark skin.

'Don't get embarrassed. It's true. You're going to have to get used to my compliments.'

'I suppose I'll have to come up with some for you now, too. It's going to be hard. I'm too used to insulting you.'

'I know that. But you know what they say, practice makes perfect.'

Nuria gave him a speaking look but said nothing.

Realising they were both neglecting the other guests at their table who were politely talking to each other, they turned and joined the conversation.

Later on he reached under the table and squeezed Nuria's hand. Nuria was busy talking to his mother and father but she returned the pressure.

Sebastián looked down at his starter, a smartly presented mix of serrano ham and melon. Before they started to eat the speeches were going to be heard, but with his stomach rumbling he hoped they wouldn't drag on for too long...

As he waited patiently for the speeches to start he heard a voice in his ear.

'¿*Contento*, Seb?'

He turned to face Felipe who was sitting next to him and Emilio.

'Yes, of course I am. Why?'

'You look it. You should be celebrating not just your wedding, but also all you've done since you bought this place. We never thought you'd manage it.'

'I know. I'm not sure I did either.'

'I think we should all of us give you more credit,' said Felipe, unwontedly humble.

'It really wasn't up to me. The staff working here are wonderful and I couldn't have done it without them. They've always gone the extra mile when they've needed to. As you did too, of course, when you were here,' Sebastián added hastily.

Felipe grinned mischievously at him.

'Oh, I've done you plenty of favours, Sebastián. Falling out with Nuria was one of them, for a start.'

'You're lucky my wife can't hear you.'

Felipe sobered up straight away.

'Yes, that's true,' he said contritely, straightening his tie that seemed all of a sudden too tight for him.

Emilio, who was chatting to Paola, turned and asked Felipe a question. As Felipe answered, Sebastián took the opportunity to look up at the farmhouse.

The voyeurs at the dining room window had lost interest and gone elsewhere.

Sebastián absentmindedly tried to remember what the farmhouse had looked like when he'd first arrived. He struggled to visualise it.

He remembered his sense of despair at the atrocious condition it was in, his desperate anxiety over his loan repayments and the insurmountable, monstrous piles of administration needing to be dealt with in his office.

But here they all were now with the beautiful farm buildings all sensitively restored, the farmland looking like an active, productive enterprise at last, and a superb, dedicated team of staff members.

Restoring Las Nevadas had been a superlative team effort. He knew that without the dedication of the people working for him he wouldn't have managed it.

As he watched his co-workers at the wedding party he was filled with pride in them, feeling confident that between them all Las Nevadas would flourish and thrive for years to come.

A breeze suddenly started up, causing the broad leaves of the palm tree to rustle quietly, as though whispering sweet nothings to the crowd below. As Sebastián turned in his seat he saw a strand of Nuria's hair had come loose and was blowing gently about her face. He instinctively reached up and tucked it behind her ear.

Nuria looked at him enigmatically for a moment, and just at the point Sebastián feared she'd be annoyed by his possessive gesture she leaned across and kissed him unselfconsciously on the lips. As their wedding party started to whistle and cheer, and as bawdy comments rang across the courtyard, they brazenly carried on kissing, ignoring their boisterous audience and losing themselves in a world of their own making.

THE END

Acknowledgements

I feel enormous gratitude for Cathy Tingle, my literary guardian angel, who has watched over my writing like a hawk.

Thanks are also due to Stephen, my wonderful husband and biggest fan, for his faithful encouragement even though he has no interest in reading novels.

My appreciation also goes to Charlotte Mouncey for her patience, wonderful cover work and all the hard graft in putting the book together.

Finally, thanks to James Essinger for his insightful, caustic and often humorous commentary, and his willingness to take on my books.